D1565230

CURIOSITIES

TULIPA XX.

Princesse des Asturies.
116.

A.L.Wirsing fecit et excudit 1774

Anne Fleming
Curiosities

a Novel

ALFRED A. KNOPF CANADA

www.penguinrandomhouse.ca

Knopf Canada and colophon are registered trademarks.

Library and Archives Canada Cataloguing in Publication

Title: Curiosities / Anne Fleming.
Names: Fleming, Anne, 1964- author.
Identifiers: Canadiana (print) 20230465285 | Canadiana (ebook) 20230465293 |
ISBN 9781039004979 (hardcover) | ISBN 9781039004986 (EPUB)
Classification: LCC PS8561.L44 C87 2024 | DDC C813/.54—dc23

Jacket design: Lisa Jager
Image credits: original painting *Bacchus* © Dorielle Caimi; (tulips): The Miriam
and Ira D. Wallach Division of Art, Prints and Photographs: Print collection,
The New York Public Library. (1768 - 1786); *Tulipa XX "Prince Des Austuries."*
Typeset by: Sean Tai

Printed in Canada

10 9 8 7 6 5 4 3 2 1

Penguin
Random House
KNOPF CANADA

To everyone who has experienced the double-take—
Is that a man or a woman?—and to the people who love them.

(Also, to the pair of 'maid'servants in seventeenth-century Delft
who dressed in the clothes of their master and mistress, popped
by a waffle stand, then took themselves to an inn, where they hired
a violinist and danced, danced, danced.)

CONTENTS

Anne's Note

Once in a very long while—a generation, a half-century, a blue moon—a marvellous confluence occurs. Things once thought separate join up.

That's what this book is. A confluence.

In researching the seventeenth century broadly, as an amateur, I came across—"discovered," as you may have it—John Aubrey, a personage new to me, but well-known to others, hilarious and charming, maybe a bit dotty, maybe a bit dodgy, maybe more scientific than we think. There is more to say about him, but for now I'll just note it was through John Aubrey that I found Lady Margaret Long.

Lady Margaret Long was (and still is) counted a very minor figure in the annals of seventeenth-century Britain, not having published poetry or memoir of note, not having made scientific discoveries, having been, in fact, in her various theories of natural phenomena, quite wrong. She was classed an imitator of the Countess of Pembroke, which she consciously was, modelling herself upon the learned Mary Sidney. A correspondent of gardener and collector John Tradescant, she was in dialogue with many of the men who would later make up the Royal Society. Her fine collection of eggs was purchased by Elias Ashmole, after he had taken possession of Tradescant's Ark and turned it into a museum (named after himself, not Tradescant; the present-day Ashmolean Museum, if properly named, would be the Tradescantian Museum, but glory goes to the donor, not the collector).

Minor figures are, to me, the most interesting, because aren't most of us minor characters? And aren't we interesting? We are. I assert this over and over. We are. Ordinary, weird. Which is to say: human. The minor figures I've come to know in this research are gloriously, stubbornly, interestingly themselves: Lady Margaret; Joan Palmer (about whom, more shortly); John Heard, who gives us a tiny view of war-scarred Bavaria in the 1620s (and a tightly wrapped view of his own psyche, which puts me in mind of the inside of a snail shell); and Tom Barrows, sailor, physician, surgeon, who will in due course carry us far from the others to Hudson Bay, where he will endure moment by moment, yearning for all he has left behind, *one* he has left behind, not knowing if he will ever return.

That I found Lady Margaret's papers at all is thanks to a lucky mistake. As a self-taught historian of the seventeenth century, a complete amateur, the fairest and most likely course of events would be for me to visit archives and parish record offices and churches and cemeteries, marvel over parchment taken from a sheep four hundred years ago and written upon by a living hand now long dead, a hand tallying a will or marking on a contract or some other document delightful to me in its small details, but find nothing of real historical significance. And so it was, when I first went to the archives at Canterbury Cathedral. Inordinately proud of my easily obtained researcher's ID card, I called forth from the deeps the catalogue of collector Isaac Barrow's curiosities, sundry ecclesiastical records of witch accusations, and random wills and deeds (in Latin, so that I could barely understand them). It was fun. But it didn't add up to much.

Next, I found in the Wiltshire and Swindon History Centre the papers of Aubrey's great friend, Sir James Long of Draycot Cerne. Among them—this was the mistake—were three letters from Lady Margaret Long. Those letters should not have been there. There is no relation between Sir James Long and Lady Margaret's husband, Sir Arthur Long. But the letters were charming enough that her name lodged inside my brain.

Then, in Somerset, spying Lady Margaret's name in the catalogue, I requested all the Long materials. And there, buried in an archive hardly anyone had looked at, were the two tales that follow: one of Lady Margaret Long herself; and contained inside that, one of her "companion" and "amanuensis," Joan Palmer.

They tell it better than I, and so ends my preface.

Anne Fleming
VANCOUVER

The Memoir of Lady Margaret Long

(DAUGHTER OF SIR HORACE GRIMES & ELIZABETH LOCKE)

*J*N 1590 MY DEAR MOTHER'S time came at the height of a Thunderstorm in mid-somer. With a very Clappe of Thunder was I born at seven o'clock in the evening, a lucky hour, near Fulking, in Sussex. I was predicted a Sonne but born a Daughter, beloved of both my parents, their first and onlie Child, my Father having alreadie six Children, all Daughters, of his first Wyf.

My Mother, a great believer in the education of Women, mayde certayne to provide for my learning, first instructing me herself, then securing for me a Tutor, the poet and astronomer Robert Sorrow. In Sorrow's company didde my knowledge increase and my curiosity grow. He found me, not to state the case o'er its merits, an apt Pupil, diligent of study and acute of understanding. My interests early ran every which way, falling from one thing to another, but in Natural Philosophy and Astronomy I maintained a deep curiosity.

My father's contemporaries twitted him that he made me unmarriageable by indulging my learning and Experiments, but my mother and I never feared for my prospects. We, as so often was the case, proved right. I didde not lack for Suitors, spurning two alreadie by the time I had twenty years of my age, when I met Sir Arthur Long. He had then thirty-five years of his age, a bountifull Man in every aspect, generous, loud in laughter, with a ready wit. We married two years later, and I removed my Laboratory from my Father's house in Sussex to my husband's in Somerset, where we continewed very happy untill the stillbirth of our first Child, a Boy, and the death, after a brief four days of life, a year later of our Daughter, which threw us very low in spirit, so for a time we could scarce rise from our beds.

God's will is God's will, however, or so we are told, and we swallowed our grief and rose again to live our lives.

I hadde a great fondness for my Nieces, the daughters of my sister, Anne, who married Sir William Tylden of Wormshill, Kent, and drew them to me for distraction and cheer. They hadde been used to come visit me at my father's House, where we would read and wander and discourse and play Musick and watch the Stars. Now I brought them to us at Longwood, near Chew Magna. We were from the first a merry company. My husband loved the house to be lively and full of life, and so my nieces made it. With them came a Maid, more companion to them than servant, having by the goodness of my sister shared their Schoolroom, where she had proved especially adept at ciphering.

It fell out that while my nieces and their schoolroom companion were delitescent with me, my Maid ran off with a Non-conformist. I pressed my nieces. Would they consent to have Joan, for that was the maid's name, leave their employment for mine? After some persuasion and discussion with my sister, I prevailed, and Joan came to live with me. As with my nieces, she was ever more companion than maidservant. I strongly suspect her parentage is not what she thinks, as I have told her oft and again.

Another year brought greater sorrow. On Christmas Day, my husband died at Table. One moment he was discoursing of Poesy, the next his face dropped into his Soup. He had a great fervour that Soup come hot to Table. I feared he would burn himself. The dish made a terrible Noyse. Broughton, a physitian who dined with us, leapt to his side, I pulling his face from the soup, Broughton clapping hand to his Neck to find a Pulse, where was none to find. He was gone. Now were my Heart and Soul plunged into darkest Night.

After we put him in the Ground, I sent away my husband's friends and refused all Company. When my sorrow had something waned, I wandered the Halls of Longwood, cold and empty where once they had been full of Musick and Wit, and was rent anew. I hadde not even the will to attend Church. The Rector called on me and tried to turn my head toward life. I sent him off as soon as I was able. Joan was my main, my onlie, Companion. She hadde, in her infancy, lost in the Sicknesse all she loved, and understood my Grief. She never asked that I again grow merry as had been my wont.

She read to me. She visited my Husband's Grave with me, and the Graves of our Children.

Spring came. The Steward had need of me. I referred him to Joan. The Gardener had need of me. I referred him to Joan. I felt a lassitude in my very Bones.

Summer came. With the change in weather came a change in me. The lassitude lessened, evaporated, and was gone. When Joan sayd, "I wonder if the Owls nest again in the wood," I sayd, "Well, let us ascertain the truth of the matter."

She did not so much as raise her Eyebrows, tho' any other soul would have. I rose, and dressed, and ventured out of doors, felt the Sun and the Wind and the Shade, smelt the Grass and the Trees and the Flowers, and felt Wonder creep back into my Heart.

———

When I am in extremis, I let my mind loose upon the page. Why? Why do I put this down? That I was born, that I was educated, that I was married, that I was happy, that my Children died, that I was widowed, that I was full of Grief?

Because by my side stood Joan. The love I bore for Joan—and, I will say it, my curiosity about the world—carried me through, more than God himself, unless Joan's love came to me by God's grace, which I must not doubt. (In truth, I doubted God's existence. I still do. But I am flawed, and irrational, as any other.) I write this because Joan, who is not a Witch, but has been called one, must be exonerated.

The whole of Joan, her goodness, is bound up together with the whole of Joan, her life, the Tale of which she told me time and again. She had a need to tell it, I a curiosity to hear it, so it was a Thing ever between us until at last it seemed almost my own.

In this manner will I tell it here.

Joan's Tale

$\mathcal{T}$he Sicknesse of 1603 took the lives of every Villager in all of
Wormshill, coun. Kent, save for two small Children, one not
above four yeares of her age and the other not much advanced, who
would certainly have dyed also but that they suckled a Goat.

The older of these children was Joan. Her mother was the first
taken. In not much more than a summer's Daye, the swellings erupted
over her mother's Bodye so you would hardly know her for the same
Woman. Her neck grew lumps the size of Apples and she shook with
fever and could not get out of Bed. Her Nan sent Joan to the garden
for Rosemary then burnt it in a Pot in the middle of the room. They
washed the floors down with Vinegar and soaked Sorrel overnight that
in the morning she might eat it, but she threw it up and in two more
dayes she was gone and buried. The fat Baby Joan loved to make laugh
followed. The days after took her stern old Nan and then Mary, her sister
of eight yeare, and her brother of ten. Joan wept anew each time one
was stilled to think what she'd lost—Mary, her hand when Nan's tongue
got at them, Jeffrey his Flute and the joie in his eyes, their mother, her
strength like a Willow. And what they became before they died—not

themselves but Husks of themselves—haunted her dreams. Joan feared to close her eyes for the Vizions that then came before them.

Each day and week brought more deaths until there were hardly a dozen alive in the village, so her father said, with fists rubbing his eyes. Others, all who had full enough purse to do so, had fled. Mary Dance had sent notice to her brother she must for the safety of her husband and children take herself to Whitstable.

The sicknesse was God's punishment sayd the Curate and they must look among themselves for their wrongdoing, but Joan could not think what wrong they had all done, and surely God had no cause to spare her and her alone. Therefore she must sicken and die in her turn. She felt her Neck and watched and waited, but it was her father who felt the Fever first. She came upon him digging a Hole in back of the Smithy.

Digge you a Grave? she asked.

Yea, said he. You're too small to get me into the Ground, I must needs do it myself.

No, Papa, you shall be spared, said she. His very precaution would spare him, she thought. It is those who think they will be spared who die. Those who expect it must not.

Death comes to us all, said he. You must call on my sister Mary Dance to care for you, said he.

She burned Rosemary again, and so smoked out the room of bad ayr. She gave her Father rue and sorrel. She cooled his forehead with a Cloth. "Bless you, Joan," he said. "You must call on my sister to care for you."

"Bless you, Joan," said he when she cleaned the sick from his chin and emptied the Bucket in the Privy. "Bless you," when she trickled ale into his Mouth. She prayed he might be the one to live. "Bless you, Joan," said he in the middle of the night when she lay awake on straw by the fire. In the morning he was worse, the fever wasting him, the

Lumps enormous and green. "Bless you, Mary," he said now, mistaking her for her sister or her mother. He rose and staggered out the door to his Grave, where he lay down in it.

Like her mother Joan's Father saw things that were not there, as if he had looked into a different world, or Hell. He put his hands up to ward someone off, crying, "No! No!" Then he fell into lassitude. His body shook. His breathing was like a creaky Bellows. And then silence. His breathing stopped and Joan's own Breath with it. Onlie when her own heart pounded did she allow that she was not dead alongside her whole Family. Birdsong came to her as strang as the sun at midnight.

She wept until she was spent, then she stood and looked at her Father, in Death. His Eyes were closed. No rest was on his Face. A pile of Dirt stood beside the Grave. She could not yet put it on the Face of her father who had been so recently alive. After some time, a Crow dropped down beside the Grave. She waved it off, but it flew only so far away as it needed and then returned, turned its Head on its side to look at her so that she thought it a Messenger. It hopped on her father's Chest. She shouted at it but it returned. For a long time, she chased off the crow and its fellows who soon joyned it. She lifted the Shovel to pile the dirt on but the Shovel was heavy and fell from her grasp. At last she pushed as much dirt in as she could with her hands. Her father's Body stayed still beneath it, though she expected it to move. She wept again beside the Grave and then left it, walking round the Smithy to the House.

The chickens raced to her, expecting scraps. "I've nothing for you, Hens," she said. "I must feed myself before I feed you." And before that, she felt she must tell someone of her father's death, for he was not well covered. In the cottage across The Street, lived the Coles. Goodman Cole was dead, she knew. There had been a service said for him at the same time as for her brother and sister. Joan heard no sound from their house where fine days would find Goodwife Cole on her stoole in the yeard calling out to all who passed, or saying to Joan I will give you peas if you run an errand. The door was open. Joan walked through, calling out, "Good morrow? 'Tis Joan Palmer. God has called my father to him at last, I suppose I must be next." There was no one in front room and no one in back, no one in the buttery. She ventured up the stairs, where she had not before been, poked her head into each room, where were only beds and close, hot air. She ran downstairs past the memory of the family at table and out into the lane. Birds sang. A cow lowed. Chickens clucked. No human sound came from anywhere, no singing, nor shouts, no one calling children in or coaxing oxen on.

A human sound made her turn, a swallowed weeping like a Chyld but it was a Man, Thomas Willes, the husbandman, she saw as she drew closer, and at his feet, a Body.

"God save ye, Mr. Willes," she called. His aspect did not change. He was looking down at the man at his feet, the Chapman at their door these many dayes ago dead where he had fallen. Thomas Willes his chin was a-quiver. Sounds issued from his mouth.

"God save ye, Mr. Willes," Joan tried again. "My father is dead, God rest his soul. He has dug his own grave."

Thomas Willes took to his heels, weeping as he went. Joan followed like a dog after a horse but it was not long before he outstripped her. Turning onto the path for Ringlestone was another figure, who turned when Goodman Willes ran past, so that Joan could see it was Bess in service to the Hazelwoods. Joan called after her but she seemed not to hear so Joan ran until she caught up. Bess drew up her shift over her nose to speak to Joan.

"I am going home," said Bess. "They may not thank me for it but I am going home."

"My father has breathed his last," said Joan, "and has dug his own grave."

"I am going home," repeated Bess. "You should not be out of your house."

"I covered it up, but the crows come still."

"I am going home and none can stop me." Tears came out her eyes though not the noise of weeping. Bess picked up her pace so Joan fell behind, but she kept on, for what else should she do?

"The Coles are all dead, Bess, the large and the small," cried Joan. "And the chapman lies in the road and the Vines are gone and my aunt is gone."

"I cannot care for you, Joan."

Joan had given no thought to herself. She only wanted help with her father. Then the sickness could take her and it would be over, God save her soul.

Joan stood watching until Bess was out of sight. Well, she must find someone else. She turned. A crow flew down from an oak onto the chapman's head. "Shoo," she shouted, running at it. Then she held her breath as she ran past, on to the church, where the Graves in the churchyard were fresh and no stones put up. No one was in the Church. Joan prayed for the souls of her family, especially her father and brother, for whom no service had yet been said. She stopped next at the curate's Cottage where was a foul smell Joan ran from, not knowing who lay there. She stopped at three more dwellings, two empty, one with a stench and began to think she would find no one to help. In the lane, she called out to any that might hear, "Are there any can help? My father has died and I cannot get him into the ground." She listened and heard Birds and Cattle and Sheep but no human sound. She yelled until at last it was a cry with no words. Then she stilled her voice and let her heart still also. A cow bawled. She followed the sound to the rectory stable with cow and heifer she turned out to forage. As soon as they found grass, they bellowed no more. She thought of their own cow still out to Pasture. Now she felt her own Hunger, and made her way back to her house.

There was no bread, for there were none to bake it since her mother and Nan and sister had died. There was cheese in the buttery, and fresh salad in the garden. She picked peas and pulled carrots and made a supper from that. The sounds of the beasts roused her at last. They must all be turned loose to find what they could to fill their stomachs.

She spoke to the Cows and Pigs as she loosed them. "It seems there are none alive but me. My mother was first taken, then my fat baby brother, John. I'd put my apron up over my face and drop it down to make him laugh."

At five or six houses she released animals. At the Willes's Cottage was a steady beating against the door of a Shed and when she opened the door out trotted a white Goat who looked at her with amber eyes. Thomas Willes had got a goat to save on a cow and had paid the difference in fines ten times over as the goat ate through hedges and gardens. Thomas Willes was a fool, everyone said, but her father would laugh and say, "Come now." The Goat bleated. Behind it came one of the twins, a Child a year or two younger than herself that had been locked up with the Goat. The Child blinked and rubbed its eyes and Joan saw the eyes were the same colour as the goat's.

"Are you truly a human child?" asked Joan even as she knew the child for one of the Willes twins.

It ran toward her and embraced her. In the child's embrace Joan wept.

"I am Joan Palmer," said she. "Which of the twins are you?"

"Tom," said the child and Joan thought it to be the boy because the girl was named Thomasina. Joan's mother had laughed at Goodwife Willes for christening her babies Thomas and Thomasina, but Mistress Willes said, when I call them, both will come. The child's Shift was filthy, its face not much cleaner, but it was a round and sturdy Face and it made Joan feel better to see it. She found she did not want to let go, so she held its Hand.

"Well, Tom," said Joan. "So there are two of us alive, at least. My mother died first, Tom, and then my baby brother, John. Then followed my old Nan and my dear sister Mary and my brother Jeffrey who played the flute and at last my poor kind Father, who dug his own Grave. How is it with you, Tom? How came you to be in the shed?"

"Papa said, In you go with Agnes."

"Agnes?"

The child nodded at the goat.

It was almost dark but a warm evening. Tom was hungry so Joan led Tom to where the Goat fed. Tom pulled out handfuls and stuffed them in his mouth. When afterwards he pulled up the shift and crouched to make water, "I see you are Thomasina," said Joan, "not Tom."

"Tom," said Thomasina.

"As you like," said Joan.

They slept together in the shed. Joan started at the sound of the Goat returning and settling by them in the straw, but Tom nestled to her as if by Habit. In the morning the goat nudged them awake, bleating. Tom's curly head went right to the goat's teat and sucked and Joan saw how she had in this way stayed alive. When Tom had done, she gestured to Joan to take her turn. First she took the teat in her hand to squeeze it but she had not the strength and so like Tom put her mouth on the very teat and so got her breakfast.

From the Goat the children suckled as kids and by her side they slept as kids and altogether lived not as human children but as young Goats. The Goat ate, the Children drank, and when they had drank enough she butted them away. They kept away from the Body in the road that the dogs and crows made free with. They played at pat-a-cake and skittles. So the dayes continued. Nights the three curled together in slumber.

One morning they heard a noise like a Spade against dirt and went out into the lane to see a ragged Figure in skirts digging a hole by the

Body. They ran up, the goat following. "Good day," they called. "Good day." But the Woman gave no answer. They asked themselves whether she be Phantom or Spirit. Certainlie, she acted as tho' they were not there. "Who are you?" asked Joan. No answer. "I am Joan and this is Thomasina, called Tom." The woman but kept on with her digging. "We have not seen any alive in all these dayes," said Joan. "Whence came you?" But she answered not again. They grew afrighted, but then, the woman clearing her nose in such a plain, human waye, it came to Joan, the simple answer. "Oh. She cannot hear."

She tugged on the Woman's skirts, struck herself on the chest, shouting, "Joan." The woman nodded and went on with her work. They took up sticks to help her. There was not much left of the Chapman. They watched as the woman dug and dug. At last, there was Grave enough to roll the Chapman in and cover him up. Joan had not known how it troubled her heart he was there until he was under ground. Below, where the Bodie had lain, were maggots. Tom crouched by them, poking at them with her stick. The woman wiped at her brow and walked off, maintaining the shovel. Joan ran after. She tugged at her sleeve and led the woman to her father's House. She had not been back to her father's grave. She had come close but the Smell was bad and she knew she had not buried him well enough. She led the woman around to the grave. The woman went to work with the shovel, filling in the grave. The Goat had followed them, as it was wont to do, and now grazed in the Palmers' garden. Joan wept and said what words she could remember from Church for the soul of her Father, gone to God.

The old woman went into the cow-shed. Joan followed and began again her recitation of her losses. "First my mother was taken, then the fat baby John . . ." The woman came out with a Rope in her hands, which she knotted and shaped. Then she pulled from her apron an apple and drew to her the goat, slipping the knotted rope now a halter over its snout as she let it chaw on the apple. Then she led the goat away.

"That is our goat," shouted the children. They chased after her and shouted, but the woman went on just as she had started, across the field to Barrows Wood, where, it was said, lived a—Joan's eyes widened—a Witch with no Tongue who would come, so said her Nan, for Children who did not do what they were told. But Tom was ahead, running on her sturdy little Legs and would not turn back, so Joan had no choice but to go on. At forest's edge, the path led down a hill, through thistles taller than themselves that scratched them and often they lost sight of woman and goat but on they went, for without their beldame how would they sup and how stay warm as the nights grew colder? At last they came to a clearing by a stream, where outside a rude Hut was the goat, tethered and being milked by the woman into a leathern Buckit.

They marched up together and when they stood just by the woman in the shadow of the hut, their hands reached out for the other's. Joan thought of her dead sister and was glad for Tom.

"That is our goat," said Joan again.

"Agnes," said Tom.

The woman lifted her eyes to theirs. Her eyes were deep in their sockets and small and brown and Joan could not say what was in them. The woman inclined her head toward the hut and took the bucket up. The children followed. Tom ran to the Goat's side and petted it. The hut was little more than stickes on three sides, with one side open, a woodsman's hut of one room with cot, table, stumps to sit on and earthen floor. Herbs hung from the rafters. From a shelf she took a jug of Ale she poured into the single mug. She pointed at the two of them that they should share. Joan did not like to eat of a witch's table, but Tom had no such qualms and Joan supposed she should keep Tom company. If Tom came to harm, so would she and so be it.

The woman built up a Fire in a brick circle outside the hut and made the children a gruel they lapped up in hunger with wooden spoons from a single bowl. As they ate, she went off again back the way they had come. Joan thought to follow but filled her stomach instead. When they were done, Joan wondered what to do. They could untether the Goat and take her back with them. But there was comfort in the presence of a grown person, Witch or no.

"Well, Tom. Where has she gone? What should we do?"

Agnes bleated. "We could take Agnes again with us. We could return to our house, for there is no body there now to keep us away."

Tom ran over to the stream, bent down and picked up small stones. She was a merry little child, and chortled now as she tossed stones and saw them splash. She stomped her feet in a shallow pool and laughed the more. Joan joined her. They stomped and splashed until they were wet to the skin.

A great squawking told them the woman was come back and there she was with two Chickens hung by the feet in each of her hands. She snapped her wrists and let them flap to the ground and spread corn from a pocket in her apron so they had reason to stay. She unbundled from a square of cloth two mugs and plates and bowls to add to the ones she already had. Joan supposed they were meant to stay.

The woman went off again and returned this time with a Coney, its neck broken. Now she set to skinning the rabbit in the yard. Tom crouched by her, watching. When they had the Coney in a pot on the fire, the old woman took off Tom's shift, took a corner of it and dipped it in the stream and washed Tom's face with it, rinsed it in the stream and hung it to dry. She signalled Joan to take off her wet skirts and dry them. She set the two on her knees to keep warm and bounced them there, so they screamed with surprise and delight. Her face in a smile was a different face, she was a different creature.

When their clothes were almost dry she put them back on them, and then they ate until they could eat no more, and then they put by what was left. Then was the old woman at her ease. Out of her pockett came a Mouse and the children cried with surprize and delight. She fedd it crumbs and corn, making small chipping sounds with her tongue. Come nightfall, the woman laid out for them straw and a blanket. The Goat bleated at her tether. The old woman did not hear it but lay snoring. Joan up and let the Goat to lie with them, untying the knot by feel and they lay together, the three of them, as was their custome.

They soon fell into their days and the goat gave milk and the chickens gave eggs and the stream gave fish and those who had farmed the fields about them were gone and the corn stood ready for the harvest. The woman was never idle but for a moment in the evening, when she fed her Mouse and bounced the children on her knee or made a hollow sound by shaping her mouth into an O and knocking on the top of her head. "Why, she sounds like a nut," said Joan. She looked like a nut, too.

"Old Nut," said Tom.

So they took to calling her Old Nut. When she wanted them, she rapped on things to draw their attention. Once, when Tom was crying, to distract her, she put a finger in her mouth and popped it out. Tom's cry turned to a laugh that shook her whole body and that made the old woman laugh, a funny loud sound from she who was so quiet. The pop sound, that became her way of calling Tom or meaning her. Her sign for Joan was a thump on the chest just as Joan had done in trying to teach her name. Joan would not have known she had attended the gesture if she had not repeated it, but she came to see Old Nut showed little and took in all. Indeed, she seemed to understand so much of what Joan said that Joan wondered if she were not deaf after all. But if her back be turned, she never heard a thing, thus Joan concluded she be truly deaf.

It did not take long for them to learn her other signs—for Chicken and Goat and Fire and Wood, for Rayne and Stream and Fish and Cat, for eat and wash and sleep.

When they had need of anything, Old Nut went off to the village and returned with it—warmer clothing for Tom, who had naught but the shift, tools and rope and salad and parsnip, for there was no garden by the hut to thicken their pottage.

The children stayed with Old Nut and drank the goat's Milk and ate what she scavenged or took. In the evening, when she was stille, came from her pocket the Mouse who ran up her dresse and in and out her sleeve and ate from her hand. She was gentile with it, slow with her movements. A brightness came into her eie at the sight of it, and she chirruped to it. After a few Daies, she let the children feed it, and they grew used to the sight of it running about her personne.

Joan was a childe who loved to talk, a childe who could not stop talking, it was her waye, as it was Thomasina's way to climbe and explore and pull things apart. One time falling from a height Thomasina set a-crying, whereupon Old Nut picked her up, rubbed noses with her and tossed her into the air. Tom squealed with delight. Old Nut threw her up agayn and agayn and so the two were fast friends. One time she caught Tom in this waye and Tom's arms went about Old Nut's Neck where her hand felt something hard as a nut behind the Ear, under kerchief and hair, bigger than any nut. "What's this?" she asked. Old Nut thrust Tom off lyke the Childe hadd struck her. Her face went hard and turned in on itselfe and she rose instantly and went off into the woods. Tom set to crying again and Joan tryed to comfort her the best she could.

Old Nut didde not play that game again. Instead she took her small knyfe and mayde Tom and Joan figures from wood, a gyrl and boy for them to play with. But Tom wondered about the hard thing behind her ear, what it was and why she should push her from her so, who loved her.

Some daies they followed Old Nut on her rambles. She did not slow or wait for them so they must run to keep up. She had Snares to check, cobnuts to gather. One day they followed her a long way up through the Woods and came out to a Farm, where there was a human sound, the sound of mowing, the sound of a man in the field cutting corn with a scythe. Joan ran toward the sound, waving and yelling. "Good day to you," called Joan but the man could not see her. "Good day! Good day!" Startled, the man looked up and saw only Old Nut. "Good day to you," she called again as she came close enough that he could see.

"You near had me slice my leg off," cried the old man. "What be you, child? Fairy?"

"I am called Joan Palmer."

"Thou art Nick Palmer's child. And truly alive."

"Alive as you. First my mother was taken," Joan said, "and then the fat baby, John, who laughed so roundly, then my Nan and my sister Mary, who held my hand, and my brother Jeffrey, and at last my father, who dug his own grave. Then I discovered Tom in the shed with Agnes and we drank of her milk and then Old Nut came and buried the chapman and took Agnes with her and so we followed and there we have been ever since."

"Well. I am called William Dorset, and keep the manor farm. My two sons died and the girl ran off and I lay sick seven days and thought I'd not rise again, but God spared me. When I had strength I went round the village. I saw the grave in the Street and by your smithy, there. There were more that I buried, the Curate and them at the Rectory. Who came, then, and buried the chapman?"

"Old Nut here. We call her Old Nut for she makes a sound like a nut but I think she is the witch of Barrows Wood."

"Barrows Mary, we call her, she that cannot hear. I thought it was she calling out to me just now. In a child's voice! That's the reason I frighted like a young rabbit. She who has no voice calls out 'Good day' like a child of six. Well, Barrows Mary," he addressed Old Nut, "you remember we've work for you at harvest."

"She gave us ale and pottage. She washed Tom's face."

"Oh, well, then, if she washed his face, all's well!"

The child did not recognize a jest. "Her face."

"Hmm?"

"Tom is a girl, called Thomasina Willes."

"Oh, aye, Willes had twins."

Old Nut was changed, Joan saw. Her eyes were cast down and flicked up in shifts to see what was about. William Dorset nodded to her and shouted as he made signs of cutting and gathering, "I'll hire ye, I'll take all hands. Come cut with me and there'll be corn in it for you and coin, too. And you, young misses, you can rake for us."

He fetched another scythe for Old Nut. "I am glad there are more quick in the village. What can Wormshill have done to be so smitten? I have been asking myself. I have seen the sickness come four or five times and take its toll, but never like this."

The days after, they came to the Fields again and cut and raked and gathered. William Dorset showed Joan how to tie the raked corn into stooks. They had their dinners in the field and worked until dark. To save them the trip to Old Nut's hut, they slept in the barn. William Dorset made them tether the Goat.

Joan chatted, William Dorset grunted and nodded, Old Nut worked, and Tom tumbled or sat in the dirt and looked at bugs. The weather was fine. It grew cooler in the evenings.

One time, Joan fell from an apple tree where she had been picking and hurt her leg so she could not walk. Old Nut being by, she got Joan up on her back to carry her. Joan, with her arms about Old Nut's neck, felt something hard against her upper arm like a stick under Old Nut's bonnet. "What's this?" said she, for as you know she was not one to stay quiet when a thought came into her mind. Old Nut turned her head to see what Joan asked. She repeated her question, feeling at the stick with her left hand.

Old Nut as good as dropped her right there. Joan wept and Tom comforted her, just as when Old Nut dropped Tom and Joan was comfort to her. Together they puzzled over Old Nut, tho' it didn't do to puzzle much or you would never be easie. Soon enough, her tears were spent and Tom lent a shoulder so that Joan could hop. When they were halfway there, Old Nut was back with a cloth to wrap the swollen ankle. She showed no kindness in the doing, but there was not her roughness, either, so Joan took it that Old Nut's temper was past. But she and Tom were curious—what was the hard nut or stick behind her ear?

One day they heard voices and William Dorset stopped swinging his scythe. "It is the Hazelwoods back at Home Farm," he said, then went on swinging. "The first news she had your mother was sick, off she sped to her sister's in Faversham, though why the sickness should spare Faversham when it spared not Wormshill, I could not say. She'll be up to see us before an hour is out."

Sure enough, Eliza Hazelwood was up to the manor farm in short order. With her came Ned, her son, who had fourteen years, and her daughter, who had ten. She and William Dorset exchanged news, she that her family had been spared, "God be praised," though Faversham had not, he that almost none had been spared but for the two children, himself, and Barrows Mary. He did not know about the folk at Norwood Farm or Park Farm or what had happened to the Dances, but he had not seen any at Yew Tree farm. Eliza Hazelwood said they had left Bess Baggillie to care for the chickens and cows and young John Cole to care for the rest of the farm, but there was no sign of either of them but for a mound in the stableyard.

"I buried young Cole," said William. "As for Bess Baggillie, I cannot say."

"She said she was going home," said Joan. "'They will not thank me for it, but I am going home, Joan Palmer,' said she."

"Where reside the children?" asked Mistress Hazelwood.

"In the barn with Barrows Mary for harvest."

"Has anyone sent word to their people?"

"Who would send word, Mistress Hazelwood, the birds of the air?"

"Word must be sent."

"Goodwife Willes was from Cornwall, Thomas Willes an orphan."

"Mary Dance is Joan's cousin, is she not?"

"See them?" The children were climbing on Old Nut. Tom grasped her thumbs, walked up her legs and spun in a circle, laughing. "They're as well off here as in receiving alms in Maidstone," said William Dorset. "Let them stay with the nutter until their folk are heard from."

Every day William Dorset wondered if he should go to Bredgar or Lenham or Maidstone to see about hiring labourers to help, and every day he thought of the work lost in taking the time to do so. They worked from dawn to full dark, ate little during the day, filled their bellies at night, and slept. Their food was meagre and not well cooked for there was not time to prepare it, but they grew used to their daies and didde not mind. Tho' Joan missed her Family still, she grew attached to Old Nut and William Dorset and Tom most of all. At night, they slept curled together.

One day Joan's aunt, Mary Dance from Yew Tree Farm, came to the manor farm with her daughter Margaret, who was almost grown. Every few steps she ran as if she could not get to them fast enough, and Margaret beside her trotted to keep up.

"Aunt! Aunt!" Joan shouted and threw herself into Mary Dance's skirts. "My mother was—"

"God save you, Joan, God save you, William Dorset. Have you seen Christopher?"

"Nay, I've not."

"My mother was first—" tried Joan again.

"Hush, child," said her aunt. "Let me hear Goodman Dorset."

After he'd lain ill, William said, he'd gone down to Yew Tree farm and found the body of John Dance, God save his soul, and had buried him, but of young Christopher he'd seen no sign.

"Oh, thank God," sayed Mary Dance with hand on chest, breathing as if she had been holding her breath. "I feared he was in the same grave as that in the yard."

"No, that is the Grave of your husband, I am sorry," said William Dorset.

Mary Dance said they were in a puzzle, for the farm looked cared for and yet no one came when she called, and she had *thought* the mound in the yard only large enough for one grave. Mary Dance and Margaret had gone to Canterbury with young John that he might take the exam at the King's School. He took it and passed it, but all was vanity, for Mary then took the sickness and fared poorly, and then young John himself took it and lost his life. They'd had word from her brother, Nick Palmer, that the sickness was come to them in Wormshill.

Joan tugged on her cousin Margaret's skirt and said to her, "First my mother was taken, and then the fat baby, John—"

While Margaret listened to Joan, Mary Dance and William Dorset continued their tales. Old Nut laboured on. And Tom bent straw into shapes.

"And these children the only ones left?"

"They suckled Willes's goat until the deaf one took 'em home with her."

"Barrows Mary?" cried she.

"Aye. They've a liking for her, the two of them."

"They'll come home with me, then," said Mary Dance. "I am Joan's kin and little Thomasina is but one small mouth to feed until we find where to send her."

So Joan and Tom went home with Mary Dance. Joan wanted to take her leave of Old Nut but her aunt was calling, "Come, Joan," and Old Nut did not look up from her labour. Joan felt sorry to leave her and pulled her hand from her aunt's and ran over to Old Nut, who stopped her work when Joan got close enough. "We are going with my aunt," said Joan, making signs to show what she meant. Old Nut's face was as expressionless as the day she took the goat and Joan felt tears at her eyes for she had thought surely Old Nut loved her but now it looked as if she did not. Tom followed Joan, but did not stop where Joan did but tried to climb up Old Nut as she was wont to but the scythe was in Old Nut's hands and she did not put it down.

"Come, Tom," said Joan as her aunt had said to her. Tom knocked on her head with her mouth in the shape of an O and Old Nut put down her scythe and made the popping sound and Tom laughed and so they parted.

On the way back to the farm, Mary and Margaret wondered what might have happened to Christopher, if he might have run off and if he had where he might have gone and what work on the farm he could do, having only nine years of his age. And Joan told her story again, who had died, in what order, and how she had found Tom and Old Nut.

At the farm, Old Rowley had watered the horses and fed them and came back now from a tour of the farm, saying he had not found Christopher, but there was corn cut in the east field. "Well," said Mary to Margaret, "we must do as Eliza Hazelwood and pick up the scythe and rake ourselves."

"We must send to Maidstone as William Dorset says to hire help."

"I will cut, Mistress," said Old Rowley.

"Then we will rake."

They went out to the field. Joan went to help rake as she had been doing the days of harvest but the rake was too large for her and Mary Dance told her to rest. She and Tom sat at the edge of the field under the trees and chewed on grass. The old man swung the scythe with ease. Mary Dance stopped every now and then to rest. Margaret raked behind them.

They lay on their backs and looked up into the trees. And then Joan saw a face in the tree, looking out at the people working in the field. Christopher. And though it was her nature to call out, she did not call out but gazed up at him as he gazed out at his Mother and Sister and the Man who worked for them and so they remained for a length of time until at last Christopher climbed down, dropped to the ground beside them and walked towards his mother, who dropped her scythe with a cry of his name, fell on her knees before him and wept as she embraced him. Joan and Tom followed behind. Mary Dance soon dried her tears and rose to her feet.

"O, Christopher, Christopher. We hoped and prayed for your deliverance. Why did you not come forth when first we came?"

Christopher opened his mouth but nothing came out. He seemed skittish and ill at ease and not as Joan remembered him a bold, carefree boy of nine years. There in the fields and again at supper his mother asked him what had happened. "Come, tell us the tale." But he would not or could not say and indeed spoke no word. So Joan spoke all the time and Christopher spoke not at all. Her aunt hushed Joan as if it were her chatter that kept Christopher silent.

That night when it came time to sleep and Tom and Joan were in a bed for the first time in many a long night, Tom tossed and turned and could not sleep and cried for the goat, which they had left with Old Nut. Even if Agnes could be got, Mary Dance would not let a goat sleep in the house or the children sleep in the barn and so there was nothing for Joan to do but try to comfort Tom the best she could. At last Tom held a hank of Joan's hair and fell asleep that way. The next day, Tom wanted Old Nut and did not understand why they could not go to her.

"We live with my aunt now," said Joan.

"I want Old Nut," said Tom. She kept starting up the Street towards the manor farm and Joan kept bringing her back. At last she decided that if she was minding Tom and Tom wanted to go see Old Nut, they should go see Old Nut. On the way, it 'gan to rain. Old Nut was in the barn. William Dorset was saddling up a horse to go to Maidstone to see who he could hire. Tom did not know who to embrace first, Old Nut or Agnes. She called out their names, ran and tapped Agnes on the head and then ran to Old Nut and right up her legs, trusting that Old Nut would catch her hands, which she did. They were like tumblers Joan had seen at the market in Lenham. Old Nut let Tom walk up her legs and do flips over and over. The two of them laughed to see each other. Joan told William they had found Christopher hiding in the trees. William Dorset set off. Tom suckled from the goat. Joan and Old Nut played a game where one person held her hand palm down over the other's, palm up, and had to draw theirs away when the other tried to smack it. The rain was just lessening as Margaret Dance came drenched into the barn, in choler. "You cannot just run off," she said. But Joan and Tom did not understand.

They were far from finished the harvest when the rains came. William Dorset wept to see barley rotting in the fields but could do no more than he could do. Old Nut was no longer at the Manor farm and when Joan and Tom went to find her at her hut in Barrows Wood, she was not often to be found.

Then one day she came to the house, wanting to trade nuts for ale. Tom squealed with glee and jumped on Old Nut as she was wont, but Christopher hid behind his mother, shaking.

"Christopher, what has happened to you? 'Tis only Barrows Mary who has come of old to beg ale and bread of us."

But Christopher quivered behind his mother as fearfull as if the Divell himselfe stood before him.

"Bid her leave, Margaret," Mary Dance said, turning to her son to comforte him.

Tom clung to Old Nut still, climbed up her skirts till she was resting on Old Nut's hip. Old Nut took little notice, as if to have Tom climbing on her were her natural state.

Margaret shook her head at Old Nut. Old Nut shook her basket, which rattled with the sound of nuts.

"She has nuts to trade," said Joan.

"We don't want your nuts, old woman," said Margaret. "Go."

Christopher whimpered in the back of his throat, the first sound he had made since their return.

"Oh, give her what she wants and get rid of her that way," said Mary Dance.

Margaret clucked and filled Old Nut's jug and gave her half a loaf of bread and hurried her on her way. Old Nut had to shake herself free of Tom, who ran after her. Joan chased after both of them, and Margaret stepped forward, but Old Nut turned to Tom and put a hand out to Tom to say stay and then a fist on her palm to mean stop here. Tom bawled.

The next time Old Nut came to trade nuts at Yew Tree farm Old Rowley chased her off with a stout stick to tell her she were not welcome anymore at the Dances, their house. Joan and Tom saw less of her, tho' Tom ran off to find her still. Mistress Dance spanked Tom and kept her in doors or hadde Christopher or Joan watch that she do her work and not run off but she could not be watched all the time and Joan tried but could not stop her running. "No, Tom, you must not go to Old Nut. She will not be there in any case. We live with my aunt now," Joan said but Tom would go anyway and if she did, Joan must follow, and the two of them be punished with switches later on. Mistress Dance oft repeated how she rued the day she had took Thomasina in. "That child has the Devill in her," she sayed, so often that it made Joan's heart sore.

One time they came upon Old Nut with her kerchief off, scratching her head and treating it with some receipt that steamed in a Pot. Before she saw them, that was when they saw the Horn for the first time. It was of a colour like to her hair, that is, a dull grey mixed with brown, but darker and flecked. It came out of her head behind her ear about the thicknesse at the base of a seven year's sapling and turned about in a spiral downwards, narrowing to a point. They both saw it and knew the other saw it and knew it was the hard thing they had felt before and they waited until she had rinsed the receipt from her hair and retied her kerchief before they showed themselves to her. She laughed and chortled and gave her usual smile to see them. It made Joan's heart glad for there was no one else in the world who took joy in seeing themselves as Old Nut.

Mistress Dance suspected Barrows Mary of causing her son to be mute. Her neighbour, Eliza Hazelwood, encouraged her in this suspicion. Eliza sayed that Christopher should scratch the witch's face and that way cancell her spell, and if not Christopher, then his mother. This they went to do, Mary Dance and Eliza Hazelwood together (for Christopher would in no way go with them), and Margaret Dance, as well, and were successful in scratching her face but not breaking the spell for when they gott home, Christopher remayned mute. But at

Old Nut's hut, Mistress Hazelwood saw mugs from her own house and plate and she knew not what else, and so old William Dorset was enjoyned to act Constable and search the hut, where was a bolt of cloth Mistress Hazelwood swore was of the rector's household and Mistress Hazelwood's very scissors, as well as blankets and the chickens, and other items that had once lived in the houses of the village. This was ever her way, said the women. She is a Magpie and a Thief. And a Witch, Eliza Hazelwood failed not to add.

"When she was young, she caused a tree to fall on her father, to kill him, for he beat her. That was her first act on behalf of the Divell."

Eliza Hazelwood never saw her or heard of Old Nut but told the story of her causing a tree to fall on her father, though it might have been the mother that did that, she was known for a witch herself, cursing those who helped her not. There were those in Bedmonton who had not been sorry to see either the man die or the woman, for it was a relief on their eyes and ears. The Atwoods in Bedmonton had taken in Mary for a servant but she had taken something of the household's and they could not make her understand even though she spent time in the stocks and lost her position. They were lenient with her and then she took to the woods and bothered them no more.

So Old Nut went before the magistrate and was sentenced to three months hard labour and they did not see her agayn in that time nor afterward for some months longer so that all thought they would ne'er see her agayn, which occasioned distress to none but Tom and Joan. Tom had the Goat again and was less wild, not having Old Nut to run off to. Again and again, the Goat ate what it should not eat, until at last Mistress Dance said it must be killed. Tom was in a fury because of it and would not speak to Mistress Dance for weeks.

When the three months and more were donne and the witch hadde not returned, it happened that young Christopher Dance, the day after the goat was killed, spake agayn. "Amen," said he when their food was blessed. His mother and sister rejoyced that his voice was restored. In time, he told them this tale:

You had been gone but two days when we heard our aunt, Joan's mother, had the sweating sickness and then the bell tolled for her and we heard our uncle buried her. Father wanted to go to see what he could do but I was not allowed to see my cousins, who were confined to their house. More dyed. The churchbell hardly stopped ringing. We were gladde you were safe away from us. We prayed you remain safe.

Papa consulted with our neighbours and the churchwardens and we shouted communication with the Palmers.

We went to church. We trusted in God.

Anne Wrightson in the kitchen was the first to sicken and her daughter thereafter. And then the same day young Joseph Rowley. He nodded here at Old Rowley, to acknowledge his loss.

And then my father fell of a fever. There were none to feed him but myself and none to work the farm but myself, so I must give him a drink and a soup before I milk the cows and turn them out and draw water and feed the horses and chickens and muck out the stalls and tour the fields, and come and give him a trickle of water and a cool cloth. I lost track of the days. He continued some time, three days or four, and then one morning my father was better. He knew me and could lift his head and drink. Came at the door a knock, the Barrows Witch come to beg of us. "We have no bread and we have no cheese," said I, "and none should come here but that wish to die for the air must be infected," and she huffed and blew on me in a strange way and in that instant I grew hot and sweated and from that time I knew I had the sickness myself and I shouted and cursed at her and then turned and my father was dead and I ran after her, not knowing what I meant to do, but she did not turn, no matter how I shouted but kept on her way. She had a shovel in her hand that was our shovel, I saw her take it, and on her shoulder was a crow, I saw her talking to it, and then she did some magic with the shovel, she jabbed it this way and that way, not like someone shovelling but as if she were marking a spell on the ground. "I will be back for you, Christopher Dance," I heard her say, shaking her fist at me and so I took care to hide. And she did come back. From the barn, I saw her again, she walked right into our kitchen and took out a pot and then she took a chicken from the yard, not even troubling to run after it but drawing it to her with magic so it leapt into her hand. I could keep a better watch from the barn than the house, and she did not return for many days, to put me off my diligence and think she would not return but return I knew she would and I kept watch until one day she came into the barn and so then I kept a lookout in the trees. I'd come down to do my chores and then go back up and I kept her away from that day to your return with my watching. Then you came home and I stopped watching and she came agayn.

It was Christopher's belief that old Nut had sent the Sicknesse on before her so she no longer had to knock on doors but could simply walk into howses and take what she wanted. See how she survived it and profited when all else around fell? His mother, feeling tender toward him, allowed it was possible. Eliza Hazelwood, already ill-disposed to Old Nut, seized on the truth of it immediately. Margaret had no fondness for the beggar but thought it more likely that Christopher's fever had caused him to see and hear things that others did not see.

In the Summer and Fall of that yeare no one in Wormshill saw or heard Old Nut, or Barrows Mary, as she were more generally known. But in winter or springe she was back, and the first to know of it was Tom. The Dances murmured darkly about whether she should be charged with witchcraft. Christopher, who still hadde his tongue, was for it, but Margaret was not, though she hadde no liking for the old womanne, and Mistress Dance was herselfe torn between the two. She feared further harm from the womanne if she truly be witch and pitied her if not. She would rather pray and that waie seek their salvation. So Old Nut was suffered to live as she hadde been wont, and recover her hut in the wood. She no longer came to beg at Yew Tree farme. Tom, who roamed the woods as oft as time would allow, gathering mushrooms and nuts and sorrel and simples and tending to Old Nut's snares where she oft tooke coneys, was the one to discover her return and leapt on her and clung to her as one returned from the dead. Mary Dance hadde great trouble of Thomasina Willes because of this roaming and climbing and being headstrong and ungovernable, so that she hadde thrown up her hands or almost washed her hands of her. If there were a man in the house, sayed Eliza Hazelwood, that child would learn to mind, but even when she were beaten, chided or constrayned, it subdued her not, so that Mistress Dance at last gave up and let her come and goe as she pleased so long as she didde her share of work and joyned them at Church. It did not hurt that Tom brought nuts and simples, and a coney here and there, that she was adept at making and mending. They hadde no word following inquiries they hadde mayde of Thomasina's relations. At first in the daies of Tom's roaming, Joan feared for her and missed her. But soon she came to understand that Tom alwaies returned. She stille slept clutching a hank of Joan's hair.

There were by then more returned to the village and some new withal, drawn thither to fill the old vacancies. When the hammer rang in the Smithy Joan took it to bee her own father and hadd a new griefe when remembrance came to her of an instant that it were not him but John Wilmott from Chatham.

So time went on. The new Curate took boys at the church to learn letters. He came round to all the village houses to flush out any boys that had not been at church. At the Dances' house he thought Tom a boy till she stepped out behind a table and even then he was disposed to ask why this boy was in girls' dress. Later, Tom told Joan she wished there had been a way to keep the Curate mistaken, for she hadde a great curiosity about letters and reading. She had snuck up once to the pulpit to look at the great Bible chained there. She'd had to raise herself up on her arms on the pulpit's edge to be of a height to see anything and then only got a glimpse of a square thicke with black shapes in orderly lines like furrows. It seemed a wonder beyond knowing that these shapes should allow anyone with the skill to decipher them understand what another had set down.

"Who's this? They tell me at the mill there are two girls here and a boy."

"Tom, Sir," said Joan.

"Tom, is it. Well, Tom, take care I see you after Matins that you may know the word of God."

"Our Tom is no boy, but a girl, like myself. Tom we call her, but her name is Thomasina, like the old queen's dwarf."

When school began, Tom followed the last boy into church on the quiet and spied on their lesson, and because Tom did so, and to satisfy her own curiosity, Joan did so also. First they said the Lord's Prayer. Then the Curate talked about knowing the word of the Lord. At last he brought out two hornbooks. He named the letters. The boys had to repeat him and put their fingers on the letters as they went. Tom mouthed them as they did. If the boys fidgeted or spoke to one another, they felt the rod.

She snuck in as many days as she could but because she could not let herself be seen, she could not learn what the letters whose names she learned looked like. She told Joan she tried to imagine them. What remained in her memory of her glimpse of the Bible was rows of sticks with bits jutting out, and so "A" she saw as one stick, "B" as a stick on a little crossways stick, "C" as a leaning stick, though soon after this her font of imagination ran dry.

She related to Joan how she tried to watch where the Curate put the hornbook that she might seek for it later. She was crouched behind the last pew and rolled under it as the boys 'gan to leave at dinnertime. She waited for the Curate to follow, and when he had done so, she came out and ventured to the front of the church and there upon a lectern were the hornbooks, upon which she traced the letters with her finger without knowing which letter were which. But soon afterward, the Curate found her spying and thought she was after the boys as some girls are, and adjured her to keep away.

Anno 1608, Ned Hazelwood with the thin head and sloped shoulders was driving their pigge home past Old Nut's hut. The pigge did not like to be ledde and the dog that drove it was a pup. In shorte, the dog could not keep the Pigge from getting into the hut and getting at Old Nut's stores. Back came old Nut making a noise lyke a bellowing cow to scare them off. If you have ever heard the bellow of the Deaf, you know what I mean. Boy and pigge and dog ran off in a terror. A weeke later, the pigge had piglets, two of them stillborne and one with two heads. The boy, his mother came one day bringing with her a crowd including Mary Dance, for Eliza Hazelwood had come with her for similar purpose before, and Joan and Tom came also, and Eliza Hazelwood brought the two-headed piglet, which hadde dyed soon after its birth, for evidence.

"Here is the womanne that didde bewitch our sow," Eliza sayed to the crowd. To Old Nut she said, "You pretend not to be able to heare but I know you hear me and now hear this: we will drive you and the Devill out."

Tom wanted to see the piglet and pushed her way forward. One animal with two heads. Sometimes when they lay together in bed or sat close in church to stay warm, Tom would not be able to tell if the limb on top of her own was hers or Joan's. We are like that pig, she sayed to Joan. They were always together and never apart.

Eliza Hazelwood tried to scratch the face of Old Nut, as Mary Dance had donne before her, but failed, as Old Nut went into a fit. Tom went to find her the next day to check on her, but she was gone. No one saw her for more than a week. Then one day, Eliza Hazelwood was struck with a palsy. "She is back," she swore. "This is the Witch, her doing. She is back." She sent Ned to complayn to the constable, that Old Nut be arrested.

"She is gone," said Tom. "She will not be found."

But Mistress Hazelwood was right. She was back. The constable, the miller from Ringlestone, brought with him three strong men to make the arrest. Old Nut when she saw them tried to run, but was tackled and brought down. She fought and kicked so that it took all four to subdue her and they must tie her hands to her sides, but at last it was done and they kept her in the Hazelwoods' barn until the Magistrate was sent for.

At Old Nut's arrest, Mistress Hazelwood's palsy stopped. Tom and Joan were certayne she had seen for herself that Old Nut was back, for her farm was closest Barrows Wood, and then affected the palsy, but no one cared to listen.

The Magistrate said Old Nut must be examined by three good women of the parish for signs of her pact with the Divell. Old Nut's hut not being constrayned, she was examined in the manor farm. A crowd gathered outside. Tom and Joan and other children tried to look in the windows. The man standing guard shooed them away but forbore to do the same with the women who took their place and called out proceedings to the crowd. There came a shriek from inside.

"'Tis a mouse! And another! Her imps are abandoning her," cried Goodwife Tibbett at the window. Mice ran out from Old Nut as they undressed her.

"The devill's imps," cried the crowd.

"They are her pets," said Tom and Joan, but no one listened. They waited.

"They undress her. They examine her. They have found something. Something on her head, I cannot see."

Tom and Joan looked at each other. They held hands.

"It looks as if . . . I cannot tell. They examine something on her head. She is subdued. She fights them not."

So they heard it later. When they undressed her, two mice had run out from her clothes. The mice could not be caught before they disappeared into the walls. When they removed the scarfe from her Head, they found the Horne, growing out from behind her ear, on the sinister side, with a base the circumference of an apple, and a spiralling down to a point four or five inches below. The horne was counted a great wonder. That the womanne hadde kept it hidde all these yeares and that they hadde not known when they looked at her that under that scarf lay not onlie hair but this monstrosity, too, mayde gulls of them. In their searching, they found three protrusions wherefrom the Divell, his imps may suck, that being stuck with a pin caused no sensation in the witch.

They allowed Old Nut her clothes agayn and made a report to the Magistrate, who came immediately to see the Horn for himself and to question Old Nut. They saw him enter. They waited. Then out came Mistress Dance. "Joan, we have need of you." Joan stepped forward. Tom followed. "Not you, Thomasina."

Inside, the Magistrate sayed to Joan, "I am told you can converse with this miserable creature. She has been brought before me ere this, but in the case of theft, her guilt was clear and went to the assizes. Now

I wish to hear from her if I can." Old Nut looked miserable indeed. She rocked back and forth on a stool, with her arms tucked in and a blind look upon her face. The clothes she wore were rags. In the woods, you did not notice. Her headdress was off. The horn showed if you looked close.

Joan curtseyed. "I know but a few of her signs, my Lord," sayed she.

He nodded. "Does she know the crimes she is charged with?"

Joan did not know how to ask this of Old Nut, but felt she must make some attempt. She stood before Old Nut and knocked on her own head with her mouth open, their sign for Old Nut herself. Old Nut continewed rocking. Joan thumped her chest to say her own name. Old Nut made no show of seeing. Joan took Old Nut's hand in her own and put it on her chest as she thumped again with her other hand. Her hand remained limp until Joan let it go. Joan's heart fled from her so her chest felt hollow.

"She does not respond, my Lord," said Joan.

The constable stepped forward from where he stood and lifted Old Nut's head so her face was to Joan. He kneed her in the back and jerked her head and shouted, "Answer, by God."

The Magistrate waved him down and asked Joan, "Has she reason? Is she an idiot?"

"She is no idiot, my Lord. Her face closes before those she knows not. I have seen it since I was a babe. When she is alone and easie she is not like this."

"The Constable found her wild and intractable and thinks she may be mad. Think you she is mad?"

"No, My Lord."

"Does she deny being a Witch?"

"My Lord, I have never heard her claim to be a Witch, my Lord, nor deny it."

"Ask her now if she deny it."

Joan stood before Old Nut, pointed to her and tried to mimic a witch's hunched stature, the stirring of a cauldron, playacting that seemed to Joan very feeble and without effect. Joan could not even say Old Nut saw her. It was as if she were blind as well as deaf.

"Ask how long she has had the horn."

How long? Joan could not think how to ask such a thing. All she could do was touch the horn, which she was nervous of, remembering the time she had felt it after falling from the apple tree. Joan stroked Old Nut's shoulder first, to let her know she meant the touch gently. Then she tapped the horn lightly. It felt like other horns, hard as bone, onlie stronger. Old Nut neither winced nor pulled away, nor responded in any kind. Joan held up fingers, first one, then two, then three, then ten, to ask how long. This close, she saw Old Nut's ear under her hair, so large and bulbous it resembled a root or a mushroom or a fungus on a tree. Tears flew to Joan's eyes and seized her throat, she could not have said why except that this Old Nut was not her Old Nut, but onlie a shell with nothing in it. For the first time, she feared Eliza Hazelwood and Christopher Dance were right, Old Nut truly was a Witch and in league with the Divell. She feared for her own Soul and for Tom's. Then just as suddenlie her fear was gone and she felt onlie sorrow.

"You say she is no idiot, and not mad, but I fear she is both."

"She is deaf, my Lord, and hard used."

"Joan!" said her aunt.

The Magistrate lifted his eyebrows. "You may go. I will send word if you are needed again."

"I beg your pardon, my Lord," Joan said, and with a humble bow took her leave.

The gathered crowd was eager to hear what Joan might tell them. She told them Old Nut was bound and made no sign, and then she and Tom walked away. "Do you remember, Tom, the day she took Agnes?"

Tom shook her head. "Tell me again."

Joan told Tom the story again of hearing the spade and seeing Old Nut bury the Chapman and enjoyning her to cover Joan's father, all so, and of Old Nut luring Agnes with an apple and leading her away. "You chased after her, shouting and shouting but she turned not. On and on she went, into Barrows Wood and I remembered of a sudden my Nan always said there was a witch lived in Barrows Wood, and I thought certainly this must be she. But you were not afraid. You were in choler because she had tooke our Goat. Then she fed us and made us laugh and I feared no longer. Think you she is a Witch?"

Tom shrugged. "I know not." Then she said, "I think people are afraied of her. It is not the same thing. When you are afraid, you see things that are not there."

"O, Tom. I fear they will convict her and she will hang. Then there will onlie be us two." And the two children put their arms about each other.

In a few days, at the manor house, all concerned were called to give evidence. Joan was present to speak to Old Nut if she could and for her. It was Joan's first time in the manor house. They were in a large room with little furniture, onlie a large table behind which sat the Magistrate on a great Chair and beside it a man with a ledger and quill. Before it stood Old Nut, with a man either side of her standing guard.

"Does the accused know why she is here?" Sir William asked first.

Joan approached Old Nut. Her eyes were turned down to her feet, but Joan sensed she had returned to herself from whence she had gone the few days before. Joan lifted one of Old Nut's hands. She struck herself on the chest to signify who she was. Old Nut did not raise her eyes, so although Joan did her best to ask the question through gesture—a tap on Old Nut to signify "you," a tap on the temple to mean "know," a shrug to mean "why," a circular gesture to signify "here, this place"— Joan could not say if Old Nut knew what was happening.

The Magistrate sighed. "I will hear from those who accuse this woman. Stand forward," he called to them.

Eliza Hazelwood stepped forward, and Mary Dance and Christopher Dance, and three others Joan did not know. She soon learned they were from Bedmonton, beyond Barrows Wood, and the birthplace of Old Nut, who they knew as Mary Grove, and said she and her mother both had been suspected of witchcraft in the death of her father, a labourer, who died under a tree when cutting wood. She was not born deaf, said they, but became so upon being struck by her father at a young age. Mother and daughter sold charms and simples and had caused Milk to sour and Butter not to set. After the mother died, the daughter could not be made to understand enough to work as a maid or labourer, and took to the woods, where she had stayed ever since, which was now two score years. She had, this speaker thought, above fifty years of her age. By and large they had found her harmless. She came by selling nuts and simples as in Wormshill, and did not like being turned away without Milk or Bread, and had twice, not an hour after being so turned away, had soured the Milk she had desired.

Mary Dance then gave her suspicions of Old Nut that she had caused her son to be mute, but told how after she scratched her, he spake not yet, and so she feared to accuse her. Then was she sent away for theft and they thought her gone for good when at last Christopher's tongue unfroze.

Christopher then gave his evidence, that Old Nut had killed his father and cursed him and cast a spell with crow and shovel.

The Magistrate stood up and came around the table. "What does the accused say to these charges?" He stood before Old Nut. "Did you

CURIOSITIES

strike Christopher Dance mute?" Joan held her hand, tapped her, pointed to Christopher, pointed to her shut mouth. This time Old Nut raised her eyes and seemed to follow Joan's finger, but showed no comprehension and gave no answer, even when Joan repeated the question.

"You have been examined," said the Magistrate, "and there were found upon you two mice that fled at your examination. Further, there were found upon you two marks insensible to the prick of a pin, whereby these imps might suckle. What say you to this?"

Now Joan had more to go on for she knew the sign for mouse. But her heart broke, for the onlie time she had used the sign before was to ask to see Old Nut's companions that gave her such joy and to which she showed such tenderness. She gave the sign for mouse and sucked her knuckle to indicate suckling. Tho' she knew it boded not well for Old Nut's fate, yet she hoped that Old Nut continewed her silence. Already Joan's trying to make the Magistrate's words sensible had the feel of betrayal.

"Have you had concourse with the Divell?" asked the Magistrate.

Joan put her fingers at her temples for horns and made a fierce, develish face, then pointed at Old Nut. To her great surprise, Old Nut responded. She drew herself up so she seemed much taller than herself and tugged as if at a coat. Joan guessed she indicated a Gentleman, who bowed. Then she turned as if taking another part, her own part, bowing her head to the Gentleman. Then she took the Gentleman's part again, suddenly pushing against her, knocking her down, and pulling up her skirts.

During this display, the Constable and his men stood uneasily by, for her actions had the look of violence in them. Her breath came loudly and her eyes inflamed as she acted out the scene. She made more crude gestures, and then gave a show of the Gentleman shaking her hand and promising her money. Then she tapped her Horn and twisted her finger to show that it had grown. The devill had come to her and had his way with her and promised her money and from that time had her horn grown.

She brushed herself off and folded her hands and seemed to be done. Now her face had not that closed look, but a defiant one.

Said the Magistrate, "I think that was a confession."

There were further proceedings. The Magistrate asked if there was anyone who wished to speak in Old Nut's favour. William Dorset put forth that she was a good worker come harvest and he did not believe any harm of her. Joan said that she had buried the Chapman and had helped bury Joan's father, that she had cared for Tom and herself when there were none other to do so, and the things she had stole were from those who had no earthly need of them. The Magistrate said yes, he had heard that defense last time and the courts had been merciful. Now was Old Nut remanded to Maidstone gaol to await the Assizes.

Old Nut huddled in the back of the Cart, bound for Maidstone, her hands tied to the side of the cart, her gaze fixed on her hands, her back rounded, her whole shape round, a Nut indeed. A man sat also in the Cart, his legs hanging over the end. The constable drove. Eliza Hazelwood cheered to see them go and Mary Dance looked relieved and Christopher looked older and more like a man. But Tom ran from Joan's side and lept upon the cart and threw her arms around the bent shape, weeping and shouting, and had to be pulled off. Old Nut raised her eyes for the first time and watched them hand Tom to Christopher, who held her wrists. Joan could not say what was in Old Nut's face. The cart trundled out of sight up the Street.

Not long after, Tom's Father came back to the village and carried away Tom, who wished not to go. "You have a Father," cried Joan. "I have none. You must with your Father go."

After Tom left, so soon withal after Old Nut's apprehension, Joan felt as if something had been torn out of her, or that she was half a person, diminished. She, who usually kept up a bright stream of chatter, went quiet, and must swallow tears at every turn. For a moment, when Tom had run from her father, Joan had been in choler that Tom should have a father and not want him, while she had neither father nor mother and wanted them both. "Go with your father," she had shouted. "Go!"

She prayed. A world of woe this surely was.

[*At this point as Joan told me her Tale she never failed to halt for a time, so moved was she by all we must lose in the world when we are born into it. Old Nut was no Witch. This she knew with great clarity. Why then would the old woman pretend she was? It was a mystery she could not crack.*

There is an awful symmetry now, but no mystery: Joan is no witch.
—M. L.]

November drew on cold, the coldest Joan had yet known. Tho' it froze her fingers and toes, she went out into it when any errand was called for so to match her dull spirit to the weather and shiver and let the tears come to her eyes.

One day came Sir Wm Tylden to Yew Tree farm to ask if Joan may be spared to serve at the manor house, an honour not predicted by Mistress Dance, who'd scolded Joan her forthright speech at Old Nut's examination. So went they up to the manor house, Joan with her few belongings, to discuss the terms and sign her name.

Tho' Joan was used to see Sir William and his wyf, Lady Anne Tylden, each week at Church and they were familiar by their presence, they hadde not before this time spoken to her directly, and Mistress Dance had made her fear what missteps she might make in discoursing with them. "Speak only when spoken to," said she a hundred times. "You are prone to chatter."

Lady Tylden was shorter than Joan. Her eyes looked tired. "You are the blacksmith, Nicholas Palmer, his daughter?" sayed she.

"I am, my Lady, he who dug his own Grave that I might not have to."

"Hush, Joan," sayed Mistress Dance. "My Lady did not ask whose grave he dug."

Lady Tylden raised her hand to reassure Mistress Dance.

"All my family died," said Joan, in her litany. "First my—"

"Hush, child, they do not want to hear your list of the dead."

"I am sorry your family was lost to the sickness, God bless their souls," said Lady Tylden, "but Mistress Dance speaks true that a mistress does not wish a servant forever chattering."

Joan ached to say all their names, remembering each one. My mother, my sister, Mary, my brother, Jeffrey, my Nan, oh, even my Nan.

"What skills has the girl?" asked Lady Tylden of Mistress Dance.

"She can make butter and bread and ale and help any way in the kitchen. She can milk and help with the cheese. She knows some simples of the old witch. She can spin and use a needle and a loom. She is quick and tidy, tho' she must learn to hold her tongue for she is inclined to chatter. There is nothing I have tried her at she has not speedily learned. She knows her letters and can read the Bible."

"You spoke for Barrows Mary," said Lady Tylden. "My husband noted you."

Joan knew not what to say to this and took counsel from Mistress Dance and said nothing.

"Well, then, Joan, seeing you are clean and well-spoken and quick, we will take you on. Can you sign your name?"

"I have had no cause before to do so."

"You may make the mark of an X or what have you."

But Joan wished to sign her name. "With what letters mark you Joan?"

So Joan took pen in hand after Lady Tylden had dipped it in ink, and wrote the letters J-o-a-n as the Lady spelled them, and after Joan P-a-l-m-e-r, and was in their employ for a period of one year.

Mistress Dance parted with Joan saying, "Be good, Joan, God bless you."

"We are a small household here, Joan," sayd Lady Tylden, leading Joan thorow the house, and with that, Joan understood Lady Tylden had come from a greater household. "We have onlie two maids of general work, along with my maid, Ellen. The other is Susan, from Faversham, who had been with us two year, and Bess was the other, she has been pressed into service as Nurse since our Nurse quit her place of a sudden, and now you. You will answer to me or to the Cook or to Ellen. Here, put your bundle here with the beds, and I will take you to meet the Cook."

In the Kitchen was a vigorous-looking womanne of middle years, who was the Cook, and also there was Susan, a lean maid with thin cheeks and a ready smile, their faces known to her from Church. Then Susan took Joan about the house to show her what she must know.

On the ground floor were the Hall, with two closets off one side, and across a passage on the other, the Pantry and the Buttery and behind that the Kitchen. Outside was a Garden and a Dairy and an Alehouse and a Store-room built into a hill, and a Privy. Upstairs were two Bed-rooms and the Nursery, which turned School-Room each day, and a Still Room, where Lady Tylden kept necessaries for the health of the household.

From the school room as they passed on their return came the sound of children, their voices, and out the door came at a run the youngest, William, a curly-headed babe who had two years of his age, laughing and squealing. After him ran Bess. "Run not from Bess," said she. This made him run the faster. Bess sighed and lifted her skirts and ran after him.

The family, as Joan knew, hadde six children. Frances and Anne were doubles, of an age with Joan. Joan hadde never been able to tell one from the other. Then two more girls, Jane, who had nine years and Mary, who hadde six, followed by the boys, Richard, four, and William.

Joan was kept busy in the kitchen. She helped Susan to set the table on its trestles for Dinner, and lay the linen upon it, and serve the meal, and brush the linen afterwards and fold it and sweep and forty other tasks, small and large, none of them new but in their location. As they worked, Susan and the Cook asked about Old Nut and Tom and Mistress Dance and her Family, so Joan could tell her Tale. The telling set her somehow in place.

Then told they their own tales. Mistress Shaw, the Cook, her husbannde hadde worked in the ship-yard, and, falling, hadde broke his neck. Then hadde she gone second Cook to another family, wealthier than the Tyldens, but not so antient, and then to the Tyldens. She hadde a sonne who was a saylor, and a daughter, married, in Devonshire.

'Twas strang that night to bed down by the fire in the kitchen, and not in the Dances, their bed. She was so close to her former life—her former lives, in plural, such as they were at Yew Tree Farm, and at Old Nut, her hut in the woods, and at the Smithy with her Mother and Father and Sister and Brother and Nan, which seemed now distant as a dream—but felt miles away, among people whose faces she knew but whose lives she did not.

Joan lay for a time feeling the heat of the fire on her face and the cold against her back, wondering how Tom was and what heaven was like and how fared her family there. Were there houses? Was there winter? Sometimes she dreamed of her mother and father. Sometimes she dreamed of Crows at her father's head. When the cook woke her in the dark, one of the cats had curled into her. "Aren't you a very ember," sayd Joan. The cat mewed in protest when Joan stirred.

"I feel the same," said Joan. But up she rose and went to work, as was her duty.

———

Joan quickly came to like where she was. It lessened her woe to become part of the household. The work was not much greater than what she was used to and Lady Anne was counted a good mistress. She could be sharp and she had days when a black mood settled on her. Then would her words be clipped and they could expect no extra kindnesses. But her good spirits returned in a day or two and she became gentler and more forgiving.

Joan saw that Anne liked to best Frances at her lessons, to be first and quickest at everything, and that Frances did not care but hated her sister to gloat.

She saw that Frances was her mother's shadow and wished always for her favour and pouted if she got it not.

She saw that Little William could not sit still and was either laughing or crying at the top of his lungs and went everywhere at a run. Poor Bess was run ragged chasing after him.

She saw Richard, his brother, was his opposite, quiet and careful.

Mary, like William, fidgeted. Jane watched and tried to get her in trouble.

November was concerned with setting by stores for winter and preserving what the Garden had grown in summer. Joan was sent to gather simples that Lady Tylden made use of in the still room. There was wood to be carted in from where it had cured in the forest, food to be put in cold storage, bedclothes to be aired and repaired, linen to be cleaned for Christmas, &c. Lady Anne's sister was coming. A room must be made ready for her, the whole house spruced up.

Lady Margaret arrived like a warm wind or a little sun. [*Joan gave it in these very words: "a warm wind or a little sun," words that warmed me as I had, unbeknownst, warmed her when young. I remain faithfull to her account.*—M. L.] She was compact in form, younger than Joan expected, closer in age to her nieces than her Sister, and inclined to do as she list. Before the Coachman could lay down a step, she leapt to the ground with a joyous cry of relief after her journey.

A good fire burned brightly in the Hall as they laid the tables. Great cheer and excitement for news. Lady Margaret brought news of home, her father and mother, and others, and of the world that she hadde heard, Christopher Newport back from Virginia with the treasures of that land, &c.

She had gifts for all. Books and baubles for Anne & Frances, toys for the younger children, for her sister thread and fine cloth, for Sir William a hood for his hawks, for the servants ribbands and kerchiefs.

After supper, Lady Margaret and Lady Anne played upon the lute whilst Anne beat a tambour. Sir William danced a turn or two with Frances. Then sang they all together. Joan hadde forgot such conviviality and felt a soreness in her throat at it.

"What of your horned Witch, Brother?" sayed Lady Margaret when they hadde tired of dancing.

"She is ta'en to Maidstone to await the Assizes," sayed he.

"A horn!" sayed she, throwing her hands on her knees and leaning forward. "A horn! Quite a Witch to have so great a sign about her."

"What mean you, Margaret?" said Sir William.

"Only that it is exceeding strang. We have been much taken with discussion about it at home. A dumb womanne with a horn! What creature is this! How came she to have a horn, think you?"

"It grew," said he. "How else?"

"But how? How? It is like to drive me mad! I must know these curious things!"

"Our new maid, Joan, was ta'en in by her after her the sickness robbed her of all," sayed Anne.

"The girl you wrote me of?" Lady Margaret asked of her Sister, "who knew her signs?"

Lady Tylden allowed it was the same girl.

"Let us have her before us, then," said Lady Margaret.

"She is here now. Come forward, Joan."

Joan did so, giving courtesy.

"Tell us all about the Horned Witch," said Lady Margaret. "How did she come to take you in?"

Joan then recounted the sickness and finding Tom in the shed with the goat and Old Nut's stealing it and learning her signs and the whole tale. Lady Margaret asked to see the signs; Joan obliged her.

"Knew you she hadde a horn?"

"'Twere hidde under her cap," sayed Joan.

"Think you she is a witch in truth?"

"I asked her the same question," said Lady Tylden. "Give us your answer, Joan."

"In truth, I know not, my lady," sayed Joan, "but I would not have said so."

"You are more of Mr. Scot's mind than of our sovereign?" said Lady Margaret.

"She knows not Mr. Scot," sayed Lady Tylden. "That will do, Joan."

Joan stepped back.

"Mr. Scot says there are no witches, onlie wronged old women," sayd Lady Margaret. "But whence the *Horn*! This is what bedevils me."

On the morrow, Bess was gone to her parents for a few days, and Joan left the care of the younger children. Jane washed and dressed herself and Richard tried to do the same, but the others must be chased and coddled and tricked and goaded into getting clean before Joan could brush their hair and make them presentable for their Aunt, who was to visit the school room.

Their mother led them in prayer and the Creed, and then they hadde turns in reciting Bible verses. Whenever Jane or Mary faltered, Anne leapt in to supply the missing phrase so that at last her mother must tell her to let them be.

Richard, his verse was very short. "Children, obey your parents in the Lord: for this is right."

"Has William a verse?" asked Lady Margaret, bending over him.

"Amen," sayed William.

"Amen," sayed they all, with laughter.

Now he bobbed up and down crowing Amen like a cockerel and Joan must collect him and take him off to leave the others free to show their learning to Lady Margaret.

She raced him to the door before he could run off and kept him busy all the morning, playing patty-cake, and hide and seek, and hide the button. She let him ride on her back and climb up her front so that he flipped over. She had joy of it but also sorrow, in remembering Tom and Old Nut.

At last William was worn out and beginning to yawn. Joan took him back to the school room to lie down, passing Lady Margaret and Lady Anne on the way.

"They ought to have a tutor," sayed Lady Margaret.

"Sir William will never allow it," sayed Lady Anne. "When Richard and William are of an age will he consider it, but for the girls he will not."

Joan slept in the schoolroom on the trundle rope cot with William, and on the bed above slept Jane and Mary and Richard, and Anne and Frances, while their Aunt took up residence in the room where they regularly slept. The warmth of William, his small body, recalled to Joan even more forcefully what she hadde lost in Tom's departure, what she hadde lost in the death of her family.

When William pissed the bed in the night she was less happy. Now she must wash the linen and restuff the tick. She saw she would have to wake herself up in the night to get William up and help him use the chamber pot.

Lady Margaret kept them all very lively and merry while she was there, and then she departed and days became ordinary again.

When Bess returned after Twelfth Night, Lady Anne called her in together with Joan to say that Joan would continew in the school room, and Bess turn her duties towards Anne and Frances as well as the house at large.

"I wish you joy of William and his piss," said Bess.

From this time was Joan much in the schoolroom and among the children. William was her chief care and she was in and out of the schoolroom with him. Richard, with onlie four years of his age, was more diligent than his sisters Jane and Mary, who continewally broke off their studies to chatter and play.

In the morning, William must stay for prayers and the creed and Bible verses. Afterwards, if he played quietly, he and Joan might remayn as the younger children reviewed their hornbooks, or learned their verses, or tried their hand, or learned a new stitch. If they learned French, or one of them read, they embroidered at the same time. Lady Anne took one or another aside to learn Musick and set Anne and Frances to teach the others. If William became boisterous, Joan must take him out, and so was separated from all she wished to be close to. She wished to learn all that they learned—each letter and verse and stitch, each song and instrument, each language, each number and cipher.

When, as often happened, their Mother were called to some other matter, she left the schoolroom to Anne and Frances. Frances would then act as much like her mother as she was able.

"Now shall we learn French," she would say, then hold out her hand, her foot, point to her knee, her nose, and ask for its name.

"Now shall we conjugate verbs."

Anne, the while, would read on her own, or work at a translation, or try to write poetry, or what she would.

On this day, Frances sayed to Anne, "I will work with Jane, you with Richard and Mary."

"I shall do as I please," sayed Anne.

"Mother wishes us to teach the younger children."

"Frances."

"Anne."

Jane covered her smiling mouth, amused at the discord between her sisters. Mary spun in a circle. Richard sat soberly and whispered to his small clout doll.

Joan had just laid William down to rest. Next she would go to the kitchen.

"Joan," sayed Anne, stopping her. "Know you your letters?"

Joan knew not what to say. She did but she was afraid perhaps she did not. "Well enow."

"Teach you Richard with his hornbook, then," sayed Anne. "And Mary."

"Here is my hornbook," sayed Richard, his face eager and proud. "I know my letters."

They sat on two stools beside the fire. "Show me your letters, then," sayed Joan. "You may draw in the ashes." She passed Mary a small stick. "You first, Mary, then Richard."

Mary drew. "Here is A, the large and the small." Her drawing was large and rough but the shapes were correct.

Joan smoothed the ashes.

"Richard?"

"B," said he, drawing the letter as well as his sister had drawn the A.

So they went, back and forth. When it was not her turn, Mary poked the fire or shuffled her feet for the sound they made.

After they had done the alphabet, Joan saied, "I will be wanted in the kitchen."

"So you will and so must you go," sayed Anne. She sighed and roused herself to take her turn with the children.

Came a day Lady Tylden asked Anne to run the younger children through their letters and Anne objected that she was in the middle of translation and could not Joan do it? "She has been doing it these three days."

"It neither troubles nor surprizes me that she should have it in her to do so," said Lady Tylden, "Mistress Dance spoke true when she saied she was quick to learn. But it troubles me greatly, Anne, that you should in this way shirk your duties."

Anne looked down. "They are well served by Joan," sayed she. "They are better served."

"That may be, but it was left to you."

"But—"

"End now, Anne, before you worsen your state."

Anne apologized. Frances shook her cap in a way that suggested she was pleased Anne had been caught. Lady Tylden set it out that Anne should teach the children herself every day for a week, and set aside her own desires in the meantime. No Lily, no Ovid, no Catullus.

The week after, Lady Tylden allowed that Joan might take a turn with the younger children, and so she continewed, half pupil, half tutor.

Proving herself reliable, resourceful, hard-working and good-natured as well as quick to learn, Joan soon became a favourite of all the household. She aided Lady Tylden in drying simples and preparing salves that they might use for burns or cuts. Her stitches were quick and neat in needlework. The cook liked her in the kitchen for she listened well and had the knack of thinking ahead and providing her with what was needed almost before it was asked for. A favourite of the younger children, she made withal a good audience for Anne to practise her Latin on that she was teaching herself from a book Lady Margaret hadde given her. Frances was easier now that Anne battled not for supremacy in the schoolroom.

Joan grew fond of all the children, William and quiet Richard, and restless Mary and quick Jane. She slept now in the nursery. William woke her each night or she woke him. She helped him find the chamber pot and use it. He fell quickly back to sleep while she stoked the fire. Jane and Mary shared one cot and William and Richard another, while Joan had a low rope cot next them. They oft ended up there, for warmth if nothing else.

In February must Joan travel to Maidstone with Sir William, as magistrate, to testify at the tryall of Old Nut.

Sir William entreated her to ride inside the carriage, so biting the cold. He patted the seat beside him that she should sit, then arranged a blanket over both their knees.

"Well, Joan," sayed he, once she was ensconced. "Are you prepared to give your evidence?"

Joan assented. "Think you," she asked, "she will be convicted?"

"Yea. The evidence against her is fourfold: she had familiars, she has a Divell's teat, she appeared to confess, and she had images for image magic."

"For my part, I venture they were not familiars but pets, and the images but toys as she made for me and Tom."

"Were these pets not strangely comfortable with her? Could it be that what looks to you like a pet might be in fact a familiar? You are wont to speak too freely, Joan."

"I am sorry for it, my Lord."

Here he patted her knee under the blanket, as if in forgiveness, then removed not his hand. Joan stilled. What was this? What should she?

He moved his hand higher, and higher still, up her thigh untill it rested by her hip.

She was still as a mouse when the owl hunts.

His hand moved no further but remayned and remayned and remayned untill it were hard to say what was her hip and what his hand, their warmth being equal. Then would the carriage shift and jostle and make her aware again the hand.

At last, as they drew near Maidstone, he withdrew it, giving no sign it hadde been there, or of anything changed.

They reached Maidstone at midday, the cold nothing abated and took dinner at the inn where Sir William would stay, with enough food withal to take to Old Nut in gaol, where Sir William thought to see her before her tryall on the morrow.

At the gaol, Sir William let the gaoler know they were there to see Barrows Mary, as she was called.

"We are doing brisk trade in the horned woman. You may see it for twopence, touch it for three."

"We pay nothing to see or touch the woman's horn," said Sir William. "She is a woman of my parish and hath been a friend to this girl."

"She? Friend?" said the gaoler. "If you call weasel friend. Or bull-dog. Or bear. She will take a run at you."

"Your pay to keep her comes from me, Sirrah, and to me you will answer."

The gaoler turned obsequious. "Forgive me, my Lord. Jest, my Lord."

He led them through the gaol. "A friend to see you," sayed he to Old Nut.

Old Nut had looked old and ragged in the fall when she had been arrested and examined. Now she looked ancient. She hummed loudly and incessantly, so that the other prisoners hated her for it. She rocked back and forth. She was held in Chains for the way she flew at people. Joan was frightened. The prison was dim and smelled bad and was cold. Their breath turned to vapour in the air and then to frost on their cloaks. They could hear her moans, her rhythmic *ohn-ohn-ohn-ohn* like an unholy chant. The stink of piss and shit assailed them. When they caught sight of her it was of a skeletal creature. The figure huddled and rocked upon straw on the stone floor, a wrist manacled from behind, a rasping of the chain with each rock forward. She shrank from the light of the lanthorn and gave no sign of lunging at them as they had been told she would. Joan knew not what to do. Had the old woman been as she formerly was, Joan would have touched her on knee or shoulder, greeted her with the knock on the head and thump on the chest that signalled their names. Now she feared to touch her at all.

"Hold the light aside that she may see the girl," said Sir William to the gaoler.

He didde, but Old Nut's head was inclined down. Her eyes rose not. After a time, Joan stepped forward.

Joan dared touch the shoulder, a gentle touch. She kept her body ready to leap back. Old Nut waved her left arm to ward her off but it was a weak, slow gesture.

When Joan touched her shoulder, she flinched, drew away, rocked harder. Joan touched her again, more gently, for longer. She stilled. Joan crouched down. She thought Old Nut's eyes came to her. She thought she saw tears. Old Nut rocked harder. Joan then wept.

Joan squeezed Old Nut's shoulder, and made a sign for eating, and showed her the trencher, but her eyes were cast down again and gave no sign of understanding. Joan laid down the trencher.

"Come, Joan," said Sir William. "We can do no more for her."

It was worse to see her like this, thought Joan, than not to see her at all, for to see her like this was to lose what she had been. Joan had to exercise her memory to recall Old Nut bouncing Tom on her knee and laughing her wheezing laugh. This creature was more like a beaten animal than that woman. What, then, was true of Old Nut? Mayhap the Divell had come already to take her soul, she was already in Hell, and what was left was only shell.

Old Nut would be tried at the court house in the morning. Sir William lodged at the inn on High Street and arranged for Joan to have a bed at the home of the aunt of Susan. The aunt had many a question of Old Nut. She hadde been to see the Horn, as had all she knew.

"The gaoler is getting rich off of this," said she.

Soon, neighbours came to call. All hadde questions for Joan about Old Nut. She hadde become a curiosity. Manie were convinced Old Nut were a Witch or some monster of the Divell. Others thought not.

"People do not grow horns for no reason."

"Apart from the horn she seemed like any poor idiot, pathetic and witless."

"She is not witless," cryed Joan.

"Perhaps she has lost her wits since you saw her last."

Joan hadde to allow the truth of that.

Joan was haunted through the night by the sound of the gentle rub of the chains and Old Nut's moaning and the gaoler's goading and the stink and the grievous condition Old Nut was in. She greatly feared the morrow, what lay ahead for Old Nut and herself, that she be obliged again to play a part. Old Nut might be witch, she might indeed, but if she were, Joan was afraid of no witch.

In the morning, Sir William called for her and they walked together to the court house, where crowds drew to see the triall of the Horned Witch.

The room was full. At a table on a raised surface sat the judge and at a smaller table a clerk. Joan saw Mistress Dance and Christopher and Margaret and Mistress Hazelwood and Ned and the women who examined her and the people from Bedmonton. The judge called for charges to be made and the prisoner to be brought forth. Sir William rose, gave the charges, and recounted what had happened when Old Nut was apprehended and examined.

A bailiff was commissioned to bring forth the prisoner, but there was a stir, a rush of murmurs.

"My Lord," said the bailiff. "The prisoner is dead this hour."

Another wave washed through the crowd, gasps and cries. "The Divell calls her to him," cried Mistress Hazelwood.

Her troubles are ended, thought Joan.

Joan had her eye on those from Wormshill assembled. Mistress Hazelwood looked angry, as if she had been cheated, Christopher Dance affrighted, his mother she could not say.

The judge called for quiet. "Her judgement is in the hands of God now," sayed he, and called the next case.

The witnesses and half those gathered passed out into the street. There was an air of disappointment. Tho' the air was bitter cold, yet people lingered in the street to have their say, that her Death was a denial of Justice or enactment of it, an Act of the Divell or a strang accident.

A young man passed through the crowd, advertising, "View the horn of the dead witch afore it is cut off!" A stream of people surged toward the gaol for this purpose.

"Cut off," sayed Joan to Sir William. "What will become of it?"

"Someone will pay for it, I am certayne."

"Has done already," sayed a man nearby, overhearing them. "A gardiner from Meopham, they say, who collects any thing curious."

Joan recalled their discovery, she and Tom, of the horn, and their pledge to tell no one. It was part of Old Nut and should not be cut from her head. "It should be buried with her."

Sir William shrugged. "She has no use of it, nor hadde she in life, come to that. If it pay her burial, a balance has been made."

Old Nut was in God's arms, or the Divell's. That was an end to it.

She would make no return from the grave. Joan was relieved she would play no further role in her hanging. But sad, too, she would make no more sign with her. God rest her.

It gave Joan peace that Old Nut was at rest and feeling no more the stripes and sorrows of this world. She hoped that Tom, reunited with her father, were reconciled to being in her right place, sorrowful as it was to be sundered from her. Now must she face the return to Wormshill and mayhap Sir William, his itinerant hand, on the way. She took her seat in the carriage to be across from him, but he brought himself close. Again the hand edged upward till it rested on her hip. Now it edged inward. She shifted away. He looked out the window. When she had somewhat relaxed her vigilance, he shifted closer. She tensed, but he kept his hand in his own lap. All this was done in silence. From that time, she took care to avoid Sir William as much as she could.

So time passed, Joan in and about the school-room, and part of the household. Once or twice a year did Anne and Frances go to their aunt's, where she gave them as much of the education their father denied them at home as she was able. Bess went with them as their maid, and came back dismissive of their smaller house and complaining of greater work.

Joan now had great facilitie in reading and writing, and had a little Latin. She was quicker than any at ciphering. Lady Tylden enlisted her aid with accompts. Those days when Lady Tylden was in a bilious or lethargic mood and took to her bedroom to spare the household, Joan held sway in the school-room.

The third year of her service at the Tyldens, when Anne and Frances again visited Lady Margaret at their grandfather, his house, one morning was Mary unusually quiet in the schoolroom, her feet not kicking, her voice not humming, until Joan worried enough to feel her forehead, where indeed she found cause for worry.

"My lady," sayed she, seeking out her mistress, "Mary has a fever." Lady Tylden gave the child feverfew and chamomile and put her to bed in the still room.

Joan carried on in the school room but none could settle. Jane kept asking after Mary. Richard grew listless and sullen, and William took Richard's doll so Richard sent up a wail, whereupon Joan plucked the doll back and scolded William, who howled and stamped his little feet and tried to take it back.

"Neither of you shall have it now," said Joan, tucking it into a pocket. "I shall keep it safe, Richard, never fear."

Joan gave up their lessons. They would not learn any more this day. She 'gan to tell a story so that they might settle. "Once a Divell arose out of a fire and spoke to a Smith as he worked the billows."

Settle they did, but before her story was even donne, her fears were come true. Richard hadde begun a-shivering. The fever had come to him. Down to the still room went he.

In the night, when Joan woke as she was wont to put William on the pot, she found the boy hot. "My head hurts, Joan," sayed he.

"Poor boy," sayed Joan. "I will kiss it and pull away the payne. Come you now." She led him to the pot, but he made no water.

"My head hurts, Joan," sayed William again.

Joan sat him on her lap. She stroked his temple, his damp curls, and kissed the top of his head. William continewed restless through the few hours left of night. Before morning, he woke, angery and froward.

She carried him to the still room, where Lady Tylden was just rousing from sleep. "O, not William, not my babe!" sayd she.

"Even he. How do Mary and Richard?"

"They have gone betwixt fever and chills all the night, God have mercy on them."

Now there were three sick, the school room turned sick room, and Jane removed to Anne and Frances's chamber.

The children's fever continewed all that day and grew worse at night. Joan and Ellen took it in turns to sit with the sick so Lady Tylden could rest.

The next morning, Mary was cool, God be praised. By the meridian, she was sitting up and taking broth. But come evening, spots appeared on her face and they knew the fever was the pox.

By the morrow, the spots hadde growne into clear bubbles across Mary's brow and cheeks, not leaving alone her eyelids, neck, arms and legs. Her eyes swelled shut so she could hardlie see. 'Twas piteous to see her cry out to her mother, "Mama, O Mama, I am sorry for my sins, why cannot I see?"

Then did the spots appear on Richard, his smaller bodie, and the same awful transformation proceed.

In the kitchen swooned the Cook of the pox, its first fever, even as she laboured.

The household turned with one mind to care for its sick.

Blisters on Mary, Richard and William disfigured their small faces, then turned to pus. Their fever returned.

Sir William, in despair, cried out to the doctor he must do something, he must let blood, he must do more, but the doctor sayed children had not enough blood for that, he could not.

By nightfall, William's breathing was shallow, and slow, so they strained to hear each breath. Joan held her own breath to listen. Lady Tylden rose up and leaned over her son. She put her cheek to his mouth to feel his breath and waited a long moment.

"William," she cried to rouse him, "William," but he roused not.

He who had been so filled with life, was no more.

"O, my sweet William, my youngest, my joy." She bent over him a long time in sorrow.

Mary whimpered and Joan gave what comfort she could, whispering, "Your brother has gone to God, Mary," while Lady Tylden wept.

The candle flickered.

Richard's breath came shallow and hard. Lady Tylden wiped her eyes and pulled a sheet over William, his face, then turned her care to Richard.

"Fetch Sir William," she sayed to Joan.

Joan ran swiftly through the darkened hall. "What is't?" cried Jane. "Your brother," said Joan.

Sir William was in the Hall by the fire and started up at the sound of Joan's footsteps. "My Lord," said she. He leapt up and pushed past her.

His sorrow filled the still room and spread through the house untill all were awake.

Mother and Father knelt beside Richard, in prayer, as Joan pulled Jane away and sent her back to bed. Then in an hour didde Richard give up the ghost withal.

Sir William carried his heir downstairs himself. Joan brought the body of William. They laid them out on the board.

Lady Tylden and Sir William wept through the night. Now were both their sons dead.

Joan took her grief out of their hearing. "Your tears are no help," sayed Susan. Joan assayed to dry them and went to Mary, her side, where at last she fell asleep. She awoke at dawn after only a short repose and rose to tend the fire and do what hade to be done to start the day. Before they broke their fast, Susan and Lady Tylden washed the bodies and dressed them in clean dress. Joan tended to Mary.

Unthinking, late in the day, Joan put her hand in her pocket. A knob there. Richard, his little clout doll. She must return it to him, he would be so glad—so thought she for the blink of an eye. Then was she rent with sorrow at what the world costs us.

Each time she loved, loss followed. First her mother, in little more than a summer's day. Then the fat Baby filled with laughter, then her stern old Nan, and then Mary, her sister, and Jeffrey, her brother, who played the flute, and then her Father, who dug his own grave. Then Tom to her Father, not Death; and then to Death, Old Nut, a Witch, and now William, who was never stille and Richard, who ever was a sweet and tender Boy, lost forever.

To her, she reminded herself. Lost to her. But in God, his hands.

After a year Joan remembered as a silent one—Lady Anne kept to her closet, Sir William rode out to his brothers, Frances and Anne with their grandfather, Mary at prayer, Jane barely speaking above a whisper—new life followed. Lady Anne gave birth the following summer to another boy, an heir for Sir William, named, in the family tradition, Richard.

In 1615, a letter from Anne brought happy news of Lady Margaret's engagement to Sir Arthur Long, knighted by King James in 1610. Sir Arthur was an ingenios and lively gentleman, who enjoyed his wyf's vigour, and loved to laugh when others were discomfited by her outspokenness. He much indulged her, even to modelling herself on Countess Pembroke and keeping a laboratory in her house, where she wished to found a second Arcadia.

A year later, Lady Margaret was delivered of a stillborn child, a boy, whose loss she and her husband did greatly regret. [*I write this with as much brevity and directness as I can summon, taking Joan, her view of it. But between this paragraph and the next, lies a world, as I have written elsewhere. M. L.*]

The summer following, she invited Anne and Frances to stay with her. Bess having left their service, Joan went with them as maid.

Everything about the place was greater than Wormshill, the house, the park, the gardens, the size of the Hall, the number of rooms, the number of inhabitants. Joan saw now how Sir William, not having wealth on this scale, asserted the worth of his five-hundred-year-old name.

Lady Margaret, who every day liked to go out into the air, hadde recently begun a collection of eggs, and it being the season of nesting, she proposed an outing to gather more of them.

The day they hadde planned for it was windy. Sir Arthur and his friend, Mr. Godolphin, walked with them across the park. Sir Arthur ambled slowly, leaning on his stick. Frances kept pace with them. Lady Margaret and Anne were on ahead, waiting for them, then getting ahead, waiting, then getting ahead. Joan and Sarah, her ladyship's maid, trailed behind, carrying baskets of things that might be needed. The boy had a basket that fitted on his back and a bag slung over his shoulder.

"You are keeping us back, my dear," said Lady Margaret to her husband.

"The nests will wait, my love," said he.

"In this wind, they may fall," said she.

"Is there a note of eagerness in your voice?" said he. "Do you wish them to fall?"

"For the birds' sakes, I wish it not. For my own—'twould lessen the toil of getting 'em."

"Tell me, Frances," said Sir Arthur. "How does your mother?"

"We left her as well as can be hoped for when her time is this near."

"She hopes for a son," said Anne.

"We all hope for sons," said Sir Arthur.

"Do we?" said his wyf.

"We cannot help it, my love. We love our daughters mightily, but a sonne carries our name and our hopes."

"And our daughters carry more sons. It cannot be done without them."

"Some carry all daughters, some all sons, as God wills."

Sir Arthur and his friend turned back at the edge of the woodland.

"Go you not with us, my Lord?" asked Frances.

"Oliver and I would slow the party down. No, you must go on alone. You have Samuel with you and my wife is most capable. Come, my dear, a sweet buss to part us."

Lady Margaret led the way, Anne hard on her heels, following first a broader path through the woods, and then a narrower one so they must go single file, and then off this path to a hornbeam where the first nest was to be found.

"How far do we go?" asked Sarah.

"I know not," said Joan.

"My former mistress never walked further than the gardens," said Sarah.

The wind blew less here. The treetops waved but at ground level it was but a pleasant breeze that kept off the gnats. Up ahead, the boy shinned up a smooth trunk and then angled out to a higher crook where from the ground a small nest, well hidden, was just visible. Off the nest flew an angry Chaffinch and began to swoop near the boy's head. Beside Joan, Sarah dodged her head in sympathy, sucked in her breath, and cried out.

"He is not harmed, Sarah," said Lady Margaret.

Now he was up above the nest and could look down on it.

"Three," he called down.

"She will be all right with two," sayed Lady Margaret.

The boy reached in and took an egg. He popped it in his mouth and climbed down. At the bottom, they all crowded round to see as he popped it out of his mouth again and into his hand. Now the boy opened his basket and Joan saw it was lined with wool. He nestled the egg down into the wool.

"My notebook, Sarah," sayed Lady Margaret.

She retrieved the notebook and pencil for her lady.

"This is Sarah's first time hunting eggs," sayd Lady Margaret to Anne and Frances. To Sarah she sayd, "And I shall need your back withal to write upon."

Sarah gave Joan a look to say, "Is't believable?" and bent her back.

"To be maidservant to me is not as most ladies' maids," said Lady Margaret. "Is't, Sarah?"

"As I learn, my Lady."

Lady Margaret conferred with Simon and made a mark upon a cart to mark the spot. Anne, as ever, stayed as near her aunt as could be, wishing for favour.

They walked on and came to a place of fewer trees, thicker brush and shrubs, which the boy pushed through, Lady Margaret following, waving at the others to stay back.

"Five," said the boy. "Mother's off."

"Come forward one by one to see," sayed Lady Margaret. So stepped forward Anne and poked her head into the greenery. "'Tis a nightingale's nest."

Joan could hear her exclaiming. "On the ground?"

"Out of the way, that is their nesting ground."

Then 'twas Frances's turn. Then called Lady Margaret Sarah to come see it, and then, "Joan, is it?" said Lady Margaret. "Come see, come see."

Joan put her head through the bush and saw on the ground protected by a low shrub a grassy nest and five green-brown eggs. Once she had seen it, Lady Margaret nodded to the boy, and he took an egg, and they all backed out.

"Will they miss it?" Anne asked. "Think you they can count?"

"She will not miss one egg of five," said Lady Margaret.

The next nest was up a hill to a dead tree with a cavity about twenty feet up.

"An owl's nest?" said Joan without thinking.

"Indeed," said Lady Margaret. "Let us search all about it for pellets."
They looked at the foot of the tree all around. "Is this one?" said Frances. She picked it not up. Lady Margaret strode over and plucked it from the ground.

"It is indeed," sayd she. She held it in the palm of her hand. "Look." They all crowded round. It was a little package of fur and bones, so compacted that nothing could be made out with certainty. "Mouse bones."

"Can you get up that tree, Samuel?" said Frances. The tree had no limbs low to the ground, and those higher up were broken off near the trunk.

"I have done it before," said Samuel.

"Not by yourself you haven't," said Lady Margaret. "Sarah, I will need you to give Samuel a leg up."

"A leg up, my Lady?"

Joan stepped forward with her hands already clasped to serve as a stirrup. "I can do it, my Lady," Joan found herself saying.

"A moment. Let us look first for the male," said Lady Margaret. "He oft stands guard nearby."

They all peered up into the trees about them and saw no owl.

"I think we may attempt it," sayd Lady Margaret.

Then Joan stood at the base of the tree and made a stirrup for Samuel so he stepped into her hand. She raised him up, he being light, but high as she could get him, it was not quite enough.

"Here. Step on my shoulder next," said she.

He hesitated.

"I am in earnest. Do't."

So Samuel stepped onto Joan's shoulders. From there he reached up and grasped the dead branch just as it met the trunk, and so pulled himself up, got his foot upon the stub of the branch and rose up so that his head was at the height of the hole. He looked in, and then was Joan's heart in her mouth, for the owl flew out, and she thought the boy would fall. But he had ducked out of her way. Now he had his head in again, and had reached in an arm. The owl swung around and came back for him, but he was already crouched down, and hanging from the branch stub, and dropping to the ground. He popped an egg out of his mouth, and grinned.

"Samuel, you are a wonder!" sayd Lady Margaret.

"I thought she might be in there, my Lady," sayd Samuel. "I was ready for it."

"I thought you'd fall," said Frances.

"I knew he wouldn't," said Anne.

"A wonder he didn't," said Sarah.

The owl's egg was tucked into the basket like the others and they went on, a merry company, thrilled by their encounter.

They stopped for refreshment, finding a sun-dappled copse where Joan spread out the blanket, then visited another three nests, found two more they had not known about, but could not get to, and came back to the house. Once there, Lady Margaret hastened them through into her laboratory, where Samuel unpacked the eggs and laid them on small woollen nests.

"Now," sayd Lady Margaret. "When we have had some rest, we will take their measure, then prick them and blow them out, and then we may paint copies of them."

"It seems a shame to blow them out," said Frances. "They shall never hatch."

"And when they hatch, their eggs are broke. A different shame," sayd Lady Margaret. "I have hatched them in years past. As a girl I did it often. I had three chaffinches, very tame, and a redpoll. But they are hard to keep alive once hatched, it takes constant feeding. I minded not staying up thro' the night when I had twelve years of my age, but now, I stay up onlie for the stars."

Lady Margaret held each egg in her hand, and shook it, and held it to her ear. "If they are too far advanced," sayd she, "they are no good to us, they will spoil."

But all of these were fine. Lady Margaret pricked a hole in either end of each egg, then passed it to Sarah, who put her lips to the hole and blew.

"Harder," said Lady Margaret. "Pass it here."

She took the egg and blew hard on it. Out dripped the innards.

Anne wished to try. Her aunt showed her how to prick the egg. When she went to blow it out, though, her fingers cracked the shell. "Oh," cried she. "Cursed delicate thing."

"'Tis not the egg's fault," said Frances.

"Never mind," said Lady Margaret. "There are more nests, more eggs. There is tomorrow. Let us take the measure of today's eggs."

"O, I am footsore," cried Anne in her room. She fell upon the bed, then her sister beside her. "Joan, help me take off my boots."

Joan unlaced them and drew them gently off, and then her stockings. "You have blisters. Let us soak them."

Frances, too, had blisters upon her feet.

"Have you any, Joan?"

"My boots are old and worn to my foot. I will get you a foot-bath."

Joan went in search of someone to ask about finding a foot-bath or a salve for her mistresses' feet and met Lady Margaret herself ascending the stairs.

"By your leave, my Lady," said Joan. "My mistresses' feet are blistered. Have you a salve that might do for them?"

"I will ask Sarah to bring it you. How fare your own feet?"

"Very well, my Lady, and yours?"

"Very well."

They had, even at that early stage of their acquaintance, a regard for one another beyond cause. Joan courtesied as Lady Margaret passed on.

The next day, Frances's feet being still sore, she wore slippers and stayed within. Anne's feet were as bad but she put her shoes on anyway. Halfway across the park, she could not conceal her limping and Lady Margaret examined her feet then sent her home. Joan made to turn back with her, but Lady Margaret suggested Sarah go instead and Joan keep on.

Now it was just Lady Margaret, Samuel and Joan. They walked companionably, in silence or speech as was meet to the moment, watching the woods around them. Joan was put in mind of Old Nut, her hut in Barrows Wood, the peace of it, the sense of home. She carried a basket for simples. They worked smoothly together, and brought home another six eggs.

They had after that manie outings as the weather was fair. Egg season passed. They visited nests to see how fared the fledglings.

They remained with Lady Margaret and Sir Arthur two months. Other guests joined them for two or three weeks at a time. When they were at home alone they moved into an easie pattern of days. Once Anne and Frances's feet were healed, there were walks, tho' shorter than their egg walk. Joan and Sarah carried stools and paper and brushes for them that they could paint landskips. Once, they went to the sea and collected shells. Once, they went to Maes Knoll, an ancient fort. On foul days they read aloud and composed verse. In the evening, they played musick, and games. At night, Lady Margaret watched the skies, and made notes of the movement of the planets.

One day she worked at some question of planetary movement and was frustrated in her calculations. Sir Arthur could not help her, Frances could not help her, Anne could not help her. "Joan might figure it," said Anne.

"Joan!" cried my Lady.

"Indeed, she is very adept."

Joan was called for and proved able to show Lady Margaret where she had erred. Lady Margaret was astonished. As she began to test Joan to see what else she was capable of, her wonder grew. She then asked Joan to sit by so she should be nearer if needed.

By the end of their time, she had come to feel that Joan was indispensable to her, and put the question to Anne and Frances, and to their mother, whether they might effect a switch, and Sarah go to them, and Joan stay with her, if Joan so wanted. Sarah was amenable, if the wage was the same.

"I find I like to have you near me," sayed Lady Margaret to Joan when she proposed the idea.

Joan found she liked to be near Lady Margaret. She accepted the arrangement.

Then Sarah one morning left word with the cook she was off to be married, and Joan filled her place as well as her own until another could be found.

The household had, that summer, a parade of visitors.

"Tell me," Joan heard Lady Margaret say to each new learned visitor about what it was that interested them, a foreigner, a diplomat, a gardener, an architect, a collector—even the joyners who built her cabinet, she questioned. "Tell me everything."

"Take care, my Lady," said their neighbour and the rector of Chew Magna, H——, "Lest you become a Lady Faustus."

To each visitor, as well, Lady Margaret showed off Joan's mathematickal prowess, to great wonderment.

Early on, Lady Margaret had asked of Joan her parentage, and Joan had told her of her father, the Smith, who dug his own grave, and mother, who had died so swiftly, and her baby brother, her sharp Nan, her sweet sister, her brother who played the flute.

Lady Margaret said nothing then, but later she could not hold back her conviction. "I cannot credit you are born so low," she sayed, "a blacksmith only, for a father. You must be the bastard offspring of some Kentish gentleman."

"Begging your ladyship's pardon," Joan would say, "I know my parents to be mine own."

"But you have such facilitie in all things, music and physick and algebra."

"And you are a woman and have facilitie in all things," said Joan in reply.

"No, that is not what I mean. Your speech is gentile and your manner withal. I can make no sense of it."

"My father is a Smith, who dug his own grave that I may not have to," said Joan hotly.

"No. No. I am convinced your parentage is better than you know."

"I tell you it is not."

Lady Margaret gave up open dispute for the moment, but Joan could see her mind was fixed.

In fall, they repayred to Sir Arthur's house in London, but stayed not long, for Lady Margaret was again with child. A daughter, born on Epiphany, brought great joy and hope to her parents, and then an equal sorrow and disappointment, for she lived onlie a fortnight. Lady Margaret was plunged into despair. Given the buoyant womanne she hadde been, Joan would not have thought it possible Lady Margaret should sink so deeply. Sir Arthur, too, was deeply affected. Lady Margaret did not rise from her bed, but for Sundays to go to Church, for six weeks. Sir Arthur came and sat with her for a portion of each day. Joan attended her faithfully. No visitors came to the house, apart from neighbours to meet with Sir Arthur, and two of Lady Margaret's sisters, each of whom came for some weeks, each of whom had lost their own children and knew the greatness of the loss. She wished to hear no Musick, no reading, no calculations. She would not look at the Moon or through the telescope. She painted nothing, sang nothing, and barely ate. "Why should I live when my child lives not," she said.

Sir Arthur found his patience running thin. "My dear, let us get another child."

Some days to this she would argew. Other days she cursed herself. "Why am I not like my sisters, who accept their fate, mourn, and rise from their beds to live again. I am not right. I am not right at all. I have been too proud, too vain, to think that my Child should live when others live not. But it should, it should, O, it should. My Childe should live!"

Joan kept by her, listening when she wished to speak, speaking not when she spoke not, encouraging her to take some broth.

At last, in Lent, she came back one Sunday from Church and lay not down again, but took dinner in the dining room, and afterward surveyed her Eggs and turned her mind to Spring. Then followed a summer very like the one before. In the fall, Lady Margaret stayed in the country when Sir Arthur went to London, for she could not be in London a year later with no child in her womb where had been one before.

He returned to her at Christmastime, but their happiness was short-lived, for at suppar, Sir Arthur, his heart failed him, and he died at table.

Now was Lady Margaret's grief greater than before. She stirred not out of her room. Her mother came. Her sisters came. Her nieces came. Her friends came. No one could pull her from her Darkness.

Even Spring could not draw her from her Bed, even the Birds, and their Eggs, even the Stars and Moon.

Joan sat by her side, listened while she railed and wailed, when she called on Death and cursed it that it would not come, sat when she was all in lassitude and cared for nothing.

Joan, meanwhile, served as emissary between her Mistress and the rest of the household. She conferred with the Steward and dragged what answers he needed from Lady Margaret out of her. She conferred with Cook, Gardiner, Groom, and Gameskeeper. The house was quiet. The footmen had nothing to do. Lady Margaret bid Joan dismiss them, they reminded her of Sir Arthur. Joan sent them away with a full purse.

Joan each day gave her Mistress account of what she could—the weather, what news from the household and village, what she had read, any small thing that might in former days have interested her. She read aloud her letters, and scribed them in return.

One day near mid-somer, Joan came back to Lady Margaret, her chamber, with a tray, to find her lady up and dressing her self. She had opened the shutters, she had opened the window. Birdsong came.

"Since Death will not have me," said Lady Margaret, "I return to the World."

"It welcomes you, my Lady," said Joan.

Life resumed, as it will do, even when we are wearie of it. Visitors returned to Longwood, and Musick, and Philosophy. Lady Margaret tracked the Stars.

In the fall, Joan woke one cold night. "Joan," Lady Margaret called from her room, "I am cold. Come warm me."

Joan rose and stoked the fire.

"Come," said her lady again. "The fire is not enough, I must have human warmth."

Joan her self was cold, the warmth of Lady Margaret, who lifted the covers, and tucked them around her, immediate. "There. That's better."

This custom continued even when the nights warmed. "Come, Joan, you will be more comfortable here," Lady Margaret would say, or "Come, give me your warmth."

They were at that time reading *De Magnete*, by Gilbert, one of Sir Arthur's last gifts to his wife. Joan's Latin had been learnt off the coattails of Anne when chance had it. Therefore their pattern was that Joan read aloud and attempt translation, while Lady Margaret supplemented and augmented until they both had understanding of it.

On a clear night, Lady Margaret wished to see for herself the variation between the north star and the magnet's north. Out they went, sighted the North Star.

"Align your bodie thus that your arm points to it," said Lady Margaret to Joan. "And Simon, hold the lantern so I may see the compass. And I will stand beside Mistress Palmer so we are almost as near as one point of origin, see, like this, and turn, and there between the point of our two sets of fingers lies the difference."

So they stood, their outstretched hands six degrees apart, as Simon measured it, Lady Margaret's back against Joan's front. Joan's breath blew across Lady Margaret's hair like the gentlest wind.

When they stepped apart, that feeling of being joined lingered, enlivened their skin as in a perpetual electrick charge.

When they had regained their chamber, Lady Margaret drew near and said, "I am strangely drawn to you, Joan, as if our bodies were very magnets."

"We perform our own Experiment," said Joan.

"My lips are drawn to your lips," said Lady Margaret. And with that she laid her lips upon Joan's. They were cool and soft and the magnetism betwixt them drew them together. The magnetism extended to their whole bodies, drawn together. Joan had never felt the like.

Later, she lay in the warmth generated by their two bodies, awash in wonder, at the stars, at the magnetic earth, at the two of them, what they had done for each other, what it was given them to feel.

Anne's Note

I break the story at this curious and wondrous moment—why, in a defence of Joan, recount the magnetism between the two of them?—to introduce a separate but, as will later become apparent, related tale.

The self-styled "confession" of John Heard comes to us through John Aubrey.

I don't remember how I came to Aubrey himself. He was just everywhere mentioned in materials from and about the seventeenth century.

How did I come to the seventeenth century? That's a bigger question.

Maybe it starts with *Rats, Lice and History*, the first book of popular history I read. It was recommended to me by my grade eleven ancient history teacher, he of the short stature, long hair, daily baseball shirts, immense vocalized yawns, captivating lectures on Solon and Pericles, essay topics like "Gory Deaths in the Iliad," and single-question three-hour exams (which I revelled in). Malcolm.

I loved the book as much as Malcolm did, and probably for the same reasons (though I hear now that some parts of the book have been discredited). It's history through the back door. Just as I love the way a train takes you along the edge of people's backyards and shows you what they hide from the front, I loved the encounters not with generals and prime ministers and battles but with latrines and rats. From antiquity until the Franco-Prussian War of 1870, the book says, disease killed more combatants than battle did. Wars were won and lost not by leaders but by cholera and plague and all the other afflictions of the time. The book showed that everyday life—hygiene, our understanding of science—matters in what we think of as grand historical events.

My grade twelve history class was great, too. What seventeen-year-old doesn't love the study of revolutions? But after I graduated, my interests changed. I did a year in music education at the University of Toronto before deciding I would be a bad music teacher, and a year in geography at the University of Waterloo before realizing the love of drumlins and eskers can only take you so far. I completed an English degree because I was reading the books anyway and might as well get the credit. I worked in outdoor education. Started art projects I never finished. Took a drawing course at the Art Gallery of Ontario that I never finished. Tried to teach myself to paint—and gave up after "Carpet Man," whose torso resembled purplish pile more than skin (I'd run out of red paint). Also, my girlfriend at the time—the word we used in 1980s lesbian argot was "lover"—was a real artist, and although she was supportive of me, it seemed pointless to make badly proportioned out-of-perspective drawings when good art was so close to hand.

I applied to do a master's in linguistics but didn't get into the program because my second language wasn't good enough.

Even as I write this list, I realize: I am a dilettante. Like John Aubrey. "Dilettante" is the word I use to describe Aubrey to people who have not heard of him: someone who dabbles, someone whose enthusiasm waxes and spurs him to activity, then wanes before completion.

Huh.

Well, let's skip a number of years (in which I meet my beloved, move to Vancouver to do my master's degree—where, after much debate, my beloved joins me—then go back to Toronto with her, where she does her own master's degree) and arrive at the time when I visit that first girlfriend in New Jersey, at Rutgers, where she's doing *her* MFA. It is there that I pluck from her shelves *Mr. Wilson's Cabinet of Wonder* by Lawrence Weschler. What a beautiful and strange little book Weschler builds around Wilson, curator of the Museum of Jurassic Technology in California—a gnomic fellow who created exhibits that mixed the fabulous and fictional with the real so that it was difficult to know which was which. For example, an exhibit on stink ant fungus (real) might lead to an exhibit on a neurophysiologist (fictional) and his theory of memory (*Obliscence: Theories of Forgetting and the Problem of Matter*). This attention to how knowledge is displayed, and how that affects what we take as true or factual, suggests the world is always more wonderful than we know, more surprising and awe-inspiring.

This book was a revelation to me, and it rekindled my dormant love of hidden histories. It also introduced me to collectors of curiosities generally—and to John Tradescant, in particular, as well as Leiden anatomist Frederik Ruysch, who made memento mori dioramas out of fetal skeletons and other anatomical matter.

What was delightful about Tradescant was the mix of items in his collection. He had miniature scenes carved out of peach pits, he had whale bones, and shells, and different eggs, including "one given for a Dragons Egge" and "Easter Egges of the Patriarchs of Jerusalem." He had beavers' testicles, fossils, rocks, gems, spleen stones, and a cherry pit featuring St. George and the dragon "perfectly cut" on one side, while the other showed eighty-eight faces of emperors.

As I went further into Tradescant's world, moving beyond the rarities of his Ark to his own writings, I fell harder for him, and for the extravagance of his spelling. Witness "A Viag of Ambusad" (A Voyage of Embassy), which is his record of a trip to Russia with Sir Dudley Digges on which "we had sighte of a great whight Fishe twse so great as a Porpos, being all over as white as snowe, wh'che they say is a great destroyer of the Salmons." I'm guessing they saw a beluga.

I began to think about writing a novel that would feature Tradescant, and maybe also Ruysch, though he lived nearly half a century later. I scrupulously avoided novels already written about him.

This meant more research on the Tradescants and their era, and this led, inevitably, to John Aubrey. I discovered that Aubrey was much more charming than Tradescant. (Ole Wurm—someone I also considered fictionalizing, for his name alone—once called the elder Tradescant an idiot.)

Aubrey is best known for *Brief Lives*, a book never intended to be a book but notes to assist Aubrey's friend, Anthony Wood, assemble a tome chronicling famous Oxford men. Aubrey began to collect first-hand—or second- or third-hand—oral histories of any man from the previous hundred and fifty years who was in any way notable. Aubrey had a huge acquaintance. He made a point of knowing *everybody*. A contemporary once said he would break his neck running down the stairs after people he wanted to talk to. He lived for company—which was just as well, given that he was forced to throw himself on the mercy of others for most of his life. As a result, *Brief Lives* is a treasure trove of anecdote and cross-reference.

My copy of John Aubrey's *Brief Lives* is inscribed, "Bet, dear, I do hope you will love him as much as I do, Elizabeth"— which makes me want to know Bet and Elizabeth, and confirms that there is a coterie of people who love John Aubrey. When I first started my research, with the haphazardness of autodidacticism, I could not find anyone on the internet who called themselves a John Aubrey scholar the way someone might be a John Donne scholar or a Philip Sidney scholar. Despite gleaning boatloads of general knowledge about the seventeenth century from his work, scholars didn't take him seriously. But the tide is turning. Recently, I've become aware of two.

Aubrey was peripatetic, always moving. He endeavoured to keep his papers together, but he also wanted other people to do the work of revising, filling in the many gaps he left when he didn't know a date or a fact, readying them for publication. There are, as we know, writers who love the act of composition and can't stand to revise; and then there are writers for whom composing is like, as my screenwriting prof once described a particularly dull book, pulling a rusty chain through your ears, but who find revision a joy. I am the latter, Aubrey the former.

Aubrey hoped that other people would take his notes and put them in order, make sense of them. Which they did in many instances—it just took a couple hundred years.

In short, around this time of research and discovery, I began to think that Aubrey should feature in my novel somehow. Maybe he would be the narrator. So I threw myself into Aubrey manuscripts. Most have been made available on "Early English Books Online," and many are in libraries. A notable portion of his papers—the ones he himself gave to the Ashmolean—are now lodged in the Bodleian Library at Oxford.

Initially, I thought I would write in Aubrey's fictionalized voice. But his own language is so much more apt than any approximation I could come up with. Who can compete with (opening the book at random) this entry, about Sir William Fleetwood, Recorder of London in the 1570s?

He was a very severe Hanger of Highwaymen, so that the Fraternity were resolved to make an example of him, which they executed in this manner. They lay in wayte for him not far from Tyburne, as he was to come from his House in Bucks ; had a Halter in readiness ; brought him under the Gallowes, fastned the rope about his neck and on the Tree, his hands tied behind him (and servants bound) and then left him to the Mercy of his Horse, which he called Ball. So he cryed, Ho Ball. Ho, Ball—and it pleased God that his horse stood still till somebody came along, which was half a quarter of an hour or more. He ordered that this Horse should be kept as long as he would live, and it was so ; he lived till 1646.

One day goeing on foote to Guild-hall with his Clarke behind him, he was surprised in Cheapside with a sudden and violent Loosenesse, neer the Standard. He turned up his breech against the Standard and bade his man hide his face; For they shall never see my Arse again, sayd he.

Highwaymen hanging their hanger? A horse named Ball? "A sudden and violent Loosenesse"? Aubrey was so much better than any approximation I could attempt. Aubrey was backdoor. Aubrey was *Rats, Lice and History*. Aubrey knew people are funny. People are weird. People have diarrhea.

Then I had the idea to build a book using Aubrey's own words. I was already reading everything by Aubrey I could get my hands on, and now added biographies and papers, including *John Aubrey and His Friends*, by Anthony Powell. This work inspired me to find out more about those friends, including Sir James Long, of Draycot Cerne, with whom Aubrey was regularly "delitescent," as he says. (The language of the seventeenth century!)

Despite Aubrey's Wiltshire origins, there isn't much on him in the Wiltshire and Swindon History Centre archives. But that is where, as I mentioned earlier, I found material on Sir James Long, and it is also where I stumbled upon Lady Margaret Long.

Something I find delightful about seventeenth-century memoirs is the way they begin with the author's parentage and birth, breeze through childhood and youth, and hop about indiscriminately through the writer's life up to the point of writing.

Look at Aubrey, for example. He wrote that he wished to have his tale "interponed as a sheet of wast paper only at the binding of a booke":

This person's life is more remarqueable in an Astrologicall respect, then for any advancement of learning, having, from his birth (till of late yeares) been labouring under a crowd of ill directions—for his escapes of many dangers in journeys both by land and water.

He was borne at Easton Pierse, (a hamlet in the parish of Kington Saint Michael,) in the hundred of Malmesbury, in the countie of Wilts, (his Mother s inheritance, D. and H. of Mr. Isaac Lyte), March the 12, (St. Gregories day,) A.D. 1625, about sun-riseing ; being very weak, and like to dye, that he was christned before morning prayer.

Compare, now, Lady Margaret's memoir: "In 1590 my dear Mother's time came at the height of a Thunderstorm in mid-somer. With a very Clappe of Thunder was I born at seven o'clock in the evening, a lucky hour, near Fulking, in Sussex."

How might my own memoir begin?

She was born in Weston, Ontario, a suburb of Toronto, to . . .

Well, no. I don't want to get into that. Too complicated. Birth, adoption, etc.

Even "she." Sure. Yeah. It works. It's fine. But also: it's not that simple.

Back to Aubrey, and the next remarkable discovery: The Confession of John Heard.

The Confession of John Heard was found in 1981 by a woman named Monica Weaver in a private home in Dorset. It might have made a huge sensation in early modern history circles and witchcraft studies had it not been almost imme-diately discredited as a forgery by the lecturer at the Univer-sity of Exeter to whom she took it. Once that pronouncement was made, no one else wanted to stake their reputation on its authenticity, though two different feminist scholars of the eighties suggested that, while assuredly fictional, the tale might have been penned by Aphra Behn or Daniel Defoe.

Weaver left her papers, including the Confession, to Cecil Williamson at the Museum of Witchcraft (now the Museum of Witchcraft and Magic) in Cornwall, where it still resides, having survived the town's flood in 2004, and where I discovered it in 2010. I don't know that anyone had read the whole thing since 1988. My initial excitement after a quick skim at the museum stemmed from its mention of Tradescant. Heard had been at school with John Tradescant the Younger! It was too long to read in the afternoon I had at the museum. I got permission from the director to copy the manuscript to read at my leisure. To my embarrassment now, given what the manuscript covers, I only read about half of it then. The bits with Tradescant in them.

There was nothing whatsoever to link the Confession with John Aubrey.

For a time, Aubrey lived with his friend, Edmund Wyld, in London. His estates were entailed in lawsuits and as a result, he had no home. He was running from creditors frequently, and there were periods when he had to keep his whereabouts under wraps. This, I think, is why his papers are as scattered as they are. He managed to have an uproarious time nonetheless. One scene he happily recounted was a dinner during which Wyld filled a dish with earth and put it atop a brazier and sowed it with seeds, claiming they would grow over the course of supper. Such seeds would normally take weeks to germinate, and Aubrey marvelled over this trick. I was reminded of this scene the other day when I read about people germinating seeds in their Instant Pots. In any case, Aubrey liked nothing better than to hang out with his friends, eating and drinking and arguing and telling stories—and then writing them down, as he says in one of my favourite turns of phrase, "tumultuarily, as if spilled from a sack."

The discovery of the lost Aubrey notes below and the letter that accompanies them was serendipitous. They were interponed in a copy of *Theophania* belonging to Dorothy ("Dolly") Long, wife of Sir James Long, lodged in the library at South Wraxall Manor, where it was found by another amateur Aubrey enthusiast I had begun a correspondence with, Carlyle Bing, in 2018.

Bing forwarded them to me. That's when I realized I had to read the rest of The Confession of John Heard. When I did, my head spun. But you will see what I mean.

Herewith: The Confession of John Heard replete with headnote from John Aubrey—and then, a third tale.

The True Confession of John Heard

Aubrey's Introduction

Wyld, et al, returning from a Tavern, were full of the tale they had of an old Man at the Three Bells. They told me the outline of his history, upon hearing the which I declared I must find this man and hear for myself, for he hadde bin in Bavaria, witch-hunting, and had known a Witch to make a mans Member disappear.

Was he a reputable Man? asked I.

He hadde been, they said, a Curate in Somerset, but now he told his tale for Drink. Each day sought he someone new to tell it to if they would keep him drinking all the while he told it. If I wanted, I should find him easilie enough, at the Inn.

There I went and there I found him, a slender Man, shrunken with age, rheumy-eyed, but clear of Tongue. I had expected a Rogue but found something closer to a Gentleman. He was clean in his person, and quick in his wit. I would have called him sober had he not spent all the day drinking. I never saw the Drink affect him, nay, not so much as to make him unsteady as he stood to piss or to cause his Tongue to slur or slip.

I put down his Tale in outline, that it not be lost, and then, pity me, lost it, along with another Packet that held many outlines.

Some year or two later, came word from Wyld—I was now delitescent in Kent with Sir J.—saying a Package had come to me. I could not at that time easily receive it, living in fear of my Creditors, so it was longer still before I was able to collect it. It contayned two lengthy Discourses. One was titled "The True Confession of John Heard," with a note addressed to me, in Heard's hand, that said, "The Tale I told was only a small part of the Truth, which now that I am Dead—for if you hold this in your hands, so I am—must be told."

The other was a letter that had been received by Heard—accompanied by another brief note in Heard's hand, saying, "I got not this letter untill too late."

Both I will relate to you now, first Heard's, then the stranger's letter.

The True Confession of John Heard

*J*WAS BORN IN 1609 IN the parish of Fynchley, fifth child of my
Father, a sadler, and third of my Mother, his second Wife, two
of us living. We were a Godlie Familiy, and I was a fervent Childe, in
awe of my Father and attacht to my Mother.

One fall morning when I had five or six years of my age, my mother
sent me to borrow yeast of a neighbour. The day was misty and wet,
there was a hill to climb, and I liked not the errand, preferring to stay
home while Mother sent our servant, Mary. But Mary was needed and
I was not and so I was sent. The road was muddy and I balanced along
a drier ridge on its edge as I walked the short distance to Goodwife
Brown's cottage. As I turned in there, I saw next door a tall Man, a
stranger to me, clad all in Black, standing at the door, awaiting admit-
tance. He turned his gaze on me with a strang intensity. My stomach
went cold, a round of ice in my entrails with a burning coldness, growing as if to take over my whole being, like nothing I have felt before or
since. I was frozen under his gaze. Then the door behind him opened,
he turned away from me, and entered the house of Goodwife Fellowes,
disappearing from my sight. Immediately, the ice in my stomach
lessened in severity, tho' it spread yet, so that when Goodwife Browne

answered her door, my teeth chattered as I told her my errand and I shivered all over. "Poor John," said she. "'Tis not so cold as that, is it?" Indeed it was not. She drew me in by the fire.

I thought to ask Mistress Browne if she knew Goodwife Fellowes, her visitor, but when I opened my mouth so to do, the shivering grew so violent that I could say nought. I had a certayntie then that the man I had seen was the Divell. I had an equal certayntie he had a greater power than I had yet known, yea tho' I had been warned of his Power every day of my life.

Mistresse Browne wrapped me in a blanket till I was warm, and filled my cup with yeast to take home to my mother. "You have an ague," she said, but I did not think so, it had not the feel of an ague but of something different, and when I was warm agayn, it was gone completely. "Run home quick now," said Goodwife Browne and run I did, not even so much as looking at Goodwife Fellowes, her place. From her yard came a great barking so I had no choice but to see where it came from and there was a black Dog charging forward. I took to my heels. The dog came following after, not ceasing its noyse. I screamed as I ran, forgetting to keep to the sides of the road where it was dryer and slipping and squelching in the muck so that I lost a shoe. I leapt up and ran on, straight into the house, slamming the door, panting and crying. "The Divell is after me," said I. "The Divell is after me in the form of a black Dog."

Immediately my mother opened the door. "No," shouted I. "You will let him in!" But she stuck her head out into the road.

"There is no Divell," said she, "nor no dog neither."

"There was," insisted I.

"A Dogge I heard," said my mother, "and I see that you are well and truly affrighted. But whatever was there is gone now. You need not fear." She embraced and soothed me and wiped the tears from my cheeks untill I could tell her my tale, but I would not go out to retrieve my shoe, tho' I were punished for it, as of necessity, I was. At last Mary was sent to fetch the shoe. For punishment, I must clean it untill it was like new.

That night as I lay in bed there came from the woods beyond the fields wild raucous cries, laughter and a tambour. The ice grew agayn in my stomach. "Hear you that?" I asked my sister.

"It is the wind," said she.

"Listen closer," said I. "A woman cries and moans."

"It is the alehouse," said she. Goodwife Fellowes, her sister kept the alehouse.

Now I listened closer. The more I listened, the more certaine was I the sound came from the wood. At last my sister allowed it did seem to come from the wood. The two of us grew more and more afraid.

We heard it again manie nights. It would stop, suddenly, and seem to have ended and then take up again an hour or two later. But it never started up when someone other than my sister or my self were in the room.

That first night, we called out to our mother, who came and sat with us, but heard nothing, untill at last we fell asleep. Once or twice a month it came. We tried my mother and my brother and when they were there, no sound came at all. But when they left it started up as if it knew. I thought the witches and the Divell wanted me. The Divell, I knew, sought out those who were weak. And I knew, even had not my father and my brother repeated it ad nauseum, that I was weak.

Our way to Church and into town took us past Goodwife Fellowes, her house, where she and her children spilled out the door. Her husband hardlie came to church, preferring to pay a fine to getting out of bed on the Lord's Day. I marvelled that Goodwife Fellowes should come to church after consorting with the Divell, but come she didde. Her face looked haggard, her eyes ringed with fatigue, her mouth set with malice. Before she emerged we heard her yelling at her husband,

Sam Fellowes, and cuffing her Idiot son, named Samuel after his Father. "Hurry, Sam. Look, here is Susan Heard."

"Susan Heard," said the Idiot. "Susan Heard, will you marry me?" This he said every time he saw my sister. She was then a pretty girl of seven or eight and Sam a boy of fourteen.

"You know I will not," said Susan.

"Stop your mouth, Sam," said his mother. "I said her name to get you moving. You're not like to marry anyone." When he looked dismayed and ready to weep, she softened. "Susan is too young to think of marriage."

The other children laughed at Sam and taunted him. Sam loves Susan, Sam loves Susan.

"Good day to you, Mistress Fellowes," my Mother said, my Father and brother having gone on before. "God save you this Day of our Lord."

Mistress Fellowes wished them good day in return. The weather was windy and fair. "Who was your visitor yesterday?" my mother asked.

"I had no visitor," said she.

"John saw a man at your door," replied my mother.

"I care not what John saw," she saied tartly. "I had no visitor." Her response, thought I, was sharper than if she had genuinely had no visitor. This was not truth but flat denial of the truth.

"A gentleman in black. With a black Dog."

"'Tis a phantasy of John's," said Mistress Fellowes. "I know none of that description."

My sister and I stood close and held hands. "It is no fantsy," said I. "I saw him as plain as you."

"I had no visitor," she sayed again with a cold, hard stare.

I could tell my mother liked not that imputation that I was fancifull and made things up but she hushed me and told me to respect my elders. "Come, children. Let us turn our minds to our Lord and his blessings this day."

My mother taught me my letters at home, and when I had six years of my age, I went to a petty school to learn enough grammar that I might be admitted later to grammar school. For this school, I must go through the town, to the church. At school and in the streets the children jeered at me, I knew not why. When they called me names, I ran, and when I ran, they gave chase, and when they gave chase, I cried, and when I cried, they jeered. Earwig, they called me, for my long legs and short bodie. "Here comes Earwig, boys. Nasty bug. Crush him." They did little more than trip me or knock me down or frighten me in other ways, tell me that the Divell was a black dog coming to get me, or take a grasshopper or worm and put it down my shirt. Each day coming and going was a torment.

My father sayed you must not show them you are frightened, but walk calmly through, thinking of Christ, Our Lord's example. "You have been blessed with a trial like that of Our Lord's," sayed my father. "Bear it as He bore it."

"Watch out. He will bore into your brain," sayed one boy as another held my head down and put an earwig in my ear. I was frightened to tears. I shrieked and panicked. The feeling of the earwig was hideous, but the fright was more aweful, for I was certain it would enter my brain and kill me.

When I got home, it was not even in there anymore, but I thought it was. I would wake up in the night, screaming. My mother went to talk to the mother of the boy who had done it. He was beaten as was right, but he only hated me more. The witch was his aunt.

Though he counted it wrong what the boys had done, I embarrassed my father by my weakness. My brother, the youngest child of my father's first marriage, who had then eighteen years of his age and was apprenticing to my father, would have taught me to fight, but my father said I must live by the example of our Lord and turn the other cheek. I must think how He bore a crown of thorns without complaint, to which a bug in the ear was nought. I must pray for strength and not shout out in the night and run to my mother.

My father smelled of leather, and spoke little. My brother said hours could go by in the shop without a word from him. He prayed in the morning and read the Bible to us—his Bible was his proudest possession—and did the same at night. He was tall and had a deep booming voice. I cannot remember him laughing.

In secret did my brother teach me to fight, or tried. I was not an apt pupil. I seemed to know how to move only towards a fist, not away from one. He had me draw myself up by a rope he'd hung from the hayloft to strengthen my arms. He stuffed a sack with straw and had me hit it with all my strength. I did not like to, but he taunted me to rouse my anger so at last I struck out. At this moment, our father discovered us, and somehow, as ever, it went harder for me than my brother, who my father always seemed to excuse.

A year or two after I saw the Divell and began hearing the witches' cries, it happened that Sam Fellowes, the younger, began to come to our house and ask for Susan and pester her. My mother must go to Goodwife Fellowes and ask her to keep Sam home. "He does no harm," said she. "I cannot watch him every hour."

"You must keep him busy," said my mother.

Goodwife Fellowes scoffed. "I'd like to see you do better," said she.

Sam would stop coming for a while and then he would start again. After some time, he began to make lewd gestures towards my Sister. One day we were passing and Sam did not call out from his yard though he was there. I was relieved but then he made a loud panting noise and we could see he was busy between his legs and then he called out Susan's name.

Our mother hurried us home, where she left us, and went back to Mistress Fellowes to say she must controll her son, he was become a danger to Susan. An hour or two after she hadde come home, my sister was taken with a violent shaking and strang convulsions and thus we knew that Goodwife Fellowes had had her revenge upon my Mother through witchcraft.

My Mother recalled my Father and older Brothers from their workshop. We gathered together and prayed and my sister's convulsions were stilled. My father met with others in the town who had complaints of the family. Other children hadde been harmed. Goodwife Fellowes' husband, a Carter, was a drunkard and alwaies at his sister's alehouse.

My sister's convulsions ceased, but she languished, and in a week, she died, through Mistress Fellowes, her sorcery. We took our case to the Constable and the Magistrate and Mistress Fellowes was found guilty of witchcraft and hanged.

In her confession, she admitted it was true that the Divell came to her on that day I saw a visitor at her door, that she was in her extremitie with care for her idiot son and her errant husband. She misliked the scorn of her neighbours for her and her sonne and in choler agreed to consign her soul to the Divell for the power to get back at her enemies and gain her heart's desire.

After her hanging, I heard the wild cries no more.

At the hanging itself, came a black Dog. It turned its eyes on me, but to my surprize, the feeling in my stomach was a coolness onlie, nothing more. The Divell had lost one soul to do his work and would never gain mine.

In that moment, I knew I would spend my life fighting the Divell. He might be racing against time to swell his ranks before the Judgement Day, and if he did, so would I, and over him the forces of God and righteousness would rule.

After my sister's death, my mother clung the more to me, which my father, being stern in all other matters but soft where my mother was concerned, gently allowed her. At last, my father having ever had in mind for me, the child of his age, that I become a Preacher, I must be sent to grammar school and university.

And so in December of 1619 I rode down with my brother to Canterbury the week before Christmas. We arrived as it grew dark, stabled our horses and saw them fed and watered, then took ourselves to the Cathedral for Evensong. Tho' we had been in the Cathedral the term before for the exam and knew to expect its grandeur, e'en so it struck us again, our smallness within it, like staring too long at the Heavens.

In the choir were the Scholars whose ranks I would join the next day. In their white surplices in the candlelight they looked benign, yet my stomach knotted. While I no longer dogged her footsteps or ran to her in the night, I liked not to leave my Mother, who wept at my departure. With my sister slain by witchcraft and myself away at School she had no children by her side. I had felt a sorrow equal to hers to ride away from her.

At least I had my brother, tho' he rode hard to make me keep up as tho' he might make me a man in two days' ride. At inns where we rested, he threw me punches, had me dodge and duck and hit back. "Harder. Harder. Come, brother. Smite me. You'll never survive school." I worked myself up and pelted him so I panted and grew hot. "There," said he at last. "Enough." I had the sense he gave up on me but my pride made me think he approved of my progress.

The wind blew cold in Canterbury and cut through our cloaks. I lay awake by my brother's side at the inn as he slept. The next night I would sleep in a room of boys who were strangers to me. I determined I would neither quail nor run away as I had with the village boys but stand and fight. In the morning, my brother came with me to the school and delivered me into the hands of the Lower Master, Samuel Raven, a lean young man with small eyes. Master Raven took the younger boys in one room.

When I had relaxed so that I was no longer quivering, I could begin to give an eye to those around me. The other new boys were a lean fellow with a long nose, a compact fellow with a bit of a swagger, a sallow boy with frightened eyes, a boy with freckles and a snub nose and three or four others. With a handful of boys who had been there since Michaelmas, we made the first form. It was cold. My fists were clenched. But by and by my muscles loosened. No fights would begin within the schoolroom. There was I safe and with this realization and my eagerness to try out my Latin and shew what I knew, which I thought would not be counted against me at a school where all had the same goal, I gave the right answer too eagerly and too often.

When we stopped for dinner, I had need of the privy, but as I left the schoolroom to make my way there, I momentarily forgot where I was and my resolve to be on guard and to fight.

"So, Stick," one boy said to me. "You are in love with the Usher."

I fetched my resolve back from where I'd stowed it. My fists clenched and my stomach withal. "Why say you so?"

"You have every answer to the ready."

"So?"

"You make the rest of us look bad," said the freckled boy.

"You make yourselves look bad by not having the answers ready."

Now we were outside and I swung around with my fists at the ready as my brother had shown me.

"What do you?" said the boy.

"I am ready to fight," said I.

"Ready to fight," said he with surprize.

"Oh, put down your fists," said the swaggering boy, and the others laughed.

A small point in me burned and grew so that I was suffused with shame.

I tried to punch the boy who first said I was in love with the usher, but he ducked easily and ran off away from me.

"I'll not fight," said he.

"Try to hit me," said another, taking his place.

I went at him, with all the shame fuelling me, but he dodged every punch, so that now a crowd had grown, eight or nine boys laughing, the older ones amused by the youngers' quarrels. Now I grew panicked, for it was apparent I could not fight anyone. I should be at their mercy all my years at school, just as I had been at the village boys' mercy. Someone *must* fight me, someone must hit me, and so end my shame with defeat. Unbeknownst to me, a boy had snuck up behind me, going down on all fours behind my knees, so that all it took was a slight push for me to tumble backwards.

"You hit like a girl," said one.

I leapt up again, fists up. "Who said that? Who?"

"I said it," said the sallow boy.

The swaggering boy said, "Come, give him a fair fight."

"The sport is too good," said the boy dodging me. "Look at his arms flailing like willow switches in a storm."

But the swaggering boy pushed him out of the way, and now, instead of onlie ducking away and dodging my fists, he came in to deliver his own. He was a little taller than my own height, and I was tall for my age. He parried my blows so I must turn to the side, and struck me a blow in my stomach as I passed that doubled me over. As I painfully straightened, another blow took me on the chin, onlie not so hard, I thought, as might have been.

I saw his face and an almost imperceptible invitation: hit me, hit me here and now, here on the cheek. He dodged once, then gave me the chance again, and this time I struck.

His head snapped away from the blow. He reeled, put his hand up to his cheek. I knew he exaggerated, and thought it was having more fun at my expense, but the others seemed not to notice.

"Go, Stick!" cried one.

He came back at me. At the last second before he landed his blow, he winked. It was a hard hit, tho' not as hard as it might have been, and I knew it was now no shame if I went down, and indeed I know not if I had any choice. Down I went.

The other boy stopped and shook his head as if clearing it yet of my earlier punch. He held his hands up. "Pax?" said he.

"Pax," said I.

He held out his hand. Grasping it, I got to my feet.

We pissed, side by side, and returned to the schoolroom, washing our hands before dinner. My heart swelled with gratitude.

I knew not yet if I had a friend, but for certain he had set me on my feet beside the other boys.

In the afternoon we were back in the schoolroom until five, when we had an hour's otium before soupar. It was by this time dark. I would not on my own have ventured out on a cold eve, but the other boys went and I hesitantly followed, not sure of my welcome. I had not their way of knowing what was next, when to move, and was ever one step behind. No one seemed to miss me or wait for me. The swaggering boy, I noted his name now, it was Barrows, stood outside and took a deep breath, stretching his arms and bouncing on his toes.

"God save your father," said he to the lean one, his friend. "See you tomorrow."

"Is he a local boy?" asked I after he had walked off into the night.

"His father is gardiner at the Abbey," said he, "and my benefactor, for he told me of this school and set his son to teach me enough Latin that I might pass the exam."

"How came you to know him?"

"On a voyage to Russia." He bounced on his toes, absently did a little jig.

"Russia?" It was beyond my imagining. "Russia?"

"Russia." He folded his arms on his chest to dance as Russians.

"What is Russia like?"

"Cold and wild with small stunted trees. Their houses were made of logs split in half."

"How came you to voyage to Russia?"

"I went all over as a sailor."

"You were a sailor?" I knew not what to say to this astonishing revelation.

Other boys drew near. "You were a sailor?" asked one.

"Where is your family?" asked another.

"I have no family. My mother died before I can remember and my father died in Virginia."

Then as now, Virginia was of great interest to all.

Gradually a crowd drew about Barrows, including some of the older boys but when he saw this, he made care, it seemed to me, to dull his answer.

"My father died when I had nine years of my age," said he. "We'd been in Virginia since I was two. The captain took pity on me. I proved an able hand and he liked me well and kept me on."

Then went we into soupar, but afterwards, as we readied ourselves for sleep, we all plied him with questions. He answered with less and less so at last the talk turned to other things. I noticed he did this often, deflected questions, turned the talk away from himself.

I could not sleep. I lay hours in the dark, hearing piss in the pot. The wind outside. All the sounds were different from what I knew. The wind was like an animal with a sharp nose. It whistled through the night. I heard sniffles from the talkative boy. The sailor, Barrows, was asleep.

In the dayes that followed, I took note of Barrows that he seemed to learn with little effort. His Latin was excellent. I rarely heard him make a mistake. I saw him turn the same eye on me when it came time for me to recite lines or read a translation or decline a verb. Tho' naturally of a ludic nature, Barrows was quiet and sober in class. Should a boy snicker or try to draw his attention away from his task, he ignored him. He did not show disapproval, he did not scowl as I did. He merely got on with his work. In the fields, at play, he was boisterous and skilled. He had neat footwork with a ball and a great capacity for tumbling. He could do handsprings like an acrobat. He could walk on his hands as easily as I could on my feet. One suspected he might have been a street tumbler, for all that. We knew he had been to Virginia and the Levant as well as Russia. At night, we asked him for tales of adventure, and he had them—of storms at sea, of pirates, of whales and sea monsters and flying fish. I admired him beyond all reason. I followed him around or watched if I could not follow. If he smiled at me and spoke to me, I warmed as if set by the brightest fire.

He was friends, as I say, with the long-nosed boy, who was John Tredeskin, since famous for the collection he maintained with his father at South Lambeth. At this time, Tredeskin, as Barrows said, was gardiner at St. Augustine, his Abbey, now in the hands of Sir —— Wotton. Barrows went often to sup with Tredeskin and stayed there on holidays and helped in the gardens. Many was the day I watched them go and wished I were asked with them. But I counselled myself to confine myself to study and prayer. When they were gone I was more vulnerable to the other boys. Pike—for that was the name of the sallow boy—might decide to needle me. But I managed. When Barrows returned, I was annoyed with him for having gone, and pleased he was back. He and I conversed easilie, and when he was there, it was easier to converse with all the boys.

Like my father, Tredeskin spoke little, but unlike my father he smiled often, a shy smile. He was an able scholar, not outstanding. I did not see what Barrows saw in him and thought onlie it must be that he was grateful to Tredeskin's father.

For his part, Tredeskin showed onlie the smallest discomfort that the boy he had taught rudimentary Latin to now far surpassed him and was become his own tutor.

One day in Spring, my feet twitched that I must walk, and I did not like to be left alone with Pike and so found myself following Barrows and Tredeskin. I followed them through the South Gate. There across the road were a handful of small houses and past them, was the Abbey, its gate.

Immediately a change came over Tredeskin. He swung his arms more easily. The two boys laughed and ran and jostled, racing across the road. I smelled blossoms on the breeze. Then they were through the Abbey gates and I was alone on the road. I decided to walk past the ruins of the Abbey and gaze on its crumbling tower and so I went round the far side of the Abbey and down the road. There was a Wall about the Abbey grounds. When I thought none were looking, I climbed it enough to look over. What a wonder to my eyes appeared, acres of gardens and orchards with the trees all abloom, a veritable Eden. It soothed my soul to look upon it and breathe in its fragrance. It gave me peace when I had not known I was in need of it. It gave me a greater peace than any I had known, yea, even the peace of prayer, so that I found myself spontaneously praying, giving thanks to God for his Bountie. After that, I often followed Barrows and Tredeskin, or at times came on my own. More than once a neighbour across the strett called me down from the Wall.

Further down the road was a bend in the wall and a small Gate. Here one Saturday post-meridian I found the gate open. Looking about me and seeing none, I passed through. Inside the gates were mounds of manure and earth, trees in pots, a cart-path and the signs of garden work. Then came the sounds of a man's voice, giving instructions, so I thought. My heart beat at the prospect of discovery, and I dodged back out of the Garden. I paused in the Wall's corner, catching my breath and feeling my heart slow. Now I heard the wheels of a cart and other sounds, clippers and shovels. I wanted to go back in, to walk through the trees and hedges, but dared not. Full of regret, heartsore beyond need of the moment, I was about to walk back to the school, take up my books, when I thought I would take just one more look, just one deep breath of the air of the garden. So I stepped through the gate again. I had forgot about the manure pile, tho', so my one breath drew nothing sweet. Now to get my one deep breath must I run lightly down the lane and peer into the patterned garden. My daring filled me with an exhilaration new to me. I ran. My feet were light. Betwixt the inner wall and the garden edge was a tall hedge, bounding the garden. This was the path I ran down, bright green with new growth settling into full leaf. Then came an opening in the hedge where I would stop and steal my glance of the garden. I had just about reached this opening when I heard barrow wheel and whistling. I had no time even to turn and run. Out of the opening came Tredeskin, pushing an empty wheelbarrow. He stopped. I stopped. Now behind him came Barrows with a second wheelbarrow.

"Heard," said Tredeskin.

"I saw the gate open," said I. "The garden drew me in." Now I turned and fled. Tears sprang to my eyes. I was wracked with guilt for my trespass. I was as bad as any of the other boys I thought myself better than. My heart tore at my chest. Back I went, and turned into the Cathedral, to kneel on the hard stone and confess and pray.

I was frightened the next day of meeting them. They looked at me curiously as they entered the school room and took their seats. I cast my gaze down. At the first opportunity, Tredeskin asked me, "How came you in the garden? Were you sent on a dare? You have never been one for dares."

My face blazed with shame, for how could I explain I had followed them? How could I explain I coveted the garden and the two of them, their friendship, and their time together?

"The garden is Sir Edward Wotton's," said Tredeskin, "and in my father's care. It is not a playground."

"My shame is Adam's shame," said I. "I wanted to know the Garden, what it was like."

"There is no shame in that," said he. "Though in sneaking in where you are not invited, shame may lie."

"Forgive me," I said.

"Heard, I understand you not," said he. "Other boys climb the wall and steal into the garden for mischief, to steal apples, or show their friends they dare. You come for Curiosity."

I hung my head. Tredeskin gave me slow consideration. At last, he said, "I will ask my father if I may invite you. He expects my friends to help, I warn you. The Garden is not for our own enjoyment but for the pleasure of our master."

And so from my shame I had unexpected reprieve. Friendship. It was beyond my experience of anything in the world, except the love of my mother, and, in truth, beyond e'en that, for there was nothing cloying or entrapping about it. I had continewally to remind myself and warn myself of the dangers of loving this life too much, when true life abided in the next. But in friendship, I had earthly Happiness.

Tredeskin was as good as his word and secured for me an invitation to the Abbey's Garden. No schoolboys could be invited to the garden unless they were workers also. The following Saturday, Master Raven excused us after our lessons to take dinner at the Abbey with the Tredeskins.

Tredeskin the Elder was lean and taciturn like his son (and my father) but greeted me so: "My son tells me you have an interest in the Garden."

"I glimpsed it as I walked past the open gate," said I, "and it was like a glimpse of Heaven, meaning no sacrilege."

"'Tis no sacrilege to me," said he.

He finished his meal in silence.

We were set to raking and clearing out leaves and sticks. To work in the sunshine was strang to me. I tired sooner than Barrows or Tredeskin. When we were done, Tredeskin toured me around the Garden. There was a grand avenue of lime trees, three patterned gardens and two orchards. I felt myself in a very dream. That night I slept well. My arms the next day felt their day of toil. I sensed myself stronger. My wonder at the garden consumed me—it was the first of the great gardens I had seen. I did not know what was ordinary to know what was wonderfull, but thought it all wonderful.

A body might have thought that Tredeskin and Barrows would be at odds, Barrows being John's father's favourite, but John's own sense of his father was secure, and Barrows made himself likeable. Looking back, it's possible to see how it was: whether he came by it naturally or trained himself to do it, he taught people to like him, and thus made his way more easy. This was not a skill I myself had. I did not know how to make myself liked. I told myself that I did not care. What is the liking of men compared to the love of God?

Tredeskin had seen himself rise and saw how usefull it was to have Latin, and saw how his son might rise also. He was not profoundly ambitious except that his work and his rarities be known. Tredeskin admired his father and honoured him and was pleased to learn from him. Here he was quick and competitive, more than at school. Barrows learned very quickly, that was one of his great abilities. He took things in at a glance. He seemed to swallow learning whole. So it was of setting grafts in trees and caring for melons and pruning apple trees and apricocks. But here Tredeskin outstripped him, and Barrows was ever the hand and not the director. All three of them had a great enthusiasm for rare plants that I confess I did not share. One plant was like another so far as I was concerned. Barrows had a good knowledge of Simples, which he said he had learned from his mother. "I thought your mother died in your infancy." "I mean my foster mother," said he. "I never knew you had a foster mother." He made a little extra money collecting them to sell to a local apothecary. I often went with him on a Saturday afternoon.

My friendship with Barrows and Tredeskin brought me greater ease and pleasure in this world than formerly, but I lost none of my conviction that my life was meant to stand 'gainst Satan. Anno 1621 was Elizabeth Sawyer, in London, accused of witchcraft, and the subject of much discussion. One day as we were divesting ourselves of our surplices after Church, didde one of our number recount the news of her arrest and what she hadde donne. He hadde a letter from London that told of it. A neighbour Mistress Sawyer hadde, who left her sope on the window ledge. Elizabeth Sawyer, her sow, ate the sope, whereupon the neighbour struck the sow to stop it. Then says Sawyer, "Strike my sow, will you? You shall feel the very blow you struck!" The neighbour that night feels a blow against her back and begins to foam at the mouth. She is wracked with payne four dayes and then dies of it, crying on her deathbed, "It is Elizabeth Sawyer who has killed me for that I struck her sow."

All the way back to the playing fields was the talk of this Witch and what she hadde done, and how she had a teat above her fundament the Divell suckt from. And Barrows sayed, "Stop this rude gossip. She is an old womanne, half-blind, they say, and, perchance half-mad. But witch she is not."

"She is, she has confess'd it," sayed Pilkinton, one of our number.

"Tell me how she didde it," sayed Barrows.

"The Divell gave her the power, I know not how."

"Any old woman gets called a witch because she frightens people."

"Would you say there are no witches, then?" sayed Tredeskin.

"I cannot say. There may be. But on the whole I am inclined to think there are none. I have not the evidence of my senses."

"You have not the evidence of your senses that God lives," said Pilkinton.

"What about the evidence of my senses?" said I, for I had told them my tale of Goodwife Fellowes. "Do you misbelieve me?"

He hesitated, then sayed, "I believe you may misconstrue."

"But the witch confessed! Like Sawyer, she confessed! She herself gave the time and date of her contract with the Divell that concurred with the evidence of my senses! She is not the onlie one."

Barrows was in the minority, tho' there were others shared his skepticism.

"How do they do what they are believed to do?" sayed he. "How gave this witch convulsions to your sister?"

"I know not how it was done, onlie that it was done."

"Well, that is not enough."

"How does a tadpole become a frog? How does air go bad? How . . . She gets her power from the Divell."

"But how does he do it? How does someone kill at a distance?"

"Poisin."

"Someone must be near enough to administer it. The poisin must enter the body."

"Perhaps the witch sends a poisin on the wind or infects the air."

It cut me to the core that Barrows should misbelieve me. It was the most important thing in the world to right the balance between God and the Divell. Each Soul was worth saving. Each Soul made a difference. Witches corrupted. Witches fouled. Witches could not live, but they could be absolved of their condemnable Sin before their deaths.

"You doubt me," sayed I.

He cast not his eyes down. "I do," he said. His gentleness in saying it put me in choler.

"Do not talk to me!" I cried. I had counted him my greatest friend. I loved him better than any. And he doubted me.

I could not speak to him for a long time afterwards. But gradually he won me over again.

It remayned a sore spot between us. Each time someone told a tale of using cunning to find lost items or sang a ballad of a witch discovered we covered the same ground. Then would he do small things to win me round again so that I should forgive him.

He had set me on my feet at school. Now I had other friends, and less need of him. I counted him my great friend even still, but was sore troubled by this difference between us, which seemed, at its root, a betrayal.

At Cambridge, I was accepted into Emmanuel College, where I found myself immediately among people of like mind. I had none of the terrible early awkwardnesses. There were many charismatic Preachers among the deanery at Cambridge and I fell under their spell. I lodged with three other young men, all pious, even to the point of zeal. We had secret meetings wherein we took turns venturing forth interpretations of scripture, debating them, testing them, were they sound or faulty. What I had concealed at the King's School, I could be forthright about now and to find myself in company that did not argue against me but with me was a heady time. I did not think of myself, I thought of Man and God, of Satan and his temptations, of the weaknesses of Man, his susceptibilities, and the cautions we must take against them. I felt my life devoted to the cause of banishing evil and abiding God's law.

On Mr. Cotton's recommendation (I had of late spent a term lodging with him), I began to correspond with Johannes Muenther, from Augsburg, in Bavaria, who had made since his youth in Nördlingen a study of Witchcraft and Demonologie. He invited me to visit, where I might assist him at the same time that I furthered my understanding of Satan, his demons and witches, furiously at work in those times in that country (as indeed they were everywhere, but where they seemed, he feared, to be making more ground). My degree taken, and no Benefice yet on offer (tho' my purse being modest, I hadde need of one within as few months as I could hope), I most eagerly assented, by God's grace, to this invitation, bundling in my wallet my copy of Cotta, his *Triall of Witch-craft*, there to guard it as closely as my purse in my travells, for a gift.

Not having much travelled in my life, I was anxious and curious in equal measure. What sights would God put forth that I should see, what people encounter? Those things that first seemed strang—people, their manner of speech and dress, even Catholicks, their spurious crossing of themselves, their monks afoot on the roads, and Spaniards—became less so as I went on. The low plains gave way to hills and woods and towns, where I banded together with other God-fearing travellers, farmers and merchants, even Catholicks and Lutherans together, to pass through those areas that brigands might hide.

Some few towns we passed through were hard served by war, with burnt houses and trammelled fields, and there were we wary, and passed through quickly under the hard eye of ones who were left, or assailed by wretches who would beg of us.

With each passing day and each set of travellers, I felt myself grow surer and less afraid, even as I looked about with the knowledge that Satan was hard at work here, and had had such success.

At night, in inns, I heard tales of witches near and far. I found it not easie to sleep, but lay awake, listening for revels. Were witches flying above my head as I lay in ignorance of them? Times were the revels— not demonic, but ordinary earthly revels—right below me in the inn. When at last I fell asleep, they mingled with my dreams, so in my dreams, I flew, rose lightly, without effort, from the path I laboured, travelled through the air with ease, and looked down in wonder at the fields and towns and woods that lay below. A weird joy, akin to terror, suffused me in this state, and I knew I must be very painefull, for by this joy did Satan tempt the weak and seduce them. I cried out in defiance of Satan. Then did I sense forms flying alongside and closing in on me, hideous forms with wild hair and twisted faces, racing to get to their Sabbat before me and shut me out, or draw me in and torment me, I knew not. This dream I had so manie times on my travels, I felt it to be a Message from God.

At last came I to Augsburg, a larger town than any I had passed through, and busy this market day. None of the first people I inquired of Muenther, his house, had any knowledge of him, but the sixth, after making an odd grimace (which gave me pause), directed me to follow a street at the end of the square until it came to an end, and there was the house, in a wall of houses against the street.

The door was answered by a stout young woman, who bowed to me in silence and went, so I thought, to fetch her master, leaving me in a small, dark hall between closed doors. Behind the sinister door I heard someone reading Latin. Then came not Muenther but another woman, this one of middle years, who beckoned me, again in silence, to a kitchen in back of the house. Here she welcomed me and let me know that Muenther liked not to be interrupted at this time, wherefore their silence. A fire in the hearth kept a large pot hot, while the young woman and a girl bustled around a table, preparing dinner.

In a short time came the call from the front room, a man, his voice. The older woman hurried out. Now came a chorus of voices together, freed from silence, and the sounds of benches against the floor, recalling to me the sounds of rooms at Cambridge when our Bible colloquium broke for a meal. I half expected to see the faces of my companions, but instead came two strang faces into the kitchen, one square and red-cheeked, another lean and pale, young men, and behind them a griz-zled bear of a man with one eye gone from its socket and the skin sagging o'er it. The grimace in the market had been in imitation of this, the look of Muenther, his face. I was, for an instant, dismayed, but then he clasped my shoulder and greeted me, *die Englischer*, with his one eye smiling, and all was well. I had a speech prepared in German to say how much I appreciated his invitation and honoured his work, but it was swept away in the preparations for dinner, the fetching and carrying of food and drink, the setting of tables on trestles. Each of the young men told me his name, but in my confusion I held them not in my mind. I felt now I had gone back in time, I was at school in Canterbury, agayn to find my place.

Their custom was to take meals in silence whilst one person read from the Bible. Afterward was I introduced formally to my fellows. The rosy-cheeked boy was Muenther, his nephew, Martin, a barrel-chested young man who bore himself with upright carriage and buoyant step. The one with light hair was Josef Hafner from Saxony. Also a thin

Bohemian with a cap of dark hair and restless manner, alwaies tapping or shifting and then catching himself and going very still before he 'gan agayn to tap his fingers or toes.

After the meal, it was their custom to walk out and discourse on what they had that morning heard. Muenther himself remayned at home for these post-prandial walks, or went his own waies. "Come," they cried to me this first after-noon. "Come." So warmly did they entreat me that despite my weary legs, I joyned them.

I sayed little that first day, but listened with interest.

Josef Hafner, the narrow-shouldered fair one, took up a subject they had clearly debated more than once, whether witches do fly through the air. "Satan, not being of material body," sayed he, "but spirit alone, as Angels, may adopt a body or create an illusion to convince he has a body, may certainly move through the air. But Witches, being made of flesh and bone, are bound to earth as we all, and may not fly."

"Birds are made of flesh and bone, and fly," sayed Muenther.

"Let us work through it another way," sayed Hafner. "What manner of things fly?"

From above came the swift flap of wings, a flock of pigeons. Muenther the nephew gestured upwards in general answer, to laughter from the rest.

Together they compiled a list: birds great and small, bats, moths, butterflies, dragonflies, other flies, gnats, midges, &c.

"I have heard," ventured I, "of fish that fly."

"Yes," cried Muenther. "And squirrels."

"What have all these in common?" sayed Hafner.

"Wings," sayed Muenther's nephew impatiently.

"The fish?"

"Their fins are as wings."

"They are all light," sayed Hafner.

Muenther: "What of a goose, or swan?"

"Some things fly not of themselves but are borne through the air," sayed Georg Janacek, the Bohemian. "The seed of the dandelion or a leaf in the wind."

"Let us categorize, then," sayed Hafner. "First we have things with wings, birds and bats, moths and flies. Then have we things light enough to be borne through the air, as seeds and leaves."

"In Holland was a cow lifted in a great storm," sayed Janacek.

"Kites and sails."

"Sheets."

"Beetles and grasshoppers have wings but fly only in short bursts."

"And what of frogs that leap?"

"Or monkeys?"

"For the time they are in the air, they can be said to be flying."

"Witches may be as these others without wings. First, they might fashion wings to fly on, as we fashion a kite. Then, too, they might employ a cape or a cloth like a sail that they might float upon it after they have called up a great wind to carry them."

"Just so."

"But that they rub a salve on a fork and fly on that I do not accept."

"Yet if they conjure a wind, if they themselves are light, yet might they—"

"Flight is an illusion given them by the Divell," sayed Janacek.

"We are destined to disagree on this, I see," sayed Hafner.

"What say you, Heard?" asked Martin Muenther.

I considered. I believed witches did fly, tho' I knew not the exact mechanism. "How a witch goes to the Sabbat is of less note than that she does," sayed I.

"Listen to the wise man," sayed Martin.

At that I found I was part of the companye, a stranger no longer. God had brought me together with men of like mind, the select.

We had by this time passed the gates of the town and walked outside its walls. The sun shone its light on us. I thought of God's great gifts, the sunlight, the earth itself, Jesus, His Son, and all of the people on earth, poor sinners, weak and sad, hurt and broken, lost and thinking themselves alone, and Satan ready to lure them from the love of God. My heart opened to God in a new and fuller way and I felt within myself a new dedication to the saving of lost souls, collecting all who had strayed from God's path, and bringing them back to him. It seemed to strengthen my very muscle and bone. With these, my brothers, I, even I, made fast against the Divell.

Upon our return, Muenther drew out a large piece of parchment on which he hadde made a cart. This he unfolded on the table and leaned over it to show how he hadde marked incidences of witchery as does a general mark a battle map so as to anticipate the enemie, his movements. There were outlying marks in England at Lancaster, in Denmark, and Sweden, in France at Lorraine, in the low countries at Roermond and Spa, and then as one drew eastward, at Trier, Waldsee, Ingelfingen, Nördlingen. The greatest cluster of all surrounded Augsburg itself.

We were in the very heart of it all.

I turned my face to him in awe when I saw what the cart implied.

"Ah," said he. "You begin to see. In our fight against that most duplicitous spirit, that corrupt master of illusion, we are at the very core. Satan is at work here, here in our very midst. Travel abroad he may and does, but here, in Bavaria, he returns. Here he schemes and plans, here he sends out his Demons, here he calls his Witches to him, to make their pact at the Sabbath, to wed them and send them to do his work. He may at this moment be greeting a woman at a well in Mainz or in her cowshed in Bopfingen. He may appear as a traveller on the road amid the weary folk at the end of their market day. He may kiss the hand of the mayor's wife in Würzburg. If we tune our ears, might we not hear him down our very street?

"*Here* must we therefore build our defence. *Here* must we stand against Satan. We must find out the witches, study their confessions to learn who else they by Satan's will and against God's they have drawn into their circumference. We must find the very Sabbat. We must find them and bring God to them."

Accordingly, Muenther sent out that evening his nephew and Janacek to seek their Sabbat. I learned that recently, between eleven of the clock and two, went out either Muenther himself and one other, or his lieutenants to wend their way to places they thought likeliest for a Sabbat, or, if it suited, to follow their ears.

"Now that there are four of you, God wills that I send you out two by two. Find we their Sabbat and we catch them all at once. Find we the Nest—and destroy it, by which I mean name them and bring them to tryall—and none may grow. So may we vanquish the Divell and honour the Lord's more perfect peace."

I could not at first sleep, thinking of Martin and Janacek out at night amidst the Witches and Demons. I remembered my dreams as if they had been real.

Hafner and I lay on our pallets. Amid the unfamiliar night sounds of a new house—creaks and groans and clicks and scuttling, a cry from somewhere—I heard his restless movements and knew he was not asleep.

"Have you been out on night watch this way?" I asked.

"Tomorrow it will be our turn, God willing."

"I wonder what they will find. Have you known Witches?"

He had. A woman in his town, a midwife, lived not far from them, and had a reputation as a witch that Hafner's mother did not credit untill his two brothers were born, one dying soon after coming into the world, the other soft-headed and slow-witted. When next her time came again, she called on a midwife from a farther town and not her neighbour. The neighbour was angry and came to their house and cursed the new childe so that she died within a week. The Witch was tried and burned and his mother's next three children were born healthy and lived.

I told Hafner of the witches I had heard as a child and that had ta'en my sister.

Sounds that when we were not talking made me alive to them now settled into something more knowable—mice, a cat, a neighbour calling out in sleep.

I imagined Martin and Janacek out in the darkness. I longed for and feared my own turn. Where held Satan his hideous revels? At the crossroads? The gallows hill? In a distant wood?

Suddenly came into my mind an image of the burnt-out town we had passed through. What a place for a witches' Sabbat. Was this a vizion from God?

How difficult this world was to navigate. What was phantasy? What came from God?

We lay awake, talking, untill Martin and Janacek returned. They hadde a long tale to tell of their peregrinations, but in short, they followed the sounds of revelry to an Inn, and then walking farther afield, heard a few distant cries but could not find their source. They hadde ideas as to where we should search on the morrow.

The next night, we set out at eleven of the clock. Muenther, after a prayer, saw us off with a God go with you, be vigilant, and then the door fell shut behind us. The spring night was chill and damp and still and dark. We first made a circuit of the town, timing our walk so that it should come to the market square at midnight. Many an account of witches, their revels, placed their Sabbats there, right in the centre of town, under the very noses of its citizens.

"How would the townspeople not know, though?" asked Hafner.

"Could be they send out vapours to induce heavy sleep," said I.

"Or cast a glamour over the proceedings. I have heard of those who wake from uneasy sleep, not knowing wherefore they were so unsettled, onlie to learn later that hadde been the very night of the witches' feast."

"I have hadde those dreams," sayed I. "I have hadde them, and wakened, and sat up wondering where, where, where hadde they come from?" I remembered then the fear I hadde felt in those moments, and immediately felt a rush of its opposite. Righteous determination coursed through me as if sent by God, and verily, I believed God had sent it. God meant me to find the witches, there to stop them in their tracks, to win them back to God even against all their own and the Divell's strength, and thence to topple lonely Satan.

So walked we slowly and attentively through the quiet streets, attuned to the noises of the night. The greatest part of the town lay asleep, but now and then came sounds to investigate. A baby's cry, not in the street we were in. We turned to each other. What witches did with babes we well knew. We cocked our heads to better gauge the direction of the cries and hastened our footsteps. Around a corner we went, down a lane, as the cries grew louder and then softened just as we drew near the house they came from, and now we heard a woman's voice, soothing the babe, and bouncing it and singing a soft song. No witch's voice, that. We walked on. We chased in the same way a woman's laughter, and stood outside the door, uncertaine, hearing more of it, and then a man's voice, words we could not hear. "If we knew the citizens of the town," sayed Hafner, "we should know whose house this is and if that be matron or daughter."

Now came different kinds of noises from the house. In daylight, my cheeks would have coloured.

"I do not think congress with the Divell would sound so," said I, ready to move on.

Hafner smothered his laughter.

"What?"

He shook his head to say he meant no mockery. "I do not think so either."

From that time, our walk was ever more companionable.

It was soon time to wend our way back to the square. We stopped a street away to tune our ears. All was quiet. We approached as silently as our shoes allowed. Our eyes had adjusted to the darkness. The square was empty. There was a low sound of pigeons, their coos in their throats, and a singular flapping, and then stillness again. Quietly we stood, and waited. Hafner's hand was on my sleeve, in a gesture to hold me back from stepping into the square, an unnecessary gesture, for we hadde stopped as one at its edge as if to step in its margins were to step into enchantment or snare. His breathing matched mine. Of one accord, we stood a long time without moving, alert to any shimmers in the air, any rifts or tears in the tent of air. At last, Hafner dropped his hand.

"Let us try outside the gates," sayed he.

Town council knew of our project, so we could pass the gates. The fear I hadde felt upon first stepping out of Muenther, his door, hadde dissipated. Now as we stepped through the gates, it crept over me again, a colder dread than I hadde felt before.

"They are out here," saied I to Hafner. "I feel it."

"God save us," sayed he. "God be with us."

"Amen," sayed I.

God was with us. God sent us. We hadde only a short way to walk to the gallows hill. A slender moon behind the clouds gave us small light. There was no sound of revelry, no sound at all other than the light stir of leaves from the trees and hedges beyond.

"If there be," Hafner said quietly, "a glamour to keep their revels from our eyes and ears . . ."

"Then must we walk through the space ourselves to discovere if it be filled," I finished for him.

We stepped forward. Our one accord made me bolder, or at least bold enough to propel my feet forward, though dread grew in my chest as we walked. What would happen if the witches were there? Would we break through the barrier of their glamour to a scene of horror revealed to our eyes? Would we *see* nothing but *feel* their writhing bodies? Such thoughts took hold of me that I hadde to remind myself again and again that God was with us, God willed us to this work, God would keep us strong.

Together we kept pace up the hill and then on its top—we felt nothing, heard nothing—across its breadth—felt nothing, heard nothing—and that was it, there was nothing more. We turned back again over what we had traversed, and laughed. "Nothing," cried Hafner. "They are not here." He laughed, a release. "I didde not know a heart could beat so fast," said he.

"You were frightened?" I asked.

"Quaking," said he. "Were you not?"

"I thought you were not." In truth, I hadde been too occupied with my own fear to even consider his. We laughed full and long, tears at our eyes. And then we calmed and thanked God and prayed and kept on. We found no Sabbath that night, tho' we heard here a cry that sounded human and followed it into the wood, there a distant, unclear sound—music? banging as of a drum or ax? As we allowed we would have no success this night and returned towards Muenther, his house, I told Hafner of my sudden sense the night before of the burnt-out town as witches' ground. "There is many a town like it," said he. "What use the Divell might make of them all! How far is't?"

It was, I thought, a journey of two days.

"Let us speak of this with Muenther."

That night, I slept a dreamless sleep.

We gave in the morning, after prayers, a report to Muenther of the discoveries of the previous evening. Hafner told Muenther of my thinking about the possibility of Satan gathering on the grounds of burnt-out towns. "Yes, I have hadde the very same thought," sayed he, and took out his cart. I knew not the name of the town I hadde passed, but it was one of manie that hadde met the same fate. His finger traced the path taken by the Spanish army through Heidelberg.

In the nights that followed, we walked in ever greater concentric circles about the town, grew more and more accustomed to the night and its sounds, found no witches, but did find old fires. And came close to a fire once, but saw it was men, travellers or bandits, may be, three of them together. Either the witches were further afield or they were expert at concealment.

After some weeks, we agreed to give up our endeavour to discover the witches at their revels. The Divell, his art of concealment was too great. We agreed, nonetheless, we would in our travells be alive to what we may find.

Muenther had correspondents all over the continent, from whose missives he added to his cart. That he gave credence to Catholicks surprized me, but he argewed we could not hope to foil Satan if Christendom stood divided. His living in Augsburg, which held both Protestant and Catholick, e'en living side by side, gave him a moderacy on the divizions of religion, where I had been used to consider it a crime. He now gave me to reconsider and see there were individual Catholickes whose goals were not unlike our own.

At this time was a great Discovery of Witches in a near neighbour, Würzburg, and Bamberg withal. He himself being unable to travel, Muenther divided up his acolytes that we may learn more, be his eyes and ears. Off went Martin and Janacek to Würzburg.

In May came a letter from Reichertshofen that Witches had there been discovered. Thither sent he my self and Hafner to assist the examiner, Kolb, his correspondent.

This was the greatest education I could have, to face directly the witches, see how they answered the charges against them, and learn whereof and how they performed their maleficence, and how bring them to confess so that they may be won back to God before their death. This knowledge would I bring back to England that had need of it.

It was nigh on mid-somer as we drew near to Reichertshofen. The days were long, but unusually cold so that crops grew but slowly. Was this the coldness of Satan, that he was near us? I raised this possibility with Hafner. Hafner allowed it might indeed be a sign of his increasing power. "Think you hellfire runs cold?"

In Reichertshofen met we with councillors to learn of the accusations and with Kolb to know what he wished of us, which was to set down a record of the trial. "The witch has no power when she is on tryall. Tho' she appear pathetic or fearsom, fear not, and pity not untill she confess and show penitence." We delivered to Kolb from Muenther a copy of his cart, which he perused with interest.

I slept poorly the night before the triall, filling my waking hours with prayer that I should be equal to the task. I should not myself be conducting the triall but witnessing and recording it, and yet there was from my childhood a miniscule echo of fear in me that shamed me. On my knees in prayer, I combatted my own weakness.

At sight of the witch in the morning I found my prayer had donne its work. I had no fear of her at all, not any.

She was a womanne with thirty years of her age, very tall and large, with a large, square, pockmarked face, which she kept inclined to the floor, seeming to try to make herself smaller by dropping her shoulders and turning them inward.

She wept and denied and wept and denied and wept and denied, and then was she lifted by her handes for ten minutes and weeping didde change in quality, becoming truer and more honest, and then didde she confess all: the Divell hadde come to her on the road between her the house of her father-in-law and her own, wearing a fine cloak, in the early evening, in the rain. He gave her three florins and promised more. "Are you bothered by the rain?" sayed he. "I can give you power to call it up or send it away, as you wish." "The rain does not bother me," sayed she, "but I wish my father-in-law to stop his shouting and blaming me for all that goes wrong." So was she won to the Divell's side, and so agreed to take his salve and rub it on a fork and fly to the revels, where she married with a Divell by standing back to back. Of the Divell she got a powder that she put into a cake for her father-in-law, whereof he ate, then was seized with convulsions and made insensible before he died. She lamed a horse and killed three cows and a bull at behest of the Divell.

So ended our first day and our first triall. My hand was cramped, my neck stiff, but my eyes open.

The next woman was recalcitrant.

"Why are you here?"

"By my neighbour's slander."

"You understand you stand accused of witchcraft."

"I am no witch and have never performed any sort of witchcraft."

"If you understand what you are accused of is my question. You must," saied Kolb calmly, "answer my questions."

The woman held his gaze. "I am no witch, tho' with being so I am accused."

This woman resisted at every turn. Even the simplest question she made difficult. Kolb gave his questions slowly, calmly and with consideration.

"The Divell has firm hold of you."

"I have been falsely accused."

"We will leave you to consider greater pliancy."

He nodded to the executioner, who led her into the adjoining room to be raised by her hands. She shrank from his touch, and as she was raised cried again and again, "I am no witch," but the resolve the Divell had given her broke at last so that her tune changed to, "I am, I am, O God forgive me."

On the morrow, Ursula Pettenbeck, the next witch, gave her age as something over three score and ten, she knew not the exact number. She hadde been a widow twenty years and lived as a midwife. Six children had she borne, five living. This she sayed with pride. The sixth had died of a fever at age twelve.

"Do you know why you have been brought here today?"

"Why, it is so you can have your way with me, every one of you."

Did she believe this or was it jest? I could not say.

We looked at each other in confusion.

"And I will have you, gladly," sayed she, licking her lips. Sickness rose in me.

"Satan has misled you," thundered Kolb. "He holds you, even now. Yet may God save you. Yea, your soul may be won for God. Confess your crime, confess it now, to save your soul."

She would not meet his eyes. She looked everywhere else. "Confess, confess, confess, confess," sayed she contemptuously beneath her breath.

"Say it. How long have you been a witch?"

"You would know the answer, would you," she warbled.

"I repeat, how long have you practised this damnable crime?"

"How long."

"Woman, you are on triall. Your life, your soul, hangs in the balance. We will have the truth from you. How long have you been a witch?"

"Oh, long and long and long and long," sayed she.

"Ten years?"

"Long and long."

"Twenty years?"

"Long and longer."

"Thirty years?"

"Now you have it." She smiled, toothless, insensible to her own depravity.

"When did the Divell come to you and how and in what season and what time of day?"

"A green day, green and long."

"A spring day, then, yes?"

"Spring, certain."

"Where were you?"

"By the coldstream."

"And how came the divell?"

"All in green, all in green."

"Like the day."

"Very like it."

"What did you at the time?"

"By the coldstream. I laid out my clothes."

"And along came the Divell."

"All in green, all in green."

"What then?"

"What then?"

"How did he approach you? With what words or promises?"

"'Will you wash these clothes of mine?' What will you give me for it? 'I will give you all that I have beneath my clothes.' What else? 'Five florins.' And what besides? 'The power to curse those that have hurt you.'"

She began attending his revelries once a week. I raced to copy down all that she sayed. She continewed all that day and all of the next.

In the night, sayed the Gaoler next morning, it seemed as if the Divell came to her, tho' he could see no one, for she writhed and called out. But the second night, after she hadde confessed all and signed her mark and took communion, she slept quietly. Then was she taken and burnt with the two fellowes who hadde preceded her.

The next witch to be tried was the daughter of Ursula Pettenbeck. Fourteen or fifteen years since, Ursula Pettenbeck importuned her daughter to come to revels in the elderberry grove, said the daughter, Barbara, but they were not Sabbaths, onlie secret dances, and at first she would not go, but her mother would not leave off, so to keep the peace she agreed to go. Her mother, she knew, set off once a week at night, for she hadde caught her at it.

This womann, Barbara Kurzhals, was wife of a baker, her second husband. She hadde a pinched, angry face, and broad teeth, which she oft ran her tongue over. Tho' she resisted more than her mother hadde donne, she was not raised more than twice by the hands before the tide turned and she were ready to confess. Then came her awful tale in a great string that continewed all the afternoon.

First we learned of the revels, of how she was married to a Divell who took the form of a farmer from a nearby town. She recognized at the revels some who had earlier confessed and since died. I could see the scene vividly as she recounted it.

To the first revel, her mother walked her to the elderberry grove, an hour's walk. As they approached, all was quiet. Then they passed through a mist and a smell of rotten egg and on the other side was music and dancing, a gathering like to a harvest dance except the season was wrong. A fire there was, and a band of musicians, the smell of roast pig on the fire, a dance underway. Farmer Schnabel from a neighbouring town greeted them, bid them make themselves merry. Then a man she didde not know, finely dressed in black velvet, bowed and welcomed her, thanked her mother for bringing her.

He gave them a cup to drink from, a golden goblet. She went to drink it, but the man stopped her. "You must turn three times and drink from the far rim of the goblet," said he. "Your mother will show you how."

So her mother turned three times, took the goblet, put her chin in it, her lips on the far rim, and bent over, tipping the cup so the wine spilled into her upside-down mouth. Then handed she the cup to her daughter, but she would not take it.

"I'll not drink of this cup," said she.

"'Tis but a game of ours," said the man. "Come. Drink. Or we shall send you home."

So she didde, she could not say why. And then didde the scene appear in a different light.

The torches that burned on posts, the lamps were the heads of babes, alight with flame that came out their eyes and merged atop their heads shooting up like hair. At centre were three great fires, one with four babes upon on a spit, another below a great cauldron, and in the third, a spirit burning, as if bathing. In and around these danced men and women and divells all in a line. There were many she recognized there—the fat farmer Schnabel, the cobbler withal.

Now she saw that the man in velvet was the Divell himself.

From the Divell at these gatherings got she powder and a salve. These she put in the porridge of her babes at the Divell's behest. After three dayes, they took a fever, and shook, and died. So hadde she killed all her children, and some others besides. So concluded the first day of her trial.

On the second day, she gave forth in a stream her years of maleficence: she dug up the graves of babes, &c. She flew out at night to revels on Thursdays and other dayes to cellars, there to drink the wine stored, and she flew, too, to the rooms of men and pressed on them as they slept.

When her first husband still lived, about eleven years since, as he slept, she took his male member in a hand that she had smeared with a devilish salve, and sayed this incantation: "Now take this penis in the name of the devil that you can no longer have your way with me." After she got it, she stored it for four days and then threw it into the river Ilm. She did the same to Wolf Widman from Gottenshofen about twelve years ago. She flew at night to his room, when they were sleeping, and took his manhood in a similar fashion and threw it into the river Paar, so that nothing could help him. She did such things at the behest of the devil.

This she revealed in answer to the question, "What other harms have you done to people, animals or property?"

We tried another two witches and saw them burnt, but it was Barbara Kurzhals who stayed with me as I was recalled to England to my new curacy. I swore I would there be vigilant against the divell's work.

As I passed through the lands I had travelled to come to Bavaria, my greater knowledge made me less afraid. Should I meet a witch, I knew how to deal with her. Should I meet the Divell, my Faith would keep me strong. If there were witches and demons aplenty at work in this world, so too were there men aplenty like Muenther and myself. Satan would not triumph.

To my great delight, I found I shared the passage from the Low Countries back to England with my old friend, Barrows, who had been lately at Leiden studying Physick. Now he returned to England, to London, there to apply to the College of Physitians for a license. He had care of a shipment for Tredeskin of plants and rarities he hadde gained on Tredeskin's behalf in the Low Countries, and was bound first for Lambeth, where now resided both father and son.

I stopped to visit my mother in Fynchley, and get my horse, and finding my mother older but in good spirits and health and well treated by my brother, then went on to meet Barrows and Tredeskin in Lambeth. In the years since he hadde been at Canterbury, he hadde amassed an even greater collection than before, and now displayed it in a great chamber called the Ark.

We hadde a merry reunion for three or four days, before I rode on to Wells.

I was ordained at the cathedral at Wells by the Bishop of Bath and Wells, committing myself fully to the word of God and to my flock, feeling the *dignity* and *great importance* of my office. "To how weighty an office and charge ye are called," intoned the Bishop in the service, "to be messengers, watchmen, and stewards of the Lord; to teach and to premonish, to feed and provide for the Lord's family; to see for Christ's sheep that are dispersed abroad, and for his children who are in the midst of this naughty world, that they may be saved through Christ forever."

Messengers, watchmen and stewards; to teach and to premonish, to feed and provide for. The words alive within me, I carried the weight of office as I rode north from Wells through the hills and down along the River Chew and up into the hills again, towards Norton Malreward, the roads growing ever narrower and overgrown alongsides, so that I passt the church not knowing it, going a long way further until stopping to ask of a man in a field, Where is the Church of the Holy Trinity?

O, you have past it, sayed he, and directed me turn around and take the first track to the left. There it was, the path I should have taken to the old church.

I had thought I would be guided to the Church by sight of its tower from afar, but the tower of Holy Trinity stood lower than the oaks about it. I tethered my horse and went in. *Messenger, watchman, steward,* thought I, opening the door of the Church.

To teach and to premonish, thought I as the door closed, *to feed and provide for.*

'Twould hold at most seventy people.

I hardly expected a Cathedral. But this. Disappointment coursed through me. And then a rush of shame. Pride, my Sin.

Hastily, I gave a prayer of Thanksgiving to God, who in his mercies had given me charge of this, his house, however modest. "When any of ye are gathered in my name . . ."

The Rectory, being across the lane, was not hard to find, a good house of two stories with stables. There was a kitchen garden and chickens in the yard. A woman came out at my call, a matron of middle age. I gave my name as the new curate.

"Thank God you are come," said she. She led me to Mr. Smallridge's closet and shouted, "Here is your new curate!" His small eyes blinked. "Your curate!" she shouted again.

"God give you welcome," said he. Then his eyes closed and his chin fell to his chest and he was asleep.

He was not merely old but in his dotage.

I gave my first Matins the next morning, for two widows, the stable boy, the housekeeper, cook, the cook from the nearby manor, and caretaker.

I spent my days in study and prayer and in composing my first sermon. I read through the parish rolls to know my flock and walked through the town, greeting all I met, of whom there were none too manie. Some farmers and their families, a tiler at work on a roof, a baker, a spinster . . . There were three families of gentle birth in the parish now resident. One man about forty, bald, inclined to talk about his horses and dogs, with a pretty wife and five children, very rambunctious (and a nurse they teazed). Another about sixty and his wife. The wife was fond of archery, which they practiced every Sunday afternoon if the weather were fine. The third a gentleman very retiring, with two daughters just coming of age.

To these families was I invited once a week, often two together, and so came to know them. I quickly grew weary of the horse-talker. I tried to steer him to other topics.

I came to know the vicar of the next parish, Norton Hawkfield. He had a wife and family. He liked to give me advice and he liked to hint at his limited means—his parish, like mine, was small and not wealthy. In short, he, too, I found tedious.

Once the novelty had worn off and I had had the same discourse five or seven or ten times, I felt I was wasted on this congregation. It suited an old and settled man. I was not so very worldly, indeed, but having now travelled a little, I knew the world to be wider than it here seemed.

All summer, the little church on Sundays was very full. In the fall, went two of the three families to London, leaving the congregation comprised of rusticks. Mr. Smallridge's housekeeper was a terrible gossip, which I could not abide, bidding her to stop her lips oft and again. E'en so, I learned the petty village gossip, who was sick, who feigned sickness, who was a drunkard, who was at odds with whom, who was lazy (almost everyone, in her view, excepting, of course, her selfe), who was falsely pious, &c.

Neighbouring Chew Magna was a larger town, a larger parish. My hopes of finding companionship with Rector or Curate there were not fulfilled. The Rector was little in residence. The Curate had six or eight years of his age more than I and a perpetual complaint he was Curate only and not Rector himself. His poverty, and all he could not afford, was his sole topick.

The holder of the benefice there was the widow of Sir Arthur Long. She was reputed to be an astrologer, and an eccentric who went tramping about the woods, collecting eggs, and haunted the Stones at Stanton Drew at dawn and dusk.

I was pleased when my friend Barrows let me know he was coming into Somerset on an errand for Tredeskin and then on to Bristol, where he would try the Chirurgion and Physician's Guild, after London had given him good answer to his exam, but not a license to practise.

He came to me in April, after I had been in Somerset nearly a year. The sight of his familiar face was so welcome it took me by surprize. I almost wished to take his face in my hands and kiss each cheek, as I had seen Spaniards do in the Low Countries. I had not known my spirits so low untill he lifted them.

He had come from Lady Margaret, the widow of Sir Arthur Long. I desiring to know what she was like, learned from him she was a curious and ingenios woman, whose great subject was the question of generation.

I mentioned local rumours that compared her to Dr. Dee.

He laughed. "People fear that which they know not."

I was reminded of our old quarrel and my mistrust. I felt it rise in me, the same anger at his ignorance, his blindness, his sense of superiority. "There is that in the world it is right to fear," said I.

"So there is," sayed he, seeing where he hadde erred.

Later that day came an invitation from Lady Long that Barrows return to dine with her the day after, and I to accompany him if I wished.

I hadde no thought of marrying before manie years hadde passed, but 'gan to notice what pleased me and what did not. I liked a woman exceedingly mild, modest, of course, patient, and not merry or froward. All men did, or so I thought. Lady Margaret was none of these things.

"How do you, Mr. Heard. Have you met Mistress Palmer, my amanuensis? How find you Somerset? Is't not the loveliest county in all of

England? Sussex, of course, where my parents are rooted, is next in my favour, but Somerset is my idyll. Have you been to Maes Knoll? Cheddar? We must have an outing. Mr. Barrows brought me the largest egg and the smallest. You must come see my collection. Come, come. Mr. Barrows tells me you are a demonologist."

"Yes, I have—"

"You must tell us all about it. Come, come, through here, see the eggs. What think you the mechanism of generation, Mr. Heard? Do not think me rude, I ask every one."

"I have not put any thought to it, my Lady," said I.

"How can you not think of it? It is the greatest event, it is the thing that keeps us going, that continews life."

"God gives us life. If we know that it happens, we need not know how."

"I see we are at odds," she said merrily. "For me, the reverse is true: if we know that it happens, we must learn how. Here we are. Now you must admire my collection and tell me how wonderfull it is. It is very wonderful, is it not, are you not filled with Wonder? An egg, say I, is the perfect shape, for in it, lies all. All future life: beak, eye, claw, foot, feather. A sphere is too neat; an egg is perfect. Joan, Mistress Palmer, may tell you the mathematicall shape of an egg."

"There is variation. They are not all the same. But most often, in an egg, a sphere meets a parabola, so that the finite and the infinite are fused."

The ostrich egg is indeed immense and the hummingbird egg very small. They remarked on how strang that there is so much variation amongst birds and so little amongst people. Lady Margaret and Tom Barrows were the principal speakers. Mistress Palmer and I said little. I was, I realized, little used to the company of women. And yet, Lady Margaret was very like a man.

"I think," sayd I, "a sphere's perfection stands for itself. A sphere is regular and perfect by its very nature."

"Ah," said Barrows. "You think 'the musick of the eggs' has not the same ring as 'the musick of the Spheres'!"

Lady Margaret directed the course of our talk. She was not as bad as my parishioner, it is true. She led us through her laboratory, saying, "I must try everything."

One side of the room housed her collection of eggs, nests, birds and other creatures. A bank of drawers held sea-shells, another stones.

One wall held books. The other side a work table of sorts, with mortare and pestle. "Here we make our paints." Beakers and vials, &c.

The meal was better than I was used to. Lady Margaret wished to hear as much news of London as Barrows could carry.

"Did you know that Joan—Mistress Palmer—and Mr. Barrows know each other of old? Both were born in the village in Kent where my sister dwelt, God rest her soul."

"No. I did not know that. I am not sure I ever heard you speak of it, Tom," sayd I.

"I left when very young," said Barrows. "And to my sorrow, never returned. But I am very glad to meet Joan again."

That Joan had a longer claim on his acquaintance pained me.

Barrows turned upon her, and then Lady Margaret, with such a look of purest pleasure that I seemed to see him anew. I had never thought him melancholy—rather, its opposite. But now I saw that his former joy had occupied not his full being. And I knew that I had never in my life known the joy he then displayed. And I was filled with a feeling—I knew not what it was—that made me call up prayer, so that I recited inwardly psalms. *The Lord is my light and my salvation; whom shall I fear?* But I felt nothing for God in that moment, no light, no salvation. The words were hollow. Where God had been was a blank, a void. Came into my mind then: *Unto thee will I cry, O Lord my rock; be not silent to me; lest, if thou be silent to me, I become like them that go down into the pit.* Lady Margaret and Mistress Palmer were them that go down into the pit. They were taking Barrows with them, the Divell was at work thro' them. So went my thoughts for a time.

I gave Barrows as many signals as I could that we should leave this place, but he was merry, and stayed, and stayed.

After the meal, Lady Margaret and Joan played a duet upon the lute, and then another, and Barrows joined in and they sang. Lady Margaret had received a new book by Lord Bacon and read from it. The evening was so much closer to what I had wished for in enduring my neighbours' boasting and braying that my weariness of it, my lack of enjoyment of it, made my spirits sink the lower. My ears heard the words of the book but my mind heard them not.

At last we rose to take our leave. Barrows and Lady Margaret kept renewing their talk rather than leaving off, so that we lingered another half hour by the door. En fin, we escaped, with an invitation to return on the morrow.

In the cool air, my head cleared and my spirits rose. I judged my earlier thoughts mere phantsy. Lady Margaret and her companion made better company than my neighbours.

"Well? What think you of Lady Margaret now that you have met her?"

"She is a very John Dee!"

Barrows laughed.

"Think you the universe is shaped like an egg?" I asked.

"A sphere better echoes the shape of the Earth, and of the Sun and Moon."

"You seem very enamored of the lady."

"Lady?"

"Lady Margaret."

"She makes a good companion."

O, and I do not? cried my heart.

We returned to Lady Margaret's the next day to explore the park and the gardens. An outing to Cheddar was planned, and another to Maes Knoll. I grew more accustomed to Lady Margaret, but my greatest pleasure was in our walks to and from Chew Magna, when Barrows and I could talk, as of old, and observe the world as we passed. He was wont to stop t'examine any thing alive or dead—toad and hedgehog, beetle and butterfly and bird.

There were some days when I could not accompany Barrows, having tasks to take care of, and then he went on his own.

"When will you to Bristol," asked I, "to try the Guild there?"

Soon, he told me. Soon. But he made no sign of going.

Came a day when I must visit a dying parishioner to give him succour. When I had done, I was to join them at Chew Magna. As it happened, the man died in the early morning. I sayed a prayer over his bodie and came away. The day threatened rain, and I thought I should be caught in the middle of it if I waited. Lady Margaret was always importuning me to join them, and so I made bold to arrive earlier than expected. But the heavens waited not for me to reach the manor, opening as I passed a cottage occupied in former days by the gameskeeper, but at present, I knew from Barrows, uninhabited. God himself, so I afterwards believed, sent the rain that I might seek shelter and see there what I saw.

The rain made such a noyze that they heard not my footsteps, but turned their heads at the opening of the door. I saw at once they were naked, Tom Barrows and Mistress Palmer, that they stood six or eight feet apart, that Joan's flesh was milky, her breasts heavy, their roundness pulled towards the floor, and Barrows, his chest as any man's, it seemed to me, tho' now covered with his hands—

In all ways was I startled, but what transfixed me was a sight I could not at first understand. Tom's yard, that I had seen him piss out of and pull at, Tom, his cock, was gone. A tumble of hair like to the colour of hair on his head there was. But nought else. In a flash, I understood.

Joan had unmanned him.

My horror must have shown on my face. My tongue was mute. I tried to put forth words but found myself bewitched. 'Twas on my tongue to say, "God save you, Tom, you are under a spell. She unmans you."

Barrows now drew on trowsers and shirt, whilst Joan, too, looked to her clothing.

I had been taken in by them, by Joan and Lady Margaret. They were in league.

All the fear I thought I had conquered bloomed again in my chest. I fled. To my shame, I fled.

I had not gone ten steps before I stopped, saying to my self I ought to have seized her, detained her, taken her forcibly to the Justice of the Peace or stopped her there. But I saw that Barrows would fight me, and that I would not, this time, when we were in earnest, win, and Joan would get away. I walked in the rain and called myself a coward. And told myself I was doing what was right. I felt as if I had been struck by lightning. I must write to Muenther and tell him it had happened here, what had happened in Bavaria. He must add to his cart another dot. I did not doubt, Joan being so close to Lady Margaret, that she was a witch as well. O, Joan, how could she have held her soul for so little to give't to the Divell? How ingenios was Satan to work thro' these women, weak with their fleshly desires.

Anne's Note

Also interponed in the book found in Dolly Long's library is this letter, the very one Aubrey refers to, accompanied by the brief note from Heard declaring it was received too late. I am bursting to say more, but nothing tops the letter itself, so I will let it introduce itself.

Tom's Tale

*D*ear John,

Now you know what I have long hid. I saw by your face you found it of great accompt but I swear it is less than you think.

When we met, you were a boy of eleven, and I a maid of eighteen or nineteen years. I hadde then already ten years' practice at keeping my sex hid and hadde come to think myself more man than womanne, boy than girl.

I was born to Thos. Willes in the village of Wormshill, in Kent, a twin. In infancy came the sickness and stole away my mother and my twin and two older siblings. My father lost his wits, so Joan said, and ran awaie, leaving me in care of a goat when I had onlie three or four years of my age.

To tell all is a great project and I have not time before I sail with Capt. Thos. James to the Northwest, but I will do the best I can.

Joan, whom I have mentioned, is my saviour. She is the girl that discovered me in our village lockt up in a shed with the goat, and freed me. And she, too, is the woman you saw me with the night past. I saw her not from the time I had seven or eight years of my age, and thought to never see again, tho' I ever wished it, untill last month at Chew Magna.

But to return to infancy.

When the Sickness struck our Village and all or nearly all fell victim to it, my father, as I say, lost his wits, lockt me in a shed with our Goat, and ran away. I knew nothing of him and missed him not. Joan, a girl little older than I, found me, else the Goat and I should certaynly have dyed. Then one day our Goat was took by an old womanne who lived in the woods betwixt our town and another. The milk of the Goat was our sustenance, and so we followed her, and found, tho' she was mute she was kind withal, and so kept us, as we hadde no Parent. Her we called Old Nut, for so she looked and so she sounded, and we were happy with her.

Then came the villagers who hadde fled back to the Village and took us away from Old Nut and into the home of Joan, her aunt, Mistress Dance, where I cried, being kept from Old Nut, and where Old Nut became an enemie of the familie upon suspicion she hadde bewitched Mistress Dance's son, who one day after meeting Old Nut was struck mute as she. I cared not whether she were witch or no. I hadde a devotion to her equal to my devotion to Joan, my saviour and my joy and onlie wished for our old life together, to which end I continewally raced off to the old woman, and was scolded and beaten for my pains but it could not stop me.

Old Nut was convicted of theft and served her sentence I know not where and was not seen in the village for a year or more. I grew less wild.

Word was sent out if there were relatives who could take me, and I was relieved that none answered.

Agaynst expectations, Old Nut returned, and I visited her as much as I could after what work I hadde at Yew Tree Farm, and learned from her how to snare a rabbit and skin it and use all the parts, the bladder, and gut and all (and became curious in how the parts of the rabbit went together), and further, learned the uses of simples (tho' not the names, for those she could not tell me), such as she collected and sold around the neighbouring villages.

I oft ran agaynst Mistress Dance, her wishes, and she was oft in choler with me, but always softened in the end and was in truth kind and charitable to take me in and try to school me in Christian humility.

Years passed. A two-headed piglet being born to a sow Old Nut had chased, she was accused of witchcraft and examined and carted away. When you and I disputed the existence of witchcraft, it was Old Nut I held in my mind, even as you held in yours the neighbour you were certain hadde harmed your sister. I have hadde a long time to reflect on Old Nut. Old Nut was ill-treated, mocked, despised, and blamed. But to me and to Joan she was tender and kind and gave us laughter.

My father walked into the village one harvest eve, as Joan and I rested in a tree, looking down over the bonfire and dancing. We did not at first note him. We were attending to Ned Hazelwood's wooing of Bess Baggillie, with which he was having little success. Then heard I my name and Mistress Dance called out for, and Mistress Dance arriving, my selfe called out for and Joan. Ned Hazelwood pointed at the tree, else we would have dropped to the ground and run to hide. Now must we drop to the ground and approach this Stranger, my Father.

"Come, Thomasina," called Mistress Dance. "'Tis thy Father, returned to you."

This struck the coldest fear into my heart that I had ever felt. I had no Father and wanted no Father. What would he with me?

Few in the village remembered him still, for old William Dorset had died and the hired man at Yew Tree had died. Those that survived the Sickness had been few and were now fewer. But Mistress Dance knew him and Mistress Hazelwood.

"God save you, Thomasina," said he. "God has seen fit to bring me back to you."

I was struck dumb.

"Come, greet thy Father, Thomasina," said Mistress Dance. Instead, I ran. I did not run wisely, but straight across the Hazelwoods' field and down the barrow wood trail to Old Nut's hut, empty now. As I lay there panting, I heard footsteps that could onlie be Joan's.

"He is not my Father," said I.

"I fear he is," said Joan. "You have something of the same look across the brow."

"I do not."

"Hush," said she, and I let loose my tears.

So came I back with Joan with tear-stained face to learn my father had plans to go to Virginia with his new wife and for me to go with him. We would leave on the morrow for London, where he was employed in helping provision the journey.

I was trapped. I could not run awaie again. Nor could I imagine leaving on the morrow all I had known and loved in this world without even knowing I loved it: Wormshill, the very place, and Yew Tree Farm and Mistress Dance, and Margaret, her daughter and Christopher her sonne, who had ever been mine enemie. Joan I knew I loved and Old Nut I knew I loved and I hadde thought them the onlie ones. Now I learned love is different from affinity. Or attachment is different from love. In any case, I would be severed from all I held dear and thrust into a strang new world with strangers.

In my absence, my father had told the Villagers his tale, of being maddened with grief and running off, of drowning his sorrows in drink, and believing for a certaynty that I must have died, too, like my mother and brothers. He slept the night at Yew Tree Farm. I must gather my things on the morrow and be off with him.

So fortune changes.

As we walked away from Wormshill and all I had known, Joan weeping and even Mistress Dance wiping an eye and Christopher Dance and Margaret Dance weeping (and surprized to see them doing it, tho' I hadde but myself realized I cared for them), and Old Nut in gaol, my father entreated me to pray. It was cold. The rain fell. I had a warm cloak from Joan and a wooden toy Old Nut had carved us and an acorn whose look I liked and a piece of flint. The weight of the rain in all made me feel as heavy in body as I was in soul. I did not want to believe this man was my father. He seemed something else.

"Well, Thomasina," said he as we walked out the Street past the bend I had never been past. "The Lord be praised, we are reunited. We must be grateful to the Lord, our God, that we are of this world, to be his servants, and for this great adventure that lies ahead."

I said nothing. My heart, as I say, was heavy.

"Daughter, I wish you to thank the Lord with me."

"You may wish it all you like," said I.

He looked as if he would cuff me, as I fully expected, but he withheld. "I will excuse you this once, for you have grown up wild, without guidance and without God. I pray for patience, but you *will* thank the Lord, here and now." He stopped and turned my shoulders to him, but I kept my head away. He took my face in his hands and turned it to him. "I thank the Lord for bringing my father to me. Say it."

I refused. He squeezed my cheeks. "Say it."

I would not say it. I kicked him in the shins and ran. He would soon be on me and it was so natural to me to climb a tree that I leapt to the branches of the closest one to swing myself up, but he caught my legs and pulled me down. I kicked. He roared for I had caught him on the lip. He threw me down, then lifted me up agayn and struck me across the face. "There is no devil in you, child, that cannot be beaten out. You will thank the Lord."

I refused still. He twisted my arm behind my back until I cried out. "Thank the Lord," he shouted, pulling my wrist higher up my back. "Thank the Lord." I was struck with the terrible comedy of the moment for I was being tortured to thank the Lord for bringing me my torturer. At last, I had no choice, and sayed the words he wanted.

"You are worse than the Salvedges. You must learn humility," he said. "You must learn prayer. It is my fault." He fell to his knees in the mud. "Lord forgive me. In my weakness, I ran from this child. I ran from Death and Sicknesse, which you brought to me and mine, which was my Cross to bear and I bore it not. I was not right in my minde and I left what I should have stayed with. Lord forgive me and Lord forgive this child. I will teach this child to pray that she may come into thine arms agayn."

He tied my hands together as if in prayer and prayed over me as we went. I thought him, if not the Divell, a very Madman.

I knew I must run away but I knew not when or how. Back to Old Nut I could not go. A boy could go off to seek his fortune or go to sea, but the stories did not tell of girls doing the same. I could go into service as Bess Baggillie had done, tho' I liked not that option, or I could maintain myself in the woods as Old Nut didde. This last appealed to me most.

In each parish, if it were convenient, my father stopped and enquired of the parish clerk if lived there widows or young women of an age and inclination to emigrate to become wives to the colonists, upright, Godly men like himselfe. He wanted none that were old or infirm, nor scolds nor degraded women nor beggars.

The Rector in one village was curious about Virginia and asked many questions. My father hadde not yet been to Virginia, but he spoke as if he hadde of the richness of the earth and the bounty of its waters. Fish lept into fishermen's nets, sayed he. Barley flew up from the ground almost as soon as it was sown. The Indians, tho' fierce, proud, strong, and cunning, were as children and would quickly come to God's side when they knew of the miracle of Jesus Christ, His Son. As he and my father discoursed thus in the doorway, I 'gan to sidle off and had made my way down a long street and was about to hop a fence into a field when my father appearing got sight of me and gave chase. Tho' I knew my selfe captured, I ran on, so that my father must jump the fence and run. His face when he caught up at last and got his hand on my cloak was red and filled with fury. He yanked me back and threw me to the ground, whereupon I lept up agayn running. He gave chase and this time tripped me and when I was on the ground took my arm behind my back as before and twisted it up to the point of pain so that agayn, I must concede. Now was his anger even greater than before, for I had shamed him in front of the Rector. I was given onlie the thinnest pottage to eat, my hands agayn tied together as if in prayer and this time tyed up behind my neck so that I might have no rest until penitent.

The punishment was not very much worse than being required to go with him at all. I saw how great my mistake to chuse that moment to flee, for I had alerted him to my flight, and his vigilance increased. I must now learn to dissemble and hide, which was new to me, and distasteful.

Given my father's vigilance and that I had never been farther than Maidstone and Sittingbourne, and those not often, and that I had a great curiosity to see London, I resolved to give up plans for escape for the present and let Fate take me there to discover my chances. I kept my eyes open to see what was about me. There were more villages and greater Towns than I had imagined. I mistrusted my father's tales of Virginia because I mistrusted him, but still I wondered what it be like.

As we drew close to the City, the road grew thick with traffick. I saw more people in a day than I had seen my whole life, carters and chapmen, farmers with pony-carts and donkey-carts with small goods for large markets, women driving geese and men driving pigges or leading cows and divers other travellers.

In the city proper, the noise and smells overwhelmed me. Though I once liked to give it forth that I took to the place right away, in truth I was cowed by its size and clamour. I did not know where to go or what to do, and it did not seem as if any one could rely on kindness. Some on the road were friendly, some were not. There were more sorts of people than I'd ever dreamed. I realized that the people I knew could be slotted into sorts, not simply high- or low-born, choleric or melancholic or bilious. People who are surly. People who yell at others. People who submit, people who defy. Now I did not think of running away, but stuck close to my father.

I noted boys who ran hither and thither, who held horses outside establishments or ran I knew not where or hitched rides on carts and carriages, boys who begged. Girls I saw not, or they clung to their mothers.

Once we crossed the bridge—itself a marvel, as the river it crossed and the boats upon it—and went into the streets we lost the sun and made turn after turn in shadow. At last we came to a house where my step-mother waited for us. She was of my father, his own stature, modest in looks and demeanour.

"What joy, husband," she said to my father. "Your daughter lives!" She greeted me with warmth, two hands upon my cheeks, such a similar posture as the way he had squeezed my cheek with wholly different intent. "She seems well."

"Her bodie may be well but her spirit is sore in need. She is a hoyden and a Heathen."

"We must then teach her." Her hands rested lightly on my shoulders and she smiled at me. She drew me in, bade me fetch bowl and spoon, and stop to thank the Lord before she fed me soupar.

My father talked as we ate of how I had tried to run awaie and how he had tied my hands and led me and prayed for me and was teaching me to pray. He spoke of people's curiosity about Virginia, the land and the selvedges. Were they naked? Did their heads grow on their shoulders as did ours, did they face the same way? Were they festooned in gold? Was the soil fruitful? Did fish truly leap into the nets?

"Watch she does not run away," sayed my father to my step-mother after he had eaten. "I go to meet Mr. Hill."

That night, though I was wearie, I lay awake, alert to the sounds in the street, so different from what I knew, and aware by her absence of Joan. I had not known it was her being by me that let me sleep. I held to my heart the Toy Old Nut had made me of wood. My throat tightened and tears came to my eyes, but I did not let them fall.

My plan of escaping to live in the woods like Old Nut no longer seemed the best course of action. I must learn more of my circumstance before I should know even how to find my way back to the bridge. So I stuck by my step-mother and gave no more sign of running off.

I soon met the man who had inspired my father to go to Virginia, a preacher with shares in the Company, and a zeal, especially to bring the Word of Our Lord to the Selvedges. He congratulated my father on renewing his paternal duties. "You fell low, Willes, but the Lord has raised you up."

"Through you, his Vessel," sayed my Father.

Gradually, I understood that after my Father had lockt me in the shed with Agnes, and run weeping from Wormshill, he hadde sodden himselfe with Drink and laboured to make what small coine he needed to buy more Drink. So it hadde gone untill he heard a Sermon of Mr. Hills, that woke him to his Misery and Sorrow and brought him agayn to God, humble and penitent, to atone for his sins. He hadde sought Mr. Hill out to tell him what he had wrought, and Mr. Hill had found work for him.

We were in London through the winter, a cold one, so cold the River froze, and the whole Town went out on it in wonder. I wondered how Old Nut fared. I wondered how Joan was. My step-mother had me hemming and stitching, hemming and stitching. We were putting by stores for Virginia. She spent a little time each day showing me sums and letters.

I felt confined, being so much in the house. I liked to go to the pump for water and to the baker for bread. I missed the trees and the fields. I missed the woods. Any chance there was to run an errand, I took it, and stayed out on it as long as I could.

The first days by my self was I taunted by boys. "Where wend you, mite?" "What's in your purse?" "If you show me your purse, I'll show you mine." I knew these to be unkindly meant, even when they were couched in kindness. Women in their doorways would scold the boys to leave me alone. I learned to answer back at some, pass on at others. There was a boy on our lane my size or smaller who threw things at me or tried to trip me until I caught the rotted fruit he threw and threw it back at him, which became our game to try to hit one another.

One route took me past a grammar school. Early in the morning they ran past me to get there on time. At noone they played in the street outside. They spoke Latin to say the rude things the other boys saied. I desired to know what it was. My neighbour, his older brother, made one of the scholars, but would not tell me. "What do you go to school for?" I asked him. "Because I must." "Why must you?" "My father desires that I may read and write, to attain a better position."

My father had attended a grammar school for two years before the death of his father required his removal from it. Now because he could read and write had he a position with Mr. Hill as clerk and factotum.

My step-mother found that I was quick with letters and with numbers. Our lessons now saw me read the Bible to her—my father had one that was a gift of Mr. Hill, which my father held very precious—to work my religious education at the same time.

The neighbour said that learning Latin was a slog. They must commit to memory long passages, else the schoolmaster struck them blows. I saw the schoolmaster outside the schole some dayes. He put me in mind of a tree, if a tree may be choleric. I liked him not and yet was I drawn to what they learned. The neighbour said with Latin may they read the ancients, Aristotle and Plato, Pliny and Galen, and I wondered at the greatness of Time and the greatness of Knowledge and the smallness of my self amongst them, and I wished to know more.

As I spent more time in the city and came to know it better, I came to like it. Every day something of interest happened, a squabble in the street, men selling ballads, singing them to sell them, tumblers and tricksters. Moors and Africans, Jews and dwarves, legless and armless, men with no noses.

One day at market I saw one who at first I thought a man, for above the waist, she wore men's dress—a man's hat, with a feather in it, a doublet, and a dagger through her belt. I did not remark her at first, thinking her wholly a man, until her whole Bodie was visible as we came round a corner and her skirts were in view. Now, looking at her face agayn, I saw how there was a womanishness I had not seen before. She stood out in other ways, for she had with her a Black servant. I am sure I stared openly. I observed everything about her. Others took less notice, which gave me to understand she or her kind were known and not worth comment, but then I did hear comments there and about.

My step-mother was kind, but I continued to hate my father. The very sight of him caused my heart to burn and if he spoke, I was incensed. We began each day with prayer and each day and almost every moment he was with us, he found ways to have me mind him. I must be perfectly obedient. I must not kick my legs as I sat and sewed. I must bow my head when spoken to. I must respect my elders. I must honour my mother and father. I must be modest and not boastful. I was seized by a sense of terrible injustice that this man had any sway over me. I had a curiosity about Virginia, but thought that if I went, I should be trapped. As I passed the school each day, I had an idea that I could enter a school. I pretended as I went to fetch water I was going to school. I would have to pose as a boy. I did not think that would be difficult, as the Curate had thought me a boy and I was always being called harridan, more boy than girl as if that were a sin, and must change my self. That did not figure, to my mind. What figured was that if I be more boy than girl, that I live that way in the world. I must needs have breeches and a doublet. Finding and securing them became the goal of all my dayes. The easiest, it seemed, was to steal the breeches off a clothesline where they dried, but the trouble was that there were too many people about. The boy across the street was of a size with me, but I never saw him in any clothes but the ones he wore. If his mother did laundry, she hung it out back, where I could not reach it.

In the square by the schole was a Tailor, but he was vigilant in the keeping of his shop. Either he or his apprentice were ever there, so no clothes nor cloth might I filch there. The thought of a Tailor made me wonder could I make a pair of breeches had I the material, although to do so in secret would be no small task. Another option was the shop where clothes were traded—but I would need something then to trade. The freedom to do this was also an impediment. And where should I stow my booty when I had it? I began to despair of having the means of escape. I wished I had been like Old Nut when the whole village was empty, simply going into each home and taking what she wished. But I could not wish plague upon the whole world or all of London. The penalties for theft I had no clear notion of. Old Nut had got off lightly, Mistress Dance said, with three months hard labour and a few days in the stocks.

So the days passed with no end to my goal. That winter was a great lesson in patience, which I had had no knowledge of before that time, being impulsive and wild. In that patience I held a hope in my heart, not a wishful hope but a buoyant, eager hope and belief that somehow, in time, I should be free of my current encumbrance, my father, and rejoined with those I loved to free them of their encumbrance.

One day, feeling unwell, my step-mother dozed off. Cold tho' it was I climbed out the back window and up on the roof. From there I could get to the next house and climb down and reach some laundry, but it was all shifts and no breeches and across the way was a woman with a hard eye watching me. I had no choice but to go back in. Agayn I had not gained my goal and yet felt I a keen pleasure in my heart beating fast and my limbs being used. The climb had invigorated me.

I continually kept my eye out. I befriended the boy in the street and the boy at the tailor shop. They thought to taunt me and call out rude names and "country girl don't know nothing, where'd you come from, country girl?" "Kent, is it? Wormshill, is it?" The older ones might say, "I'll put my worm in your hill" to which I would return, "You do and that's the end of your worm."

My father interviewed indentured servants and prospective wives for the colonists. He believed he could sniff out a woman of poor virtue, and indeed there were manie that were not hard to detect.

The day grew closer to our departure in May. My step-mother 'gan to show she was with child.

In May, our stores ready, we went down to Woolwich, there to board our ship, the *Diamond*. Seven ships bound for Virginia with the Third Supply ankered at Woolwich. The largest was the *Sea Venture*, which took the admiral and governor of the colony.

The week before the ship was due to sail was spent at Woolwich.

My father had much to do to ready the ship for departure and to ready its cargo. My step-mother helped manage the women who had been recruited to emigrate, ensuring that they had adequate clothing and supplies. Each woman must have needles and thread, pots for cooking, bottles and blankets. In the bustle, it was easy to slip off. I had no clear plan, but imagined if I could secure boys' clothing I would sneak off, as I didde now, hide myself in cart or waggon bound out of town, leap off it, take to the woods, change my clothes and emerge a boy.

At Woolwich were many boys about the docks. I had learned in London not to be afraid of them, to answer bluster with bluster. They didn't mind talking if you didn't keep them from their work or if you brought them small beer and their masters weren't looking. At Woolwich were ships bound for the East Indies, Holland, Spain, &c. Now I postulated I could get a position on board one of these ships. But when I asked how the ships' boys come by their posts 'twas all by virtue of their father or brother or uncle or mother or cousin being kin to the master or mate or gunner or cook.

One day I cried "Ho," to the master of a ship. "Look you for boys to hire? My brother wishes to ship." "No," sayed he, "we have our crew."

My father helped direct which settlers went aboard which vessels and what stores went with each ship. This busyness absented him from my step-mother and me. My eye and heart kept watch for ways to escape my Father and the trap of the Ship. I had a vizion of my Father and his Wyf sayling off while I was on shore, free, but the moment I saw the fleet at anchor, I was curious and wanted to try my feet aboard those great ships to see where they might take me. So now I was of two minds: continue patient and hopeful and board the ship or escape and find my way some way else. I kept the two possibilities open.

The other boats loaded, my father standing ashore with a list, directing. We loaded the *Diamond* last. The sailors formed a chain to pass our stores up to be stowed below decks for the voyage.

At last the ship were ready for people. It rained as we walked up the plank, which bent beneath us. Women cried out and put hands to their chests in surprize and fear, grasping the rope that ran alongside. As he had swung the other women and children before me, a robust blue-eyed mariner swung me down from the railing onto the deck with a wink and a smile and I was aboard my first Ship. This same fellow took our trunk and led us to the deck where we would sleep in a room sectioned off from the rest of the deck, already crowded with women and children. From the moment I stepped on the Ship, and felt the deck rise and dip ever so slightly with the lapping of waves, my Heart rose in me. The very structure of the Ship itself occasioned Wonder, its great masts rising taller—so it seemed to my young eyes—than the tallest trees, the bewildering Rigging spun like so many Spider-Webs from Mast to Rail, the mariners at their ease like mice or rats or insects upon this Great and Strang Vessel. I loved to see the men work the Ship, especially to run up the rigging and loose the Sayls, but allso to put their Chests to the Bar of the Capstang to raise the Anchor, or haul on a rope to shift the sayl. Even coyling a rope seemed a greater Skill than I had formerly considered it. Little of that did I see right away. We were sent below deck to be out of the way, and indeed the deck was crowded with groups of Men who made the viage with us. There we re-met our Companions on our Voyage. There were not manie women on our Ship, just ourselves and three other families with children, three or four young women who went as servants, and the gentlewoman one of them served, with her Husband, who stayed in the Cabbin on deck.

In our Cabbin, such as it were, for it were not truly a Cabbin, but simply a Section of the deck set off by canvas, were four families including myself and my Step-Mother, tho' we could barely make them out in what little light reached us from the open hatch. I smelled straw from the pile of straw pallets we would spread out to sleep on, and pitch. My Step-Mother introduced me to the others there, Mistress Bagwell, with two young children, Mistress Gibson with a little girl and a round-faced boy about my age, and Mistress Oakum, with a daughter of sixteen years. There were, in addition, two maidservants, and two unmarried women, also servants, who lodged in a smaller Room adjacent to ours. None hadde been at Sea before. "I wonder if we shall see Grampusses or Whales," said the boy.

"At last we are on our way," said Mistress Oakum.

"God grant us safe passage," said my step-mother, holding her hand to her belly.

They went over again their stores, what they brought with them, if they had enough for the winter. How mild was the winter, they wondered, and spoke with wearie bones of the winter just endured. While the women were thus engaged, the round-faced boy and I first poked our heads out of the doorway of our Room, and then edged out of it, first I a little, turning back to see if the women noticed, then he a little, turning back, too, then smiling at me, then I a little, untill we were out, and, in our escape, Friends.

"Tom," cried one of the mothers, I know not which, for we both turned back.

"What, is your son called Tom?" asked my step-mother. "My daughter is Thomasina."

Tom and I laughed at this, as did we all. Then in my heart was a clutching, for I thought of my twin called Tom.

"Come closer," said the other Tom's mother to me. She examined my face and said in wonder, "They as like as two peas! The face is almost the very same!"

"We are going on deck," said Tom.

"Keep out of the way of the saylors," said his mother.

"Mind you are sober in your conduct," said mine.

The rain misted our hair and faces. Now the smells were of harbour. My eyes were drawn up to the masts and yards and all the ropes and tackle that managed them. I could not see how they would work. I hadde seen smaller sailboats on the river in my time in London, but nothing like these great ships. Then came noise of a crowd approach on shore, a singing and calling and jeering of men who have spent the whole night in drinking.

Men aboard the ship came by the rail to see what was afoot. My father stood at the foot of the plank with a roll of names.

"We are bound for Virginia," said they.

"You are drunk," said my father, who stood on shore with a roll of names to check against. "And late come."

"Well met," said one. "You are discerning."

"The captain mislikes drunkenness. We could turn you away yet."

"We are leaving all we know for all we know not. If we raise a glass to send ourselves off to be eaten by selvedges, who'll blame us?"

The one who spoke was a compact young man who carried himself lightly, despite his drunkenness, the kind of lightness that may quickly turn. He was the man to make a gybe with jovial face and then sneak an insult after you had already laughed. The others were ragged and blearie with drink. They carried nothing with them but what they wore.

The sailors paid no attention to the young men, but went about their business. They paid almost no attention to any of the passengers. But for the one who had swung me down, I could scarce distinguish between them. They were figures who performed mysterious tasks.

The drunken young men were the last of the passengers. My father called out to the steward so and came up the plank behind them.

We had already hid a little from the drunken striplings, edging further forward on the ship.

Now, hearing my father's footsteps, and not wishing my father to tell me to go below or have cause to say anything to me at all, I ducked around the hatch and dropped down in a crouch to be out of sight. I had to peek out to see my father going up to the poope deck with the steward. Out from the cabin came Mr. Hill and a man I assumed was the captain. Mr. Hill was an investor and promoter of the project of Virginia, but did not sail with us. My father spoke and showed the rolls, passing them over. The other men heard him, the captain received the rolls, then turned away. My father, his job was done.

Now he came down amidship and passed by us to a group of men of like age which stood farther on. I could hear his voice saying we were all aboard now. I could see, too, his desire for importance, especially now that it was gone.

"Is that your Father?" asked my companion.

I nodded. "Yours?"

His face clouded and angled down. "He is the lean one, there, with silver in his beard."

He stood in the same group as my father. I guessed through their dress they were the guildsmen though my father were not one.

"Has he a trade?" I asked.

"Cartwright," said he.

There were groups of these men all over, huddled now in the rain. The young men had found more like themselves. Tho' two had fallen insensible and lay curled under a smaller boat upturned on deck, the others crossed their arms and slouched. One had a little ball he tossed and caught, tossed and caught.

Another group were the soldiers, who had a lean and tired look.

Then came a command from the poope deck, the Master to another, and he to all of us. "A-deck, a-deck! The Captain gives his address." The women were got up from below, passengers and crew all assembled.

The Captain gave a speech on the glory and promise of our endeavour, and gave us to understand what rules we must abide, which the Steward elucidated. No gambling, no taking the Lord's name in vain, passengers must not interfere with the work of sailors. He named the punishments for infractions.

"We live in close quarters," took up the Captain. "Therefore we must alwaies and actively love our neighbour, as our Lord admonishes."

Then Mr. Hill gave a sermon and a prayer and went ashore.

Now sailors I had not even noticed swung into action. Six drew up the gang plank. Gangs of four took great poles and pushed off from the wharf. Those of the passengers who had been below came up on deck to see what was afoot. Another command and one of the smaller sails up front went up to help us stand off from shore.

The rest of our flotilla lay at anchor in the Thames where they hadde been as the *Diamond* were loaded. Now they cheered to see us stand off. But we must wait for the tide, now, to go with it.

At last the tide was right. The command went out on the *Sea Venture* to weigh anker. Up went the yards. Down fell the sails. Cheers went up with each sailing. At last it was the turn of the *Diamond*. Now could I see how the capstang worked, as a crew of eight drew up the great anker, walking round in a circle, leaning into the bar. I began to see how this rope pulled that corner of that sail so it caught the most wind, how that rope raised the tops'l yard, this small one let down the furled sail.

The sails caught the wind. The great ship moved. I had always sensed the wind had power, but I had never imagined it like this. A joy rose in me. And a great Wonder at the ingenuity of the men who had made the boat that so moved across the Water, and carried us, and at the shores of the Thames and the boats upon it and all that was new to me and all that would be new to me. I wished for Joan to tell all this to. I wished for Joan at my side, the way I was used to have her at my side when I wanted her, eager to hear what I might say, her chatter that was like a clear stream, bright, and sparkling, and cool. She would be saying out loud now what my heart was saying, the words my thought spoke: Look how the sail becomes a creature, alive, something different from what it was before, how large is the world, how many live in it! And so Joy and Wonder and Sorrow all lived intermingled in me, for Joan was not with me and I was not with Joan and Old Nut where I belonged but here with a Man strang and unpredictable and a Womann kinde but not my mother and a round-faced boy his character yet unknown.

"Look how the sail becomes a creature," said I to Tom.

"A creature?" sayed he. He squinted at the sail and cocked his head.

The project of our journeying to Virginie in these Ships seemed grand, ambitious and brave, but my mind skirted the prospect of staying in Virginie. There was in me another thing that was like a cage around the heart. Fear.

Tom and I being too short to see over the rail, pulled ourselves up on it, so our chests rested atop the rail, our arms over the side, our heads out over the water. We watched the water swirl below us, the wider shore revealed to us. Then a great cry went up from Tom as of a sudden he was dangling up-side down o'er the water. His father had him by the ancles. He howled in fright.

"Draw him in! Put him down!" I cried.

"If he will put himself in danger for no reason, he must learn what God and Fate might serve him."

Then Tom, his father, lifted his son up and drew him back over the gunwhale and as good as dropped him on the deck of the ship, gasping and panting in subsiding terror.

"Pick yourself up, boy, and stop your womanish tears."

This Tom endeavoured to do. He stood and tried to quell his sobs and in a few moments succeeded passing well. Now his eyes changed, cast down tho' they were, and his face stilled and hardened so it almost shifted shape from round to long.

A crowd had drawn round. The young men scoffed. My father stepped through the crowd, cuffed me and held me by the ear.

"Make not a show of yourself, hoyden!" hissed he. "I will not have my daughter climbing like a monkey or a sailor."

Thus were we both chastised and sent back to our mothers.

As we stood down the Thames, some few of our numbers expresst discomfort at the motion of the Ship, including my step-mother, who was indeed, she hadde recently told me, carrying my younger brother or sister.

"These are flat waters," sayed my Father. "Save your ill feelings for the Sea!"

When we did come to the sea, my poor step-mother fared worse, and could not even take consolation that my Father was as bad as she.

My friend and I, by God's providence, were spared, which allowed us to avoid our fathers and roam about the deck and befriend the mariners.

At Plymouth we took on stores and our convoy swelled in number to nine Ships. When at last we weighed Anker in Plymouth, we seemed a great Congregation, taking Brittain and Christianity across the Seas to a New World. The Ships were in good Trim, and full of Hope. Tho' my Father was sick at Stomach, he squeezed my shoulder. The sun shone upon us. We were at last truly on our way.

"Thomasina, what bright future lies before us, by God's Grace. We are reunited, Thomasina. I am heartily sorry I left you behind once. I will not do so agayn."

My heart for a moment softened a little towards him.

As I now took care to be seen to be praying and bending my Head, and as I now loved my Step-Mother enow to desire her ease by my help,

I appeared a better Daughter, and my Father was less harsh. The weight of his earlier Treatment hung yet round my heart. I neither loved my Father nor trusted him. I saw he was a weak man, small of stature, trying to act large. He enjoyned me to attend to my step-mother while she lay ill. He nearly threw up himself in the saying of it, yet he sought to hide his own illness. I took care to bring her water, to empty her chamber pot, to see to her comfort, but when she seemed to sleep and have no need of me, I ran off to play with my friend about the ship.

Our bright sense of embarkation was tempered soon enough by contrary winds that kept us another week sheltering off Cornwall, not crossing any ocean, but waiting to cross an ocean, which is dull work.

In the time the others were sicke, Tom and I had become favourites of the mariners. One showed us how to make a whistle and how to blow it and taught us tunes. The blue-eyed mariner I knew as George never failed to call out to me or to wink. I reminded him of his sisters at home, sayed he. He was young, I adjudged, eighteen or nineteen. The drunken landsmen were the same age, and no one's favourites. They broke out in fights regularly and had to be disciplined by the Captain.

At last winds turned in our favour and we weighed for Virginia.

As it was with the sun falling below the horizon, so it was with the disappearance of land. It was there and then it was not. Unlike the fallen sun, land gave off no glow, no reminder of its having been there. The Sea seemed ever more vast. Our voyage, we knew, would carry us through two moons, and now I saw how far a day took us, at what great speed, and had an idea of the vastness of the Sea far greater than I had ever imagined. The World was round, sayed one of the mariners, which accounted, in part, for the loss of the sight of land.

My father's Sea-Sicknesse abated in five or seven dayes time, which was a blow to me for he wished me sober, not running the decks, playing a wooden flute or consorting with mariners. But even my father softened after a time. After morning prayer and breaking our fast and cleaning and tidying the space in our cabbin, there was little left to do, and we must all find ways to amuse ourselves. I spent time looking out at the wind, waves, water and sky, indeed could spend many a long hour so doing. My mariner friend trained my eye to squalls and shifts in the wind.

Tom and I played tig and hide and seek and what games we could devize of a moment.

On a day of sunshine, steady wind, and modest waves, Tom and I amused ourselves climbing the rail and the lower part of the rigging, just high enough to stand on the rail itself. Tom, mindful of his father's dangling him o'er the side, hopped down ere he climbed the rail, while I stayed as long as I could, my father not being by to see me. I loved the pitch and dip of the Ship as it rode the waves. What would it be to climb higher, right up to the look-out atop the mast? My limbs longed to try it.

I said this to my friend.

"I am not sure I should like it," said he. "I fear my heart might fail me."

Just then was the boat swayne passing, and not far off a group of the men, including our fathers. I hopped down swiftly before my father saw me up there.

"You have a mind to climb up?" the boat swayne asked Tom.

"I am not sure," said he.

"If you want, if your father approves, you can."

"Go to, Tom," cried his father. "I'll wager any sum you get no higher than ten feet."

So Tom started up the rigging. As his father had sayed, when he reached ten or fifteen feet, he looked down, cried out a little, and paused.

The men laughed.

Before they had done, Tom climbed on, looking only upwards now, until he reached the bucket of the look-out. I noted he gripped the rail tightly, but he stopped a while and looked out. Then came he down to general praise.

"Wc should have took your wager," said the other men.

"I am glad you did not," sayed the cartwright. "The boy surprizes me."

Then moved they off together.

My friend flopped down upon the deck, hand to his heart. I sat beside him.

"How was it?"

"Terrifying," he said.

"I would not have been scared," said I.

"No, you would not," said he. "You are braver than me."

"I hate I cannot climb that I'm a girl," I said.

"You are very like a boy," said he.

"What saw you up there?"

"I hardly know," sayed he. "But that the Ocean is vast, the ships of our convoy like to dots upon it."

We rested in silence for a time, and then I said, "My father will marry me to one of the settlers one day. It will be as if I am trapped on this deck my whole life. I must find a way to run away."

"Run away!" sayed he, looking around.

"Once we are in Virginia, idiot," said I. "Where then, I know not. If I were a boy, I might run anywhere. Before we came aboard, I thought I might turn sailor and be ship's boy."

There were two ship's boys aboard the *Diamond*, both twice our height. One waited on the Captain. The other was a hard-looking boy with a missing tooth who spat continewally.

"I fear I have missed my chance," said I, glumly.

"I would marry you," sayed my friend.

"Truly, I must run away," said I.

He punched my shoulder.

We had in that moment and in many moments a perfect companionship.

After some time, most of those afflicted with the sea sicknesse 'gan to recover themselves, while others yet lay sick, unable to rise from their pallets.

One of these dyed, a Man, sayed my father, who ne'er looked well, a Debtor of middle years. The Chaplain gave a service for him, attended by all who were upright, and his Bodie, wrapped in cloth, was consigned to the Sea. Two sailors took cloth by head and feet and heaved. A small splash on the sail-shadowed waves and he was gone.

Word ran round this was not Sea-Sicknesse, but a Fever, gained in London or Plymouth. Any who hadde been sick strove to rise to prove they hadde it not, and for two or three dayes, it seemed as if we might be free. Each morning and eve at mast we prayed fervently for health and God's mercy. Weather and wind continewed fair.

Then one of our number, a Cooper, failed to rise of a morning, but lay sick. Then one of the serving girls who slept by us. Then one of the Cook's boys. Then three or four a day newly sick, including Mistress Oakum and her daughter, two of the young men, some of the soldiers, another of the serving girls, a Gentleman, his Wife.

After a se'en-night, the Cooper died, but not the serving girl, a week later, Mistress Oakum, but not Agnes, her daughter, one of the young men, one of the soldiers, the Gentleman *and* his Wife, and others in a pattern of increasing frequency, so we grew accustomed to the funeral service and the sight of bodies disappearing beneath the waves.

One night as we lay sleeping, the cries of Tom's young sister, a babe, wakened me. She did not quiet in her usual way when her mother gave her suck and by this we all understood it was her turn. Her mother rocked and hushed her as if by her care she could keep the sickness at bay. The next day, Tom stayed close by the two of them.

My father insisted we keep ourselves as far away from the Sick as we could, which of course was not far, our whole world being but sixty feet long. That night we slept on deck, the three of us in a row, a state I preferred to sleeping below. We felt the wind and heard the sails and the creak of the masts in their steps, saw the moon and stars, and were less opprest by foul odour.

My step-mother, now large with child, exclaimed at movement inside of her. She took my hand and put it on her belly to feel the babe's kicks and punches. My father, on her other side, put his hand there, too, and said a prayer.

Moans and sighs and cries could we hear above deck and below, but the sky was full of beauty. It seemed to me incongruous that all this human misery moved along in a rounded box, as if the ship itself were a coffin moving through I hardlie know what, a heaven.

The day that followed we learned from Tom and others that his sister was worse and like to die and his mother sick withal. Midday next we heard a wail that let us know the babe hadde gone to God. Before supper the Chaplain spoke the funeral service for the babe and the words "Man that is born of a woman hath but a short time to live, and is full of misery," cut through us all, truer for this Soul than any other consigned to the deep.

"He cometh up, and is cut down, like a flower; he fleeth as it were a shadow, and never continueth in one stay."

The babe's form, in its tiny shroud, was this very shadow upon the surface of the sea, and then sunk below it, and gone.

Tom's mother in another day or two gave up the ghost and we stood once more hearing, "O Death, where is thy sting?," an ever smaller company. Tom stood by his father with his face cast down. I knew that it was not onlie love for his mother that filled him with grief but that now his life was in the hands of a man who hated him.

We hadde not dispersed from the service when my step-mother stopped in her tracks and cried out, her paines upon her. Below her skirts a flood, the breaking of her waters. Mistress Bagwell took charge, walking her up and down the deck till she could walk no more, then taking her below decks to the gun room for her confinement.

After doing what I could to help, I wearied. Night fell. My father stayed awake on deck and sent me to sleep below. I know not where Tom's father slept, but Tom himself lay curled up, weeping and a-shivering. He clutched in his arms the bag that held his family's belongings. All the mothers were absent—mine to childbirth, Tom's to death, Mistress Oakum to death, Mistress Bagwell to childbed. The men slept adeck. There were five of us where once had been fifteen. The serving girls did their best to comfort Tom, drawing a blanket over him. One sang him a song. I crept up and lay down beside him. Once we hadde been forced to sleep touching one another. Now we didde it for comfort.

We shifted through the night, lifted and dropped on the waves, waking and sleeping, hearing my step-mother make noize I would not have thought could come out of her, hearing the wind come up.

In the morning, it was clear Tom had the sickness, and that the weather hadde changed. We climbed higher upon the waves and fell more violently. Tom was hot with fever, his head aked, a flush rose up over him. Even in the dimness of our enclosure, methought the look of his eye different, not of this world. But he roused and spoke to me. From the bag he had clutched through the night, he hadde drawn trowzers, blouse, doublet, and cap. These he thrust at me.

"For your escape," sayd he.

I fell out into tears and passed them back. "You will have need of them."

He thrust them at me again. "I have the clothes I wear. Take them," he insisted.

I took the clothes and bundled them into my mother's purse.

My head aked. Had the sickness come to me? Why had I thought it would not?

The others were rising. "The waves are greater than they were," said Treena, one of the serving girls.

"How fares my mother?" I asked.

All three shook their heads. None of us said we heard no cries, not of mother, not of child, but mayhap the wind was too strong now, as indeed I found it, going on deck.

Aloft, saylors took in sail. The ship pitched heavily. I made my way forward past bleary-eyed groups of men to the forward hatch to get to the gunroom where my mother lay. Outside it my father hadde his hands over his eyes, his shoulders shaking, that told me the story as much as I later learned. The babe, a boy, was born blue, and ne'er took a breath. His mother hadde just moments ago given up the ghost and followed him.

My father saw me and wept the harder. He pulled me to him. I endured his fierce embrace, drawing no comfort from it. Now were my friend and I in the same boat—motherless, with fathers we hated or endured. Misery overtook me, and then, of a sudden, fury. I wrenched myself from my father's grip and shot up the ladder as fast as I could, crying my rage to the wind.

There was nothing to be done.

The wind increased still more, so that caps flew, hair blew straight out, and words flew off like streams of words on paper. My step-mother received an abbreviated service, during which we were adjured to put our hands to some fixed thing. Briefly, the Chaplain, his left hand clutching the edge of the boat overturned on deck, sayed words I knew but could not hear, and then two saylors took their ends of the two bodies, wrapped together, and heaved, but a wave hit just then, and they stumbled, and the bodies hit the rail and fell to the deck. On the next toss we were at the valley of the wave, and in they went into the Sea, who swallowed them up as she had swallowed the others (the sea's Mouth appearing onlie when it had something to swallow) the shroud unwrapping a bit so I had a glimpse of the bloody naked blue babe and my step-mother's hand. The next wave towered so high above us that for a minute it seemed our ship was something for the sea to swallow. This was the first time I didde not like the Sea and wanted off it.

Now passengers were sent below to be out of the way as much as to be out of danger. I found my friend much as I hadde left him, that is with sweatie brow and lustreless eyes. Our cabbin came closer packt again. I lay next my friend. Beyond him sat the girls, sorrowful at the loss of my mother and brother. My father came close beside me, the guildsmen behind him. The young men crowded into the other parts belowdeck separated from us by canvas, their bravado bellowing outward from them.

The storm continewed. Someone had brought the chickens below. They ran around squawking and defecating. The rooster crowed. The other livestock, likewise, were uneasy, and bellowed, squealed or grunted as was their wont. The decks were filled with the sound of prayers, shrieks, gasps and weeping, when we could hear anything, which was onlie when immediately beside one who yelled. The beams of the Ship creaked and groaned. They shuddered shudders that shook our very bones. The roar of the wind and water, the buffets of the wind with like a hundred cannons.

I was sick in Bodie and Soul and drifted in and out of consciousness as wind turned to storm, my father's prayer like a canvas wall behind me. As the ship pitched, so pitched we. I know not how long this period continewed. A night and a day, for certayn, but it might have been two. When I woke fully, my fever broken, it was yet dark and the men who hadde crowded our room were gone. To the pumps, I learned. Agnes Oakum had insisted on taking her turn withal, so for the moment it was just Tom and me and the three men that lay too sick to performe any duties.

The room stank worse than ever. The bucket that served as our chamber pot hadde slopped thorough its lid.

If it were day outside we could not know it, the hatch being covered, the storm still blowing.

I did not immediately realize my friend had lost his life. I hadde for some time without realizing it been half-aware of his heaviness falling against me and then away with the movement of the ship. At last, his limpness and the coolness of his skin led me to understand he was no longer among the living. I think it was at this that I came fully awake. As I did, it came to me of an instant. I could dress him in my clothes and me in his. I could live on as him, he could live on in me! In the darkness, none would know I had effected the change.

Freedom!

It was not easie to get the clothes off Tom and harder still to get mine back on him, yet I persevered.

In another day was the storm blown out. The hatch covers came off. Even the dim light that resulted from this seemed bright to us. The smell of our enclosure was of sicknesse, excrement, and death. Treena and I emerged onto deck squinting, our heades aking. Then it came to me—my father would know the difference between me and Tom. Even if others were fooled—all had marked our resemblance throughout the voyage—my father would know the difference.

The mainmast was gone, or rather, was a stub. Exhausted men lay sprawled every which where. The sun shone hot. Under power of the sail on the forward mast, torn, though it was, we sailed on.

Seated together with one of the young drunkards (now sober) I had not taken note of before were Agnes Oakum and the other serving girl, Elinor. They discoursed at their ease, erupting now and then in laughter, in the manner of people who have together fought through difficulty.

"What news?" sayed they. "Where is Girl Tom?"

"Dead," sayed I.

"Like her father, poor soul, and yours."

"What?"

"Making his way to the forward pumps in the night, her father let go a rope and was swept overboard," sayed Agnes. "Your father reached out for him and was swept off in his turn."

The convenience of the deaths o'erwhelmed me. I dropped to the deck, stunned. Agnes gave me a look like an augur. She knew who I was and what I hadde done, as she later showed.

The mood was changed aboard the Ship. The Mariners had an air of having known it all along, that Hope and Expectation is alwaies dashed or worn down. They alone seemed unchanged by our losses.

I am out of time to tell you all, but let me say when first I donned the garb of my Friend and posed as him, I was in a terror of being discovered. Surely it was not hard to know us apart. Tho' Agnes made a worthy accomplice I feared it would not be enough.

As I encountered first one and then another of those who had known me, my heart beat mightily for the moment I should be discovered and questioned.

First we hadde the funeral of myself.

"Forasmuch as it hath pleased Almighty God of his great mercy to take unto himself the soul of our dear sister, Thomasina Willes, here departed," intoned the Chaplain, "we therefore commit her bodie to the deep—"

Watched I one last time the sea open its mouth and swallow a Body I hadde loved. The Chaplain remarked not that I resembled Thomasina Willes more than Tom Gibson. The Guildsmen remarked it not. The sailors remarked it not. The rough boys remarked it not. The Cook, the chirurgion, the boat-swain. None of them.

What magick my trowzers and change in cap worked! The onlie one who gave me a long look was the blue-eyed mariner who hadde been a friend to both of us. But he said nought. Not then.

We hadde lost our convoy after the storm, and could not be certain of our position. I longed for sight of land, to get off the ship and away from those who had known me as Thomasina Willes, for discovery was every day possible.

The biggest difficulty I faced was the problem of pissing. Sailors were forbid from pissing over the stern of the Ship, being the Masters' Quarters, and over the Rail, and must piss where they shat in the Beak Head, where was nothing strang in pissing below the seat o' your trowzers when you had dropped them. In a cabbin, they pissed in pots, standing unless seas required otherwise. One thing in my favour was that tho' I saw manie a man piss, I rarely saw his Yard while he did it, it being obscured by hands or shirt tails. Thus, if I could find a way to piss so it ran not down my leg but shot forward, then I should be in a good way to go undetected. I needed a funnel, or tube, which I could press to the area and direct the stream. There came to my mind George whittling the wooden flute. A flute was too long and too broad, but a smaller piece of wood—with the middle hollowed out and one end carved to make a seal over my nether parts, the other to convey the liquid in a stream—could serve. Then it came to me that I might use the toy Old Nut had carved for me, the rough figure of a boy. To hollow it out I would need something long, thin, and sharp. A nauger would be best but I could not get close to one. And so I worked away at it when I could find a moment with a nail and a needle. I had a piece of sewing I kept about me and worked on the device under its cover. 'Twas harder to work with the knife.

I kept my Device on a string round my waist. When I needed it, I fished for't, pressed it in place, shook off as I had slyly seen others do, and tucked it away agayn, almost as if it had been attacht to me in the natural way. The fear of discovery was aflight in my chest, but once I had pissed a dozen times without discovery I felt myself more secure.

At last, eight or ten days after the storm, we came in sight of land and of two of our other ships, storm-battered like us. A day and a half later, we were sailing up the river to the Jamestown settlement. Already were three ships moored there, but not the *Sea Venture*, which we must now assume lost. The gates of the fort opened and out swelled the people to greet us and learn our fate.

The land rose up strangely to us when we set foot upon it. For a brief time, I hadde a sort of Landsickness that made me wish I were still at sea. For all that I was curious to see this new land, I hadde a powerful feeling I didde not wish to remain. In my mind and in my heart, I thought of Wormshill, and Joan.

I stayed close to Agnes Oakum & Elinor, who took me under their wing, and I endeavoured to call as little attention to myself as possible, while letting everyone know that I hoped to sign on as sailor. I preferred any Ship other than the *Diamond*, for aboard her was alwaies the risk I were recognized.

I stayed in Virginia less than two months. A great deal happened in the colony in that time, which you already know of, and I will not recount. In October four ships were returning to England. I went to the master of each ship to say that my parents hadde dyed and I hadde no coin to pay passage, but could work my way. Green though I was, I'd be quick to learn. But onlie the master of the *Diamond*, who hadde lost a boy to sickness, would have me.

The blue-eyed sailor vouched for me. "He is quick as he says."

The master said, "You are the boy who went aloft. Well. You know what life at sea is like now. Yea, I will take thee."

Thus was I then part of the Crew, who made me welcome in their way, as if I hadde crossed a line.

I slept where I could find space and learned to keep apart from gropers.

When the Ship sayled, like the other saylors I was happy to be under way again. It was better to be working on the ship than to be a passenger. I preferred work to Idleness. I took my turn aloft. I almost forgot on my first time up the rigging that I was supposed to have done it before, and nearly exclaimed my great delight. The winds blew fresh, reminding me of the stink below. My field of view increased. And it was a chance to be alone. I could relax what remnants of vigilance I needed to remayn the Boy I had become. So I sayled back to England.

To be paid at the end of the voyage, pittance that it was, was a welcome pleasure. I still held the thought of Wormshill in my mind. But when in Plymouth I stepped ashore I saw what I hadde hitherto been blind to. If I returned to Wormshill, I must return to girlhood, and the end of my liberty.

I did not return. I told myself I merely deferred, nothing was decided yet, I could return any time I wished. But in not deciding, my decision was made.

I stayed a mariner eight years, making three more voyages to Virginia, two to the East Indies, and more between England and the Low Countries. When I could, I changed from company to company so they should not be suspicious of the way I remayned the same, and didde not become a Man.

Oft I wondered what had become of Joan, but liked not how lonely I was left when I did so.

I gave as my age twelve on my first voyage, not knowing the exact year I was born. Tho' I reunited with my Father, I never asked him, but it must have been 1600 or the year before. I know not what month or season.

Eight years later, I gave my age as fifteen.

On a voyage to Russia with the Muscovy Company, I met Tradescant. He was a lean man, and a practickall one, a patient bargainer, curious. He was charged with provisioning the voyage. For his part, he strove to bring home every foreign plant he might, and if he find any other thing strang or curious, to bring home one of those things all so.

I was by then anxious to find a life that was not at Sea. Tho' I loved the pull of the sayls and the pitch of the deck and the wonder of strang shores, I no longer set out on each voyage with a light heart but rather a dread of long voyages and of keeping up certayne pretences. I would not visit a brothel nor drink as the other men. I hadde no family to visit on shore. I tired of fending off men who sought me out for one comfort or another. I hadde heard myself spoken of as mysteriously unchanging, bewitched. I must make a life apart from the Sea, though the longer I was at Sea, the less I knew how.

I hadde a great liking for Tradescant and made myself useful to him not for any cause other than that I wished to. To him, I confessed my desire for a life on Land, and he, unexpectedly, told me of his son's going to the King's School and raised the possibility that I might also.

The rest you know: I sizared at Cambridge, went into debt to go to Leiden for my M.D. Met you on the return. Brought home plants, &c., for Tradescant. You went on to Somerset.

———

I had need of money, and could not get it by my trade without a License from the College of Physitians. Nor was the Barber-Chirurgions open to me, as I hadde not apprenticed (tho' I hadde served chirurgion's mate on two voyages). The usurer from whom I had borrowed now called his loan in. I liked not to borrow from friends, nor never hadde, but now, I took money from Tradescant to pay the usurer. More than ever I felt I must repay what I owed. I offered myself as scribe and secretary.

Tradescant had a correspondent in Somerset, Lady Margaret Long, who had a collection of eggs, sayd he. She, having duplicates, had sent him some, and had long requested, should he come into them, any unusual egg. Tradescant had received of a sailor both an ostrich egg and a hummingbird egg along with its nest and skin, and these he desired me to take to Lady Margaret in Somerset, being very close to Bristol.

I made my way by coach, continuing to the house with the box of eggs and sundry skins to the estate of Lady Margaret, whose messuage was a fine large house of two stories. The heavens opened as I drew near in a great downpour. I knocked on the door very wet and was answered that Lady Margaret had been expecting me but was out egg collecting. I was led into a fine hall, wainscotted and dim, and a fire lit for me to dry out by. When I had dried out sufficiently, I drew a chair by the fire and dozed. I was awakened by the clatter of hooves outside and the entrance in a great noyze and breeze of two Ladies, one tall, one short, and a Boy with a Basket he carried on his back. The butler met my Lady and told her of my presence. She, the short one, it turned out, came and greeted me most warmly before excusing herself to change out of their wet things for they had been caught in the same downpour. She entreated the Butler to show me into the drawing room where I might be more comfortable than the draughty Hall, and where were drawings and books and a spinnet to occupy me while waiting.

There I perused delicate drawings of eggs and flowers and beetles which were laid out on top of a case of flat drawers.

They returned, in dry clothes, with fresh faces. Lady Margaret was most eager both to show me the eggs she had in her collection and to see what I had brought. "When we bring home eggs, the light is best in here to paint a copy of them, and then they go into the collection." She did not introduce me to her companion, who I thought must be her sister or cousin.

"Come," she cried, and led us through a door to a room that housed her collection. It was a miniature of Tradescant's Ark. On shelves lay rows of nests and eggs and manie birds, preserved. "Here you see my collection."

The nests had eggs in them, but there was a row separate, eggs only, and in order of size. Above this, the bird, so that the size of bird and egg could be seen to be relative, as only made sense. The smallest egg she had was a tit's, the largest that of a Swan.

I carried with me the chest, lined with wool, that had within it two smaller chests, also lined with wool. I went to open them, but Lady Margaret in her eagerness held out her hands, took the larger box and laid it on the table, slipped the latch, lifted the lid, pulled away the wool and there lay the ostrich egg, of a size to fill a man's hand. She lifted it delicately out and held it before her in wonder. She turned to the eggs and birds she had.

"I have measured, Mr. Barrows," she said, "the size of an egg relative to the bird, and it is not always the same, but it is in the range of one-tenth. If you take the length of an egg and add its width and divide by two, very often it turns out to be one-tenth the length of the bird. Joan, get the measuring stick."

I had met so many Joans in this world that I no longer started each time I heard the name. A hundred disappointments led me to take less notice. And yet, I turned my eyes on Lady Margaret's companion for the first time to reassure myself that once again, I would be disappointed. We were far from Wormshill, far from Kent, where if she lived, she surely lived still.

The light in the room was dimmer than in the drawing room, and she was turned away to take up the measuring stick, but in her movement and gestures was something familiar, and when she turned back, I saw the shape of her face was something like the shape of Joan's face.

Lady Margaret laid the egg atop a sheet of paper on the table. Joan carefully traced its shape upon the paper, then Lady Margaret set the egg back in its wool. Now Lady Margaret measured the length and breadth of the outline. Her head and Joan's bent over the paper.

"The length is . . ." sayed Lady Margaret.

"Six inches," sayed Joan. Was that her voice? My eyes remained fixed on this Joan.

"And the breadth is—"

"—a little over five."

Lady Margaret raised her head. "If this be one-tenth the bird, then the bird is—"

"Fifty-five inches."

"Almost my height!" She beheld the egg in renewed wonder.

"A bird the size of you." Joan laughed. "I cannot imagine it."

Now she must have felt my eyes upon her for she turned and looked at me directly and in her eyes, large and blue, in her cheekbones, in her small chin, the truth of herself was there. 'Twas my Joan, indeed.

"Joan!" I breathed, not knowing I did it.

"Know you my maid, Mr. Barrows?"

"Maid?" sayd I.

Joan looked at me curiously now, to see if she should know me.

I wished her to know me without being told.

I wished to weep and throw myself upon her.

I closed my hand to make it into a fist to strike myself upon the breast—her name, in the language of Old Nut—but before I did so, recognition came across her face.

"Tom," she sayed. She put her hand to her mouth with a great intake of breath that she held and held untill at last she exhaled, and wept.

Tears ran freely down my face.

"But Tom was a girl," sayd Lady Margaret.

"I had a twin, Lady Margaret," sayd I, just as Joan sayd, wiping her eyes, "The Willes had twins. You have heard me speak of the girl. The boy I never mentioned . . ."

The ease of our answer made the truth behind it stand in for the true truth of it.

Joan wept anew, contained herself anew. "What news of your sister, Tom?"

"She died," sayed I, "on the ship to Virginia. With our step-mother, of an illness, whereafter was our father swept overboard in a storm. Then was I truly orphaned."

"O, Tom. I thought never to see you again." Joan was again overcome.

"Nor I you. Every 'Joan' for twenty years have I turned my head."

"Twenty-one," sayed she.

"You must stay to supper," cried Lady Margaret, "and continew this happy reunion. Where do you stop?"

Each word from Lady Margaret was an interruption.

"I have left my things at the inn," sayd I. I had to tear my eyes from Joan to her mistress, but found I could not keep them there. "I had plans to continew on tomorrow, to my friend Heard's, who has taken up a curacy in Norton Malreward."

"I have heard of Heard." Something in her voice told me I must counterfeit my desire to drink in Joan with my eyes and ignore all else. Lady Margaret must be paid mind.

"What hear you?"

"That he is very young and very zealous."

"We were school-fellows," sayed I. "At the King's School."

"In Canterbury?" sayed Joan. "So close?"

I gave my apology with my eyes, with a turn of my hands. Wormshill was not a day from Canterbury. The whole of my time at the King's School, I watched the market, listened for news of Wormshill, but either there was none, or I heard it not. (Later, we worked out Joan had bin already in Somerset a year or two when I was at the King's School. Thus was my not visiting Wormshill a lesser sin. And I could not return as Tom Barrows, when I was known there as Thomasina Willes. Tho' this, too, I realized I had bin wrong in. I could easily have said my twin lived, and I was him. 'Twas now my exact story.)

Lady Margaret turned her eyes from one of us to the other, one of us to the other, and again I knew I must deflect her.

There had sprung up between Joan and me something greater than a meeting of lost friends.

"You have not seen the other box," sayed I. I lifted the case that held the hummingbird, its nest, and its egg to her.

As she opened the case and examined them in wonder, lifting out first the tiny egg like an elongated pea, then the tiny nest like half a small pine cone, and at last the tiny, brilliant-coloured bird with its beak like a needle, Joan and I made a compact with our eyes.

I stayed for supper, making sure to turn as much of my attention as I could onto Lady Margaret, and Joan doing the same. I told my story to Joan, much condensed, and she to me, with many interjections from Lady Margaret, ending with, "And then did I steal her away from my nieces, and here she has remayned ever since, my amanuensis.

"You find us very quiet here now, Mr. Barrows. 'Twas not always so. In my husband's time, we had great parties. Musick and hunting and natural philosophy. Our pursuit of musick and natural philosophy has continewed, tho' we are fewer in number. Let us invite your friend, Mr. Heard.

"Tell us of your travels," sayed she.

I obliged her with an account of some of the things I hadde seen on the Barbary Coast, ostriches themselves, the birds belonging to the great egg, with their strang serpentine necks. "They are as tall as I am or taller," I sayed, "so your estimation is not far off."

All the while, I stole small, sideways glances at Joan. A smile perpetually pulled at her lips. Her eyes filled and filled with tears. She gazed at me with something like thirst. I do not think she heard half of our talk. I knew not half of what I was saying.

I longed to be alone with Joan, to hear unadulterated her voice, her thoughts, to tell her mine.

Lady Margaret plied me with questions of all sorts—what news did I bring of London, how did I find Leiden, did I meet this gentleman or that with whom she corresponded.

All the while I felt Joan's eyes upon me, as Lady Margaret remarked. "You will eat our visitor up with your eyes, Joan."

"I marvel at fortune, my Lady, that brings me Tom again, when I thought all connections of my infancy lost."

At last, Lady Margaret sayed, "Here. You shall not stop at an inn. I shall send for your things. You will stay here." She rang a bell.

After suppar, we took a turn in the garden, there still being evening light. "We have not so manie rareties in the garden as has Tradescant," sayd she, "and yet I find it pleasing."

"And we have a good store of healing plants," sayed Joan. "Which may interest you, for physick."

We walked the gardens until the light grew dim, whereupon we repayred to the drawing room. The butler lit candles. Lady Margaret played upon the lute, Joan beat a tambour, and then they played together.

Lady Margaret had a telescope, which had been, she told me, a wedding gift from her husband. The moon, she sayd, would be up some time after eleven o'clock. If the sky stayed clear (the wind having driven off the clouds), she should show it to me through the telescope. Each night she measured the passage of the planets. She herself, and then, at different intervals while she slept, Joan, and her boy. The telescope was set up in the gallery.

When the moon rose, the boy lit the way up to the gallery. The telescope, being almost the length of a man, was much longer than the type of spy-glass I had seen. A seat at its base allowed the viewer comfort and help to still the eye. Lady Margaret demonstrated how to put one's eye to the end, and turn for focus. The boy helped her adjust the machine so that it gazed upon the moon. As they did this, Joan stood behind me, and quickly pressed my hand (I had them clasped behind my back). This touch enflamed me in a way I had never known.

Lady Margaret gave up her seat at the telescope for me. I put my eye to the telescope. Lady Margaret had the boy put out the light, the better to see. The moon was not quite full, and I hadde seen through better telescopes that gave it more clearly, but it was wondrous all the same to see with such clarity the marks and depressions and mountains of the moon, wondrous that the light of the sun shone with such force that its mere reflection gave this much light, wondrous that Joan had touched me.

I exclaimed in a way to satisfy Lady Margaret's pleasure in showing me her prize, but I was thinking only of Joan's touch and where she stood now and how I might feel that Touch again. We stayed some time gazing at the moon and stars while Lady Margaret demonstrated use of her Astrolabe until, at last, she began to yawn. "But we must sleep," sayed she. "Does it not irk you that it should be so? How much we might discover if we hadde no need of sleep!"

I lay awake long into the night. Hearing a noyze in the gallery, I rose in case it should be Joan, but it was the boy, taking measurements. I sat with him a time, discoursing quietly, and then to bed, where at last I slept.

After I had risen in the morning, a tapping came at my door and in came Joan with water jug in hand. "I have brought you water," she sayd.

Water stood already by the basin.

"I give you thanks," sayed I.

We stood six feet apart, not moving, our eyes alive.

"Joan," sayd I.

"Tom," sayd she.

In the mere saying of our names was something as large as the night sky.

"I lay awake all the night."

"As did I."

In the connection betwixt us the bond of our infancy was like a pip in a cherry. In the cherry itself, sweet and sharp and filled with juice, was something else, something new. Our mouths watered. She took a step towards me.

Then came footsteps through the adjoining chamber, a maid for the pot.

Joan sayed, "I brought you water but I see you have it. I will leave you to your ablutions," and went out, taking my heart with her.

I had been warmed by the affections of girls who professed to like my features, tho' I ever fended them off for fear of discoverie. Now and then a saucy wench would reach between my legs in a hallway. I made sure she always found something to please her. I knew from boys' talk and communal lodging that a yard lengthened and hardened. Mine, being false, was always soft. Fine for the odd grope, but not fine for anything further, and so I left it, always drawing away if things got to that pitch. Alas, this only drew them to me more, as they understood it to be my consideration for their own virtue on the one hand, or coyness on the other. Here and there a girl supposed I was one to go hard for boys.

From that time were Joan and I forever seeking small moments that we might draw near to one another.

I went to you, Heard, thinking only of Joan and how I should get back to her.

Our instinct was for secrecy, for we sensed Lady Margaret jealous. But one day it came over me with a force like to knock me over that we had not need for so great a secrecy as this. We might be married. I was a man, she a woman. We could wed our fates together.

When you discovered us, we were discovering each other.

In Bacon's *New Atlantis*, from which, as you recall, Lady Margaret read to us, it is proposed not that a man and wife should see each other naked before they marry, but that a friend so view them, at Adam's and Eve's pools, that they ensure no hidden defect, that each may upon this report know what they marry. We had no proxies, Joan and I, but showed ourselves to each other in solemn custom. This was terrifying and exhilarating. I had for so long hid my bodie from any eyes, that to lay it bare was an act of consequence with manie layers of meaning, one being this, to Joan: I reveal myself to you, and only you. I lay myself bare, my Bodie and Soul.

Your coming in upon us was a violation of this deep ceremony.

We had not yet told Lady Margaret of our intent to marry. First, must I get to Bristol and see about my examination. Hither have I repaired since your discovery of us, and at the Guild Hall, met a chirurgion bound to a long voiage, who wishes me to take his place as he has—o Fate!—fallen in love and cannot stand to be parted from his beloved! My own situation exactly, but for the one difference of you having sighted us when you did and discovered my anatomy. I have told him I will give an answer by nightfall. I must know if you will keep our secret. If I hear nothing, I will sail, and trust to Fate.

I hope you will hold my Secret for the sake of our friendship. I am no different than you have known me to be.

Or if that is not strictly true, the Man you know me to be is the Man I have always been.

If I were not born a Man, I have become one by being one, by living. I have hopes of happiness, of professional success, of philosophical investigations.

If you say you will hold my Secret, I'll ship not, and stay, and make my life as I had planned it, with Joan, who is blameless, and Beloved. If not, or if I do not hear, I take my leave and give you another year to change your mind.

If I am undone, I am undone. I leave it in your hands.

Thos. Barrows

Anne's Note

"If I am undone, I am undone. I leave it in your hands." That could not be the end of Tom's story!

How could I find out what had happened? Could there be a written record somewhere? I renewed my search of Somerset history. There is no record of a witch trial in Somerset at this time, no sensational pamphlets describing the Strang Discovery of Joan Palmer, Witch of Chew Magna. My small success with Joan's Tale by Lady Margaret Long galvanized me to explore every new avenue for further "discoveries." But nothing more turned up.

Then I asked myself: Who would have received Lady Margaret's papers, given that she had no direct heirs? Why, Frances and Anne Tylden! I did my best to track down their descendants, eventually sending a Facebook message to a Maureen Tilden, now living in Rhode Island and teaching nursing at Brown. She referred me to an elderly aunt in Kent, Elizabeth (Bibby) Iannopoulos, who was the keeper of family records. I sent Bibby a letter, and heard nothing back.

That was that, I thought. Dead end.

Well. Okay.

What I had already was amazing. I could be satisfied with that . . . Mostly. Almost. Not quite. Or: I could accept being forever not-quite-satisfied. That is the truth of history, after all—whether private or public. We will never truly know it. It will always be partial, in both senses of the word.

Then, six months later, I got a letter from Bibby. It was gracious and typewritten, explaining that she had been in Cyprus, where her late husband hailed from and where she spent half of each year in order to spend time with her grandchildren.

She had been intending, she said, to take stock of the family archive. She relayed a convoluted tale of family squabbles over who should have what, what should be kept and what discarded, and so on. There was a sister who would have packed up most of it years ago and dumped it in the parish records office. But Bibby had always felt there was something more to be done with the archive before it went out of the family. Even now, she wrote, she was casting an eye around for the person who might be best bequeathed the papers. Her own good intentions had come to naught. She had macular degeneration and would not be able to read for much longer. In short, would I consider visiting to help her go through the papers?

Why, yes. Yes, I would.

For this endeavour I stayed with Bibby in her seventeenth-century cottage in the Kent Downs, not far from Wormshill. The papers were in eighteen banker's boxes from, I judged, the 1960s; a steamer trunk; a plain wooden chest, possibly once a blanket-box; four hat boxes; two filing cabinets; many shoe boxes; three or four tin boxes; six or eight wooden fruit boxes; a deep enamel washbasin (or, I guess, a small bathtub); and two desks. None were labelled. Many were grouped roughly by time period—the shoe boxes mostly held war letters, for example—but others were a hodgepodge. The steamer trunk had Victorian baby shoes and christening gowns, a WWI uniform, a stack of *Punch* magazines from the 1920s, a fez, estate papers from the 1840s, a will dated 1703, and television licences from the 1970s. And the containers held not only Tilden/Tylden family memorabilia but that of generations of in-laws, whose connections Bibby outlined easily with a deep knowledge that was impossible to follow—Collinses and Greenhoughs and Davises and Mazzas. She herself had been a Drinkwater before she married Smaro Iannopoulos. It was her mother who had been a Tilden.

Even without the prospect of finding some memento of Lady Margaret Long, I was happy to be there, pulling documents out of boxes. There were so many surprises and delights (also: junk).

We realized we needed a system. And a large room.

We began organizing by family and time period, but I quickly found that Bibby was congenitally unable to sort. She stopped, and marvelled, and told me stories. If I'd had four months to spend with Bibby, I would have been perfectly happy to stop and marvel with her. Instead, I learned to keep going while listening with half an ear. Blah, blah, blah, blah, scarlet fever, hub, bub, hub, bub, scandal, jail term, divorce, love child.

After a week of this, I was convinced we would find nothing related to my own purposes. Why, I asked myself, if Sir Arthur and Lady Margaret's fonds resided at the Somerset Heritage Centre, would I expect any of their other papers to survive elsewhere? Why had I bothered tracking down Maureen Tilden and Bibby Iannopoulos? Maybe instead I needed to go back to the start and hunt for further material on John Heard, through Aubrey, rather than follow the faint trail of Lady Margaret?

And that is when we found an account book from Sir William Tylden, Joan's Sir William of the intrusive hand in the carriage, the one who died in 1613. And there was Joan's name entered into the rolls! That one name. I can't explain what it meant to me, the comfort of cross-referencing. I suppose it's very simple, but it feels huge: the trace of a person's existence.

And that was all.

I helped Bibby re-box and label the documents. Found the number to call for the Kent Archives. Had them come and assess what they would take. Stayed with her as they shipped it out into a van. Said my goodbyes.

At home I tried to catch up on the things I'd set aside—my tax return, my Jane Siberry manuscript, my critical summer-camp memoir. I resolved to sort through my family's shoe boxes, which I have stored in the basement, but then, of course, I didn't. Nine months later, a parcel came from England. Bibby had found inside an unlabelled book cover on her shelves a curious—and heavy—item.

"Dear Anne," she wrote, "The leaden packet you find here enclosed—opens! Samantha, at the archives, tells me it was once common to keep things protected, sealed and dry, to wrap them in a sheet of lead, and so it is with this. It contains what seem to be letters, or a diary, in some kind of code which I am counting on you to crack.

"I have been having a wonderful time at the museum, with Samantha, a student at Sussex, on a study term here, going through the collection, as she calls it.

"Knowing how you love puzzles, I thought you would enjoy these. And who knows? They may pertain to our Lady Margaret!"

I ran upstairs, shouting to my partner, "Oh my God, you won't believe this!"

"Sorry, something going on here," she said to the people on her video conference call, and muted her mic. "What is it?" she said.

"Sorry. Forgot you were on a call. Tell you later. I just got something great in the mail. Like, super great."

"What?!"

"From Bibby," I shouted, running back downstairs.

I felt awe and reverence for the leaden package. It was letter-sized, and flat, a bit thicker than an album cover—more like a double-album cover, or one of those multi-record sets, *Jesus Christ Superstar* or *The Well-Tempered Clavier*.

I spread out a tea towel to protect the dining room table and laid the lead packet on it. It was folded over at the edges. Should I wear gloves? I didn't know. With the tips of my fingers, I pulled up the folds and opened the package. Inside was another protective lining, this time an oilcloth. And inside this was a stack of folded-together pages, a folio—oil-stained, water-stained, with patches worn or eaten away on the end pages—in a closely written, messy hand, and cross-written, as letters often were in times of paper scarcity. The writer would write in the usual way, and then turn the paper ninety degrees and write across what they'd already inscribed.

With a little bit of study, my heart in my throat, I could make out the first word—"Joan"—and the first few lines—"I write with no hope of my words reaching you. No hope, truly, of living beyond tomorrow."

And then: the writing changed. I couldn't read it. The marks looked like hieroglyphics. Code. And I had no idea what it said.

Something old and incredibly exciting lay in front of me, and I could not read it.

But after a bit more study, and some googling of "seventeenth-century shorthand," I realized the code was only shorthand— not *easily* deciphered, because of the stains and holes and tonal differences in language, but decipherable nonetheless.

I began the task of translating the folio. Some of what I have recorded is reasonable guesswork. Some is pure conjecture. I have remained as true as I can to the original, but inevitably modernized some of its expression. What was not readily apparent on the first page, because it was most heavily damaged, became clear: the writings were framed as a series of letters to Joan.

They told the story of Tom's journey after writing his letter to John Heard (a letter, it is clear, that went unanswered)—a journey by ship to Hudson Bay.

Letters from Hudson Bay, Never Received

*J*OAN,

     I write this day in March, with no hope of my words reaching you. No hope, truly, of living beyond tomorrow, which is a near certayntie, and tomorrow's tomorrow, a lesser certayntie, until whatever in the end takes us—ice, fire, sea, scurvy, accident, another man's hand, or, God forbid, our own. I cannot be parted from this life, and from you, without addressing you again. To see you before me in my mind's eye as I write. The look upon your face when you knew me. The look upon it each time our eyes found each other again. In the lanthorn light in the hall. In the light of dawn when you brought me water. In the darkened cottage before Hurd so disastrously came in upon us.

And after he left, the certayntie of it when you sayed, "You cannot stay. You cannot live in skirts. You must fly. Hurd cares more for his own righteousness than for you. He will think it right to expose you, no matter the love he bears for you."

And in Bristol, through that night at the Inn, you wavered not that I take Billson, his place with James, while I quavered at the prospect of being parted from you and laid down my pen from my plea to Hurd time and again.

And when I had writ the letter and sent it off to Hurd, those few hours we had t'embrace and lie together as we awaited a reply that never came. I carry those with me in my skin.

It matters not what I write, tho' while I am at it, I may as well tell you my tale, such as it is, this past year. For which I must miniaturize as well as code my hand, that it fit what pages remayn.

We are halfway thorow March, the cold that 'gan in October nothing abated.

We lodge ashore in cabbins made of wattle and sail, lined with beds stacked two high and hung with more sayls and curtains to make a semblance of rooms or closets. A fire burns in the middle. Smoke rises to a small hole in the sail, which we must from time to time clear of snow, else be smothered.

There are ten of the stacked beds, but now it is so cold, we sleep two to a bed. The warmth of another body does more than ten blankets. The dogs sleep with the cook and Nick, one of the boys. My companion is Cole, the carpenter.

Through the night, groans. In the morning, groans.

"Good morrow, men," says James. "God keep us this day."

The men give good morrow, and complaynt.

"Divell take this cold," says one.

"Divell take me to Hell, where it's warm," says another.

"Where you will roast your flesh, like Leggat."

Leggat's foot had froze so it had no feeling (as all ours have done at one time or other) and in that condition he had put it in the fire and burned it before he knew it was being burnt.

I rise, swing my legs over the bunk, adjust the rags about my feet, add another coat, tuck the blankets round Cole, draw cloth across my face, put logs on the fire. I cannot light a lanthorn. We have not the fat for it, which must be conserved for Cole and the building of the pinnace.

Van Rijn is up and in the next hut building up the fire.

Will attends me as I make the round of the teeth and toes. Will is patient and quiet and observes well.

Mr. James insists I go not in order of rank, but in order of infirmity, and so I start with Palmer, the boat swayne, who was the first to complayn of the sickness and for a time complayned the most, and now we fear for his life, for he has not got up for three days. We have a saying that any of us who stays abed more than three days will not rise again, and for this reason even the sickest rise on the second or third day.

Palmer's gums bleed at the slightest touch. He has lost three teeth. He had three fewer than most to begin with. He lets me pare away the black from his gums with little comment now but a moan and a cry. His eyes open and close.

Next, my bed-mate, our carpenter, Cole, little better than Palmer. I cut away his gums, dab at them with clean linen, give a balsam-balm to rinse with. "I sit, I sit, I sit," says Cole, not sitting yet. He reaches out an arm and I pull him up. Will checks Cole, his feet, then wraps feet and lower legs in cut-up blankets and cross-garters them round.

Then it is Ugganes, with his prayers, and Hammon, with half his great nose gone from frost, Marsh, with his bets, and Leggat, Snigge, Price and Clement.

Rance wants me to rub his joints with salve. He could do it himself, but his mind tells him the physitian has gi'en him something greater. "Ah, that's tonic," testing his knee as if an oiled hinge.

By this time, Nick has got up and wrapped the blankets around the dogs. It's his turn to take out the chamber pot, which is not pot but crossed boughs of fir. The difficulty we have is that a pot freezes away from the fire and stinks near it. Nick, tired of thawing the muck to tip it out where we have made a latrine, wove a mat of fir branches to shit on that may be heaped on the pile.

Wardon has been to the cook-shed, brings back for Palmer some pottage, feeds it to him. "Eat. It will warm you and keep you alive."

"Let me die."

"Nay, friend, that we will not do."

Wardon, the mate, has become loquacious. I would have thought him the hardest nut of us all, but he has tenderness in him.

Second to last, I see to Clement's teeth. Lastly, Mr. James. Then Will sees to mine own, and our day has begun.

Survive the winter we may, most of us. But whether we shall get home is another question. The ship lies sunk a mile from shore. The foreshore is shallow and wide. I travel in my mind across it, imagine the ship raised, the ship flying across waves like a bird, up the bay, down the strait, o'er the north sea to Bristol and to you, all in one swift flight instead of the faltering, plodding days and weeks and months even a sound ship would take. Each night, I make the same trip before sleep in hopes I will dream my return to you.

Cole works on a pinnace from the shards of our shallop and boat. We all attend to it, for on it we pin our hopes. We are down to our last tools, with no way to repair them. We cannot get a fire hot enough to work iron.

We had all thought we might see salvages, but so far we have not, no, nor signs of them neither, or at least signs that are not old. Nor have we found signs of Hudson.

Each night I afford myself one memory of you. (Others arise unbidden when they list.) I savour most especially the moment in which you recognized me, the look on your face a wash of tenderness, fury, astonishment, wonder, terror, and love.

I regretted my decision to sail as soon as I set foot in the boat that rowed me out to the *Henrietta Maria*. Here was Mr. James, crying, Well come, Mr. Billson (for under that name, as you know, I sailed), well come. He is small of stature—of a height with my self—energetick, with a sprightly step, and bright eyes. O, I am not well come, Mr. James, a voice within me chipped. I am . . . I am . . . but I could not say what I was. I tamped the voice down.

James gave a dinner for the investors, and a speech, extolling our Ship, our Stores, our Men, his Mind, his Mathematicks, his Instruments, in short, every Thing connected with our Journey. Then they drank. To Mr. James, and the Investors, and the Ship, and the Masters, and the Men, and the Stores, and the Chirurgion and Physitian most expertly well-provisioned and good-natured, and Japan, and the China Sea, and the King, etc., etc. The next day, our heads aching, a Sermon was read, the ship blessed and the investors set ashore.

We stood down the river. At last, up went the sails with a roar from the crew and a sinking in my stomach.

And yet, when the wind caught the sail and 'gan to propel us, that same part of me that saw the great ships at Woolwich lifted. The wind was a wonder and man's putting it to use a greater one. The sea, too, was a wonder, a world apart, a creature in itself, a Heaven or a Hell.

Our ship, the *Henrietta Maria*, was no sleek barque, but rather lumbered through the waves. We would win no races in her.

"How she sails, men, how she sails," cried James. He clapped his hand on the back of his lieutenant, Clement, a fair young gentleman with close-set eyes, who gave a great grin.

Those of us who knew a good ship from a middling one exchanged a look that said we knew James to be no seaman, despite his six voyages, nor Clement, on his second. The *Henrietta Maria* would do. If she proved strong against ice, she'd do well. But that was as far as it went.

Just as love of sail and the sea came back to me, even against my will, so came other memories of things forgot. One was that I, for reasons you know, must find friends among the crew, and know them all, that I may stay safe.

Price, the master, I liked the look of. He had a pockmarked face, a crooked nose, and eyes like the sky. He was always watching—sky and sail and men, ahead, behind. He was alert to danger, to good work, and to bad. Price had the smallest cabbin, a closet, no more, to himself and there was no room in it for anything more than himself, lying down, and his chest, stowed beneath him.

I lodged in a cabbin with the two mates, Wardon and Whittered. Wardon was hollow-cheeked and close-mouthed, as quiet a man as I have known. Hours at a time, he said nothing. Marsh, the leadsman, an Irishman, 'gan to lay bets when Wardon would speak.

Mr. James had the largest cabbin, where we dined, and where slept Clement, and Will, James his boy, the nephew of one of our investors, on his first voyage, and the dogs, deerhounds Mr. James had brought so that we might have fresh meat.

The Cook was a Dutchman, van Rijn, inclined to superstition, but good-natured.

The Steward had the look of a bulldog and was very painful. He kept a strict tally of our bread and meat and sack and slept by the bread room withal. The Boat Swayne was his equivalent in care of our sails and ropes and tackle. They are not men to befriend, thought I, but not men to fear.

Marsh was dexterous and light-hearted. Edwards, the gunner, had a downy cheek and a so sweet a voice that Sweet became his name among us. Barton, his mate, sang the lower part, and was just as sweet. Hammon, bashful and amenable, had the greatest nose I had ever seen. Rance was a boyish ox. Ugganes, the cooper, I could not say anything of at first, but later found he was next to Cole in his skill with tools.

Whatever we thought of James, it seemed not an idle boast he had hired good men.

No sooner had we sailed than we were hit by adverse winds and a great storm, which the Cook called a bad omen. We sheltered under Lundy, and waited, day after day, for the wind to turn. My heart was sore with missing you and wondering how Heard received my letter. Again, I regretted sailing. I peered at the water I could not swim, at the shore, asking myself how I should free myself from this rash bondage and return to you, so recently returned to me.

Then went I over the same reasons we had gone over together, concluded the same conclusion. In a year or less I would be home with the pay to clear my debts and join my fate to yours.

And I felt then that I could not leave the company without a chirurgion.

At last, the wind blew from the east and released us, and we were on our way.

After two weeks of fair sailing, we drew close to Groynland. The weather closed round with a thicke Fog and light winds.

James, from his measurements of latitude, and our speed, had us more than a day off shore, but he must have erred, for that night, those of us as were asleep were jolted awake by a thud and a great Wrenching that made us fear we hadde been staved. All hands flew to deck.

There, in the dim twilight of the northern night (it being around two o'clock in the morning), we could discern little, as the Fogge continewed, but that we had struck a low peece of Ice. Around us towered other peeces of it, one as tall as our tallest mast. Wardon sent men to try the pumps, but they were dry. We were not staved. The band of iron that reinforced the *Henrietta Maria*'s cut-water had indured its first test and proved sound.

"By God, she's a good ship," sayed Mr. James.

The wind was light, and Mr. Wardon had struck sail to slow our passage. More great peeces of Ice appeared out of the Fog. The boy, aloft, had no more advance warning of what lay ahead than we, on deck. Mr. James stood on the poop, crying out each time Ice appeared from the fog, charging men to fend it off with grappling poles that broke in the effort. Cole cursed to see the pieces stick in the ice or drop in the water. "We may have need of that wood."

All that night and all the next day and the night that followed, we sailed thro' Fog and Ice. We passed narrowly betwixt two great peeces, breathed a sigh of relief and then our hearts were shaken by a sickening crack as the ice that had missed us closed on the Shallop we towed behind us.

Below we carried a boat that had now to be brought up and sent out to retrieve the peeces. "Ah, well," said Cole. "Now I will have work to do." But he had not been without. On so small a ship, all of us were part of a watch, and served more than one role.

So ran a stretch that seems almost a dream now, days of ice and fog, ice and fog, fog and ice, till at last we rounded Cape Farewell (which is the tip of Groynland), and crossed Davis's Strete.

We woke again to a great noyze, this a groaning or gnarring of some immense beast, which we supposed to be ice being ground against rock. Then, a rush as of an enormous volume of water falling in tumult, both louder than any sound I hadde ever heard.

The Overfall at the mouth of the Strete? Whittered leapt adeck. I was not far behind.

The light was that dim twilight that passes for dark in summer. Fog, in patches. Our rigging looked strang to my eyes untill I understood it was coated in ice. Our breath came out as fogge.

We could not see lande, onlie hear it.

Mr. Price after the last encounter through the ice near Groynland had argewed with Mr. James that we go not so close to shore. "But then we add nothing to the Maps, nothing to our knowledge of Tides. We learn nothing that is new," sayed James.

"Then we are not shoaled, nor crawling thorow a field of perilous obstacles," sayed Mr. Price. "The ship will encounter Ice enow in the usual run of things. We need not expose her to more."

Mr. Price thinks first of the ship, Mr. James of knowledge. Now did Price suggest standing off farther from shore untill light came, and Mr. James agreed. Price told Wardon to give out the command to drop sayl, sound depth, and anchor.

And so it was, we saw as light touched the sky near four o'clock above the fogge stood Resolution Iland, a misty scrim of barren cliffs, past which lay the Stretum Hudson and our way north.

On our sayls and rigging, ice. All about us, ice.

There are two kinds of ice: high, which comes in great crags and pieces, as we sailed thorow off Groynland (whose roots, like an iland, go far far below), and low, which floats about in flat sections and extends not so far below the surface. These mash up agaynst one another to make a continuous sheet, which was about us now. It was segmented enow that we could make some unequal progress thro it—now quick, now slow—but we hadde nothing like full freedom of movement.

There, ahead of us, to the South of Resolution Iland, was the entrance to Hudson Strete. We wished to assay it on the stand of the tide, that is, the highest or the lowest, just before the turn. In seas with a narrow entrance to a bay or strete, the standing tide be not so straightforward as in open water. Our best tactic was to start thorow two hours past low tyde.

In the end, we hadde no choyce. Ice compacted around us and encased us, and the wind gave little help. The tyde flowed toward the Strete. "Put up more sayl," sayed Mr. Price. "We will bash our way thro."

But even with all sayl, we made little way against the ice and were blinded by fog withal. The Iland we could no longer see. Mr. James turned to his compasses to check our position, but they flagged and would not spin.

For the next four hours, we flowed toward the strete, marking our progress agaynst the tip of Resolution Iland, when we could see it. Then we slowed. Then seemed not to move at all. Then back, and back, and back we went. By low tyde, we were not quite back so far as we started but near to't.

Marsh had laid bets on when we would get through. "Six tydes," sayed he.

"We will get thro on this one," sayed Will, but everyone laughed for they could see we would not.

"I'll take that bet," sayed Marsh. "What odds will ye have, Will?"

A big roar of laughter went round agayn. Will blushed but had the sense to not take it amiss.

The wind dropped. We were even more at the mercy of tide and ice.

Tho' we knew we would not pass, yet no one left the deck. We were compelled to watch and watch. Anyone who turned his eyes away for a moment, to the chess piece he carved, or the rope he lashed, or the whistle he blew, he turned them right back agayn as swift as may be. The watch changed. The men relieved thereby went not below to sleep or take their ease but remayned on deck to see if we should pass it on this tyde. The time drew near. Talk died down. We watched, and listened, and felt the small swells beneath us. "This is the change now," sayed Wardon, reading the glass.

"So I mark it," said Mr. James, with his charts and graphs.

For a moment there seemed almost perfect silence but for some creaking of the rigging or the cry of a sea bird. Then felt we the backwards movement. We let out our breaths. Talk started up agayn. Heads went back to their carving or lashing or whistle. Marsh called for a song from Sweet, who gave one, all joyning in on the chorus, and one or two dancing.

Now we would drift back untill low tyde, some time after midnight. The next high tyde would be in the morning. Mr. Cole and I played backgammon untill our heads were heavie enow to sleep, and woke in time the next morning to watch the same sad slow progression.

We 'gan to feel doomed t'our entrapment. The Cook recalled to us our inauspicious start in a storm.

"Dam up your superstitions, van Rijn," said Price, "else they flood us."

We past the boat-swayne Palmer's guess of four tydes, past Marsh's of six, past Rance's eight, and were now approaching the Cook's ten, two full dayes after our enclosure in the ice. 'Twas seven in the morning. Full high tyde was still a few hours off. All hands were once agayn on deck. All watched Resolution Iland, the southren tip, whose cliffs we were heartily sick of.

"Are we past?" said Palmer.

"That we are," sayed Mr. Price.

So went up a great cheer from us all. The very ice seemed to loosen.

Just then, the wind came up and sent us—and ice with us—toward shoare, where the tyde made great whirlings amongst towering Ice. No Sayle could fight this current. It was like the hand of God or the back of a great sea monster, some enormous force beyond the human.

The wind had been coming over our starboard stern quarter and the sayls set to catch it. As we passed the Cape came as sudden a wind as I have ever felt, which blew the sayls backwards. Out goes Whittered's command to change our tack, and the men on the larboard side loose their sheets while on starboard they haul. But now we were in the grip of the enormous sea cyclone, which spun us so hard that we all fell to the deck as it was whisked out from under us and thrown toward the rocks and ice near shoare. I leapt up, raced forward to take a hand with the sheets. We whirled. The sayls flapped madly, catching wind this way, then that, then this. The wind pushed us harder to shoare. Now goes the cry to trim the sayls. With the main course, which is the principal sayl of the ship, raised up to the yard, and the fore-course allso, the wind could do less to force us on the rocks, but neither did we have the power to free ourselves of the current. We were under force of the tops'ls, the jib, and the mains'l. We were like a cork upon the sea and tossed agayn up agaynst Ice and rock by the shore.

At last we were out of the worst of the current, into a rocky, Ice-ridden backwater, with onely five fathoms beneath us and the tyde on the ebb. We made fast to a grounded piece of Ice high as our yard.

Mr. James sent out the Shallop, being now mended, to look for a bay or other area to shelter in, but then the Peeces of Ice brake away. We signalled to the Shallop to return but now she was entrapped in Ice, so the crew must needs get out and haul her along the ice to open water again.

Still in danger of being thrown upon the Rocks, we made more sayl, which put us in danger with the Ice. Mr. James surmising that shelter lie betwixt rocks and shore, hadde us sayl over and through Rocks that we could see them beneath us until we ran right into a great piece of ice, near spearing her with our bow sprit as if we were a Unicorn of the Sea. Our beake head broke off and with it some Rigging, but no other damage.

We had no sign, though, of the Boate, which had seven men, or a third of our crue, aboard it. At last we spied them and they were come safe to us, even bringing the lost Kedger.

As the tyde ebbed away from us, the ship lowered and lowered until she were careened on her side and we unable to stand in her, so that we all went on a peece of Ice and Mr. James set to pray for God's mercy. The boatswain hadde attatched the cables high on the mast to high on the rocks (to allow for the wandering ice below). Twice were

208

there sudden shudders and we dropped a foot or two at once, untill at last we were full careened and the ship in danger of taking on water. Picture twenty-two men on a peece of ice beside their beached Ship earnestly praying for the deliverance of their lives, and one of them a carpenter with an eie to the damage he must repair on the beakhead. Even as the ship lay on her side, I was thinking of the shallop, of what we might carry in her, and of how long it would take us to get back. Three weeks, say. I almost wished the damage to the ship were worse that we could take that course, and thus reverse my folly in leaving you. Yet the shame for Mr. James, returning six weeks after he had left, I would not wish on him, and I had a superstition against calling harm down on the ship.

You may trust the tyde turned, and imagine us back aboard now after thanking the Lord.

The next day goes Mr. James ashore, and with him myself and Sweet with a fowling piece and a few others of our company. We took the boat and got close to shore and landed on a shelf of ice. We took a stake to measure the tyde and left Marsh in the boat to keep an eye on it. Since you have never been aboard a ship, you will not know the sensation of coming on land after being at sea. The land pitches as the sea did. (My mind puzzles how this should be.)

From a rocky beach, the land rose in a cliff, barren. In small crevices of rock where there is protection were there some small, dainty grasses and plants. I would have liked to take some for Tradescant, as he would be curious to see them, but they would assuredly not last our voyage. Then we come upon a place where Salvages once had fires and there were a few bones, Mr. James thought fox, also whalebone. Fourteen fox skulls we found. Fox gives not a good yield of meat, and therefore we surmise the furs may be the object. We saw no live fox. We have not seen a whale. No fowl for the gunner to bag us. We are disappointed not to take any fish to supplement our diet. I took a whalebone for Tradescant. There is no wood. What they made fire with, we cannot say. Driftwood they had carried here?

We climbed higher to look out and saw we were in the bowl of a bay that grows narrower as it moves inland. "Let us gather rocks and build a tower to mark our passing," sayed Mr. James. He felt a sort of schoolboy elation in saying, "We were here," which I recognized, but joyned not in, for wishing I were not there and rather back in Somerset with you. There were plenty of rocks for the purpose, we had no distance to get them. Sweet and Barton were like children with the pleasure of piecing it together.

When the tower were donne, Mr. James sayed, "I name this the Harbour of God's Providence, which verily, He has shown us here." In his eye shone a fervour for naming.

It is one thing to be aboard the ship and look out at the land of rock and the sea of ice. It is another to be on that barren shore with no comfort in miles, no personnage, no animal, and to look then on the ship, so foreign to the landskip, the only thing made, fashioned by human hand. The life I left behind now seemed very distant. Unreal. Our company was become much more.

And now, these months later, we are drawn even tighter together. We have no choice. I once thought I had no love for Palmer, or Mullins, but as Palmer draws nearer death, I can no longer say so.

I have bin out to gather my share of wood and be free of the thickness of the smoke-laden aire and stench (which, thank God, is smaller for the cold) of our lodging. I have bin in to keep Cole company as he and Ugganes add to our pinnace.

James has bin out to measure the height of the sun above the horizon.

'Tis dinner time. I will lay down my pen and sup, then gather snow to wash my bandages and instruments. I send a prayer to God and my soul to you.

(post-script: Palmer sits up! He has put his feet upon the floor. He rises.

"Mr. Palmer," says James. "Ye shall live another day, God willing.")

My fine Joan,

Mr. Palmer yet lives this 20th day of March in the year of our Lord 1632, as do all who were alive last I wrote. From that you will surmise we have lost some ere this. Palmer lives but he has fouled himself. His breath is shallow and stinks. All our breaths stink.

We are putrid. I begin to think human flesh a scourge upon Nature. But the stink informs, all so. By it I know how dire infecktion, etc.

Rance and Marsh help me lift and strip him and the bed below him and bathe him. He weeps to be touched.

Now Cole is close to him in pain and lassitude. He says he will take this Sabbath day for rest (as Mr. James insists we all do, insofar as we can) and will be back at the pinnace tomorrow. He and Ugganes are close to a full frame, lacking onlie seven or eight struts before the planking goes on. Ugganes now does most of the work, while Cole directs him, and Hammon assists.

I cannot call to mind England's green that must be before your eyes now. I forget I hadde any other life afore this. Neither can I foresee one. 'Tis unbearable, and so the mind sequesters itself, and we have only what is here and now. These cold fingers, this dim light, these sore joints. But then a vizion of you comes. I feel your propinquity, your touch. I see the brightness of your eye.

In the evening, it is the round of the teeth again, and then the round of the feet.

When first we landed on this ile months ago, 'twas not with the intent to stay, but onlie to gather the wood we needed for our fire and for our carpenter. The iland has a long foreshore, as I have sayd, more than a mile, that we traversed by boate for the collecting of wood. The water so thickening with Ice that we made no progress with oars required that the men take it in turns to push the boat thorow the icy water, arriving at the Ship blue and almost like statues so stiff and cold were they. We stripped them of their wet clothes and bundled them in blankets and put them near the fire. When they learned it was all for naught—on this ile would we stay, to shore would we transport all the wood just brought to the ship, and all our necessaries—Ugganes roared. Rance, who began the voyage so hot-headed you might have predicted he would have been the worst of them, simply lowered his head a minute, slapped his thighs and set to again. Six of them. Two pushed at a time. When they could no longer manage, those in the boat hauled them in, had them huddle together, and the next two went out.

To take up the tale of our journey: the ordeal of the Overfall donne, up the Strete we went, thro' the low Ice. The ice makes a noyze against our hull, a bumping and smashing we grow used to.

We hadde dayes of sun. What melted in the daye froze agayne at night. We woke to mist and rigging thick with ice. Then sun burnt off the mist and made puddles on the low ice. Its edges dripped into the sea. The low ice giving us occasion to inspect the ship's hull, we sometimes got out onto it. Mr. Cole, working with two or three, including my self, tarred & repayred what he could. Which gave our feet a soaking and the ice-water so cold it was a kind of payne to our feet untill they grew numb. Mr. James cupped his hands to try the water, was it salt or sweet? And found it sweet. Then we knew the ice had not bin formed with sea water.

One hot day brought us a rain-bow which put us in good spirits. "God shows us His covenant," sayed Mr. James. "He forgets us not, even here, in so lost and barren a land."

Afte noone the same day was a strang sight new to me, as if the Sun hadde two miniature Suns, one on either side of her, with a glare above and below them like an hour-glass.

The cook declared this, like the rain-bow, a good omen. "Our fortunes have turned," sayed he.

Price, beside me, snorted, but not so anyone could hear.

Since our ordeal at the mouth of the strete we hadde cohered, accepted one another's foibles. Now we made way with few difficulties and smooth running of the ship, by and large. We knew Sweet, his songs, and Marsh, his wagers, the Cook, his ruminations on death and the stars, his affection for the dogs, Mr. James, his recounting of Purchas, his prayers, his reading his instruments, testing the tides, refining his maps. We knew the Steward's losses at backgammon, his calling for Will when the dogs have shit again, the dog pissing on Cole's toolbox.

Two weeks of this untill we were farther up the Strete than any before, near 65 degrees N. The ice closed in like land. Northwest from the topmast is nought but Ice, Ice and Ice as far as the eye can see, as farre as glass can see, which makes it twenty leagues or more. No current indicated a passage.

James and Price and the mates conferred, James himself going up the lookout, eye to the glass, then back down. The crew feigned disinterest in their conference, but all ears turned to the poop deck, for the next command would tell us whether we hadde given up the Passage.

"Set a course West South West," sayed Mr. James to Wardon.

"West-Sou'-West!" called Wardon.

Ugganes pushed the whipstaff away.

Our course was changed.

Tho' I will not say James didde not regret fayling to fulfill our investors' mission, the switch was mayde in a moment. *That* cause were lost, for now. But he wished to *learn*, to discover what the land might tell us. Now that our end was foyled, he were free to explore. Into this he moved with such a quick will that I wondered if there were not some secret planne behind it.

I soon suspected then, and am convinced now, he alwaies intended to o'erwinter. And this turned me against him. A new year would make no difference. An ice-filled passage is no passage. He hoped he would find the River of Canada and make his name by that Discovery. Or failing that, make an early start at the Passage the following year.

My heart was sore. I hadde much better have stayed and talked to Hurd my selfe. We hadde much better stolen away somewhere, you and me, to Lancashire, or the Low Countries. Anywhere.

The morning after our turn away from our goal, Mr. James made at the mast his prayer, then announced half bread rations on flesh daies. No sound of disapproval was made, but no man looked at another, and this not looking told the tale of their hearts. In twos and threes they left the mast and turned to their tasks.

The Boat Swayne, with a face that put me in mind of a fish, and Mullin, the Steward with the bulldog face, lingered.

"My joynts ache like the devill," sayed Palmer. "And my teeth start loose. And the spots have started."

"The same," sayed the steward.

"We must look for scurvy-grass ashore," sayed I. Both men were older than the rest. They knew this dis-ease. "In the meantime, I will make you a salve."

If in the season of high summer ice stoppeth our progress, thought I, and if, as is the case, each night doth shroud our tackle and rigging in ice, I warrant there is no passage thorow the ice any time of year. Was it free and open in June, when we were in Davis's Strete and beset by Ice? In May when we were sheltering by Ireland? What good is a Shippe full of China's wealth or Malay spice when it is shut in Ice? I began to see our journey as a fool's errand. There is no passage thorow the ice. We hadde taken an oathe to say no Word agaynst our errand. None would I say alowd, but here in privet, to you, I say this. It was a fool's errand and has always been. We got not through the ice last year. We will not next year, if we live that long.

Clement, James's lieutenant, was a gentleman of about five- or six-and-twenty. We had taken to playing chess. That evening, our breath clouding the air, our fingers tucked quickley under our arms after each move, he sayed, "Think you the ice ever melts here?"

I gave him a quick look, but he kept his eyes upon the game. We both knew this edged on what we were not to say.

"I am amazed at it," said he. "It is beyond my imaginings."

"Not enough of it melts." I did not finish. And now he looked at me with a penetrating look.

"Precisely," sayed he.

And I knew we understood one another. That is to say, he had had the same thought as me: our journey from here is bootless, we will not get through next year. Therefore, let us hope that we return home this year.

James's greatest fear, as befits the leader of any journey that follows Hudson's, is mutiny. I entertained no thoughts of it myself; I was merely alert to discontent amongst the crew, as were we all. Here in Clement was some measure of discontent. He was not the proud acolyte of James he had started out as. Nor was he any enemie of James. It was only that his own discernment increased.

"It has a strang beauty," sayed he, "the ice, and yet it weighs on me like a fever dream I had as a boy, wherein a great blanket of nothingness and yet of unbearable weight, presst down on me. I have ne'er felt so small upon the face of the earth as when looking out on't."

I made a rash move in the game, taking his bishop, and he put me in check.

The weather continued foule, the seas high, and we continually struck ice. The switch to half rations let all know who hadn't surmised already that we were likely to stay out another year. A yeare never stretched so long ahead. I had to put thoughts of you out of my head or I should go mad. But at nights onlie thoughts of you gave me peace to rest.

Last year on July 21—the height of Summer—we were fast in ice. The men were dispirited. James, Clement, Price and Cole surveyed the ship's damage from the ice. She was much bruised and battered above and belowe the iron plate that protects her hit-water. Two knees she had before, to strengthen her, spoyled and torne. Her wounds were extensive but not such to sink us. We ploughed on like a wearie old ox.

For another week was our progress fitfull: We sayl thorow ice. We hit ice. The wind comes contrary. We anker. The wind comes faire. We way. We hit ice. James goes ashore, James sends the boate to check the tydes. Fog descends. The boate cannot find her way back. We sound a gun. We put in hooks and take no fish. We see no salvages, nor any beasts. We growe wearie of one another's companie.

One night, Mr. Whittered, his watch, when the wind died, trimmed not the sayls. In the morning, wind came up, the sayls filled, a sight and sound to make a heart gladde. The fogge lifted. And we saw we are once agayn fast in ice, faster than ever before. When I said "fast" afore this I meant not well and truly fast. This day were we in the fullest of full sayl and budged not an inch.

At the mast, after prayers, Mr. James addressed the company. "Fast in ice are we, so fast we make no way with full sayl. And so I say, if we are fast, let us descend from the ship, and desport ourselves upon the ice. Mr. Palmer? Found you material to make a ball, as I bid?"

"Aye, Mr. James." Palmer held up a ball made of sailcloth wrapped round scraps and rags.

"To the ice," cried James.

Hammon and Ugganes threw the ladder over the side.

Whooping, we swarmed off the ship like rats (if only the rats had done so . . .). Rance did not wait for the ladder, but leapt off from the deck, and ran for very freedom, shouting and stretching out his arms. Where he leapt, others followed. For myself, I stepped up on the railing and somersaulted off.

We had sunshine. The weather warm, the top of the ice covered in puddles of meltwater.

We threw snow, played at kick ball, our faces glowing, the ball become a hard, wet smack to dodge. We divided into teams whose goal was to take the ball to the other side of the ship: Mr. James, his team going from fore to aft, and Mr. Clements the other way. I passed to James and for a moment no one wanted to oppose him. "Come on!" he called to Will. "See if you can catch me."

Will went after him. Mr. James waited until he were almost upon him, then feinted right and ducked left, but slipped and fell on his ass and laughed loud. Will took the ball. There was no one to pass to. Hammon ran after him, but he hadd too much of a start and carried the ball across the line of the bow-sprit to score the first goal.

Palmer did not run, his joynts too painefull.

Our feet were soaked in no time, and cold, but the rest of our bodies warmed with our exertion. Faces grew red. The aire felt better. There was a warmth in the sun. We played on, Mr. James now merely one of the players, Mr. Clements the same. They faced one another. Mr. James was quicker, and better at feinting. Mr. Clements was the better defendor.

At last, our initial energy spent and our bodies and hearts warm, we paused as one, like a flock of birds, and turned and looked back at the ship, not a soul upon her, and she in full sayl.

My heart lurched in the knowledge that if she made sudden way through the ice, we should be left behind, idiot men on a field of ice, she off for some unknown adventure.

Our breath came and went. The wind sounded in the sayls. The hull creaked and groaned. We waited for one of us to crack, to run to the ship and be up the ladder 'fore she sayled. Then turned we back to our game. Mr. Price passed the ball to Mr. James, Mr. James to the boy, Nick, the boy to Whittered.

When next we paused in our games, the ship seemed the very picture of futility. The game grew fiercer. Men tackled one another, went down in the wet ice together.

When we were spent, Mr. James called on the steward to bring forth rum and portion it out that we might drink the King's health. He mayd a speech—"We are here on the most magnificent business of his highnesse" etcetera. "Long live the King." Even I was stirred, for a time.

Dear Joan,

March is almost past. How fare you now in Chew? What birds have nested? What is your life with Lady Margaret? I stayed not long enough to know, or to ask all I now long to know.

Has Hurd spread word I have not that piece of anatomy he thought I had? Or has he kept my counsel? Keep I the name Billson upon my return, or am I safe to be Tom Barrows again?

See how I speak of return? See how I conjure hope out of air?

Our days are little changed from what I last described, though it is almost April. The boat swayne yet lives. He sits up most days, gets to his feet one out of three. Sleeps. Recites Verse and Psalms. He has walked thro' the Valley of the Shadow of Death a thousand times.

Cole can work no more on the pinnace. The last two days, he has asked to be carried to the hut to do't, but he can neither keep on his feet or the stool but swoons away. We carried him back to bed, where he now stays.

I left my tale last time in mid-summer, upon the Ice, in the Sun, sweat cooling on us, hearts at rest after th'exertion and abandon of our frolick. How I wish to leave us there still, as in a painting, our momentary pleasure and contentment suspended for all time.

Among the crew then was easie chatter as we regayned the ship, proving Mr. James wise in his decision to abandon all for play, the ship never being in danger of sayling in that ice.

My heart was heavy to regayn shipboard, tho' I endeavoured to conceal my ill ease. The chatter dwindled. We had no wish to go back to our confinement after our freedom. We did not want to resume our pique at Palmer and Mullin argewing over backgammon, we did not want to play draughts, watch Hammon chew, hear Crossin's tales.

For myself, I was sick of tidal measurements, Mr. James's mathematickal instruments, the compasse that worked but fitfully, Mr. James's zeal.

The next day, still caught fast, we took it in shifts to have at the ice with mawls and crow bars, while seven men a side take ropes over their shoulders and pull the ship like galley slaves. Sweet led us in song. I have ne'er sung "I'll go no more a-rovin'" with greater heart. At the first movement forward, what energy suffused our limbs! We drew the ship along with our own strength! With strength like this, what might we not do? Such was the spirit of our work that morning. But hours later, to look ahead and yet see only ice, ice and more ice, and then to look behind and see how short the course we had come for all that effort, our high spirits waned. Still, we kept our shoulder to the ropes.

After noon, the ice on top softened, and our progress grew easier. One smash could break the ice, a good haul carry us ten or twelve feet.

In late afternoon, from the top-mast came Nick's cry, "Sea ahead!"

Our irons swung the faster and our heaves renewed. Mr. Palmer called out, "Heave!"

"Ho!" cried we as we pulled. Hope rose in us. If sea were at the end of it, joyfully we pulled. Mr. James kept us at it untill night fall. But at the end of the day we remayned fast in ice as ever, the open sea lost in the dark of night.

We kept this up.

Some eight days in, we felt the sea swell beneath us. Hope rose agayn: a swell it must mean the ice will break and loosen and we will agayn find a path thorow it.

The ninth day, we felt no swell.

A grimness settled over us. Unspoken was our fear we would remain stuck, which would mean death, for when we ran out of coal, we had not enough wood to keep cooking, even if we start to burn our boats. In the mornings, James prayed we be released from our entrapment. Prayers and curses were on all our breaths.

Two weekes we were in the Ice before regaining the open sea, where we gave our most fervent thanks to God.

Smaller misfortunes followed: we sailed upon rockes, sent the boat to find a way thorow them, lost the boat, regained the boat, lost an anker, went through a great storm, sailed upon rocks, sent the boat, lost the boat, regained the boat, lost an anker.

The land, when we saw it, was low and flat with shallow shoalding waters near shore that kept us three or four leagues off. Mr. James called all on deck, had cook and steward pour out draughts. "I name this land in the name of the King, The New Principality of South Wales, for his son, Prince Charles. To Charles, Prince of Wales!" and gave us all to drink. His naming gleam.

———

CURIOSITIES

From using our stores, our Ship lost her trim. In heavie seas we pitched and lurched in dangerous fashion. We knew we must find a time to anker and redistribute our load.

We were so pitching the night of August 21. We hadde been at anker, but seas grew higher and we felt ourselves run. Palmer was wroth, afeared we hadde lost yet another anker. We had not so manie we could lose them so freely.

Clement and I were at our game. We hadde something in way of a secondary game or dare that we remayne insouciant and playing the game no matter how dire the conditions around us (so long as we were not specifically called for).

A great lurch sent us off our seats and sent the game-board flying, even the pieces out of the peg-holes. We cursed, but forgot ourselves in the terrible keening on deck.

Lanthorn to hand, and I with small kit, we raced to the site of whatever accident had befallen. The wind was high, the temperature low, the ship bobbing and plunging in waves.

At the capstang we found great Confusion. Round its circle was a pile of men sprawled, cursing, heaving, bloodied. The keening came from Sweet, who held the lower part of his leg. Beside him Price sat shaking his head as after it has been smacked, something in his hand. Looking down now in the light of the lanthorn as Clement held it above us, we saw the something was Sweet's foot. It had come off at the ancle. Price 'gan laughing and could not stop but laughed himself breathless and weeping.

They had been drawing up the anker cable, which came up so easie they thought they had lost another anker, when it suddenly caught. The capstang rods were ripped from their hands and wrenched backwards. They hit Ugganes on the head, Rance on the chest, but Sweet, his leg had got between cable and capstang. The flesh were all torn away and his foot had come off at the anchle.

221

Seeing this, Sweet swooned, which state was the better for him. I wrapped a bandage tightly about the bottom of his leg.

I got Sweet brought below and gave him Sacke to calm him and put a ligature around the leg above the place I would need to cut, and while his leg was numming, tended the other men, and hadde the Cooke make me a poulder to put on it afterwards, to my receipt.

It took four men to hold Sweet. To cut flesh it must be done and done with all speed and the bone be cut through in the space of a breath. This I did. Clement, still holding the lanthorn as he hadde donne this whole time, now swayed, dizzy.

"Nick, take the light," sayed I, as Clement swayed again and nearly fell.

"I am fine," he cried again, then slumped in his place.

The boy, Nicholas, proved a steadie hand in his stead. Barton kept up a stream of chatter at Sweet's head. "A gunner don't need a foot anyhow. Cole will make you a fine new one, the finest you have seen."

When Sweet were stitcht up, the poulder apply'd, and bandage affixt, I could tend to my other patients, Ugganes, his cheek, which had a gash. John Rance had broke a rib. Mr. Price, his leg was strained. His laughter waxed and waned. He kept essaying an explanation why it was funny. Mr. James sanctioned drink for them all.

I sat with Sweet thro' the night. Gave him sack, while he talked in his delirium. The downie hair on his face. The smoothness of my own.

Dawn came. Barton had slept there in the gun room as was his wont. Now he woke. Sweet groaned and whimpered in a haze between sleep and consciousness. "If he wakes, give him sacke," said I. "I am going to see who else needs tending, and then to sleep."

In the aftermath of emergency is a calm, in which the surprise of the violent injury or accident remayns at play in the hearts of men. And following that, the desire to comprehend how the thing came about, who is to blame or not to blame. Each man feels the need to

222

recount how it happened to them. So it went, and so it was gone over, again and again. We had lost so many ankers they all assumed it had happened again. 'Twas Wardon's watch, but th'anker was coming up under Palmer's direction, and Mr. Price was part of the number that put their shoulders to the capstang and could have o'er-ruled the others. Who had set the anker? Who had tested it? So the talk went.

Mr. Price joined not in the talk. He brooded. He asked Sweet's forgiveness for his laughter. Sweet gave it, but Price was not comforted.

It is April 1. Easter. The days grow longer. We have had no thaw. Palmer now has two molars on either side, top and bottom, for his sole teeth. Cole must be carried to his work of a morning. Rance and Leggat make a palanquin of their arms and raise him upon it. He hardlie has the strength to lift his arms up and over their heads to rest on their shoulders as they carry him. But he'll say something to make 'em laugh as they go. The pinnace has a keel now and twenty-seven struts of thirty-four. Then the sheathing goes on.

To return to my tale of last summer: the accident that cost Sweet his leg—the bad trim of the ship —brought spirits low, and as on the day James adjudged spirits should be revived by desporting on the ice, so he adjudged this day, when we spied higher land than we had seen, a day ashore, a change, would lift men's hearts. Those unwell might find vetch, and take game, and so better themselves. He sent the boate— and the greater part of our company plus the dogs —ashore to gather wood, shoot game if they could, determine the tyde and learn a bit of the land. Clement led the shore party. Left on board were onlie James himself, Wardon, the chief mate, me and my patient, and Barton, his mate. Sweet's wound still wept, but his pain had lessened.

The shore party were meant to return at evening but failed to do so.

At eight o'clock, Mr. James ordered a shot set off. Barton fired the shot, and we all looked toward shore for its return. The sun was low in the sky and would soon go down. The shore was a dark line of trees, and behind it, a ridge. Smoke from our shot lifted in the air.

We waited.

No shot answered ours.

"What has happened?" worried James. "They may have suffered an injury." He repeated this tune. "What could have happened?" "They may have met selvedges. They may have been attacked."

James worrying about salvages was a veneer o'er his true worry—that those ashore conspired against him.

"We are like to have heard something were that so," said I.

The sun touched the horizon. In two glasses darkness fell.

"Let us send up a false fire," said James.

We sent up the false fire, and watched the shore for its return. There was no return.

"What has happened?" said James.

"Their powder may have got wet, sir," sayed I.

In my heart, I considered: He'd hired none but those without bonds of marriage and family, so their hearts would not be pulled toward home and weakened to mutiny.

He'd hired none that hadde prior knowledge of Baffin, or Hudson, his bay, that none should be able to say, "I know more than he. Follow me," and mutiny.

He'd shipped more food than we needed, so none should be hungry, and mutiny. He'd shipped warm clothes that none should complayn of cold, and mutiny.

At last, we spied smoke from a fire upon the shore, but it little consoled Mr. James, whose mind still ran to salvages, that it was their fire and not our own, else why had our party not returned our shot, which they surely must have heard.

"We have not men enow to sayl the ship," sayed Mr. James. "Not even enow to weigh anker."

If we hadde to, I thought, we could sayl her. We could cut away the anker. We could set the main course onlie, or the main and one other. One man at the helm, two for the sayls. The same two could throw the lead and the knot and read the glass.

James grew more anxious as the night drew on. At last I went to bed.

The sound of voices above oars plashing in the water and the boat drawing alongside us woke me in a few hours. Tho' I ne'er believed Price or Whittered or any of them'd mutiny, James's nervousness had infected me, for I woke alert, and waited to hear more. Then the roar of their voices told me they were drunk, some of them, and not upon us with weapons.

We learned next day that after their landing the tyde had dropped so farre, they could not get back. They had taken fowl and had tried to bring down a deere. They'd found vetches and boyled them and drank the soup. Ugganes had filled his barrels from streams they hadde found. They brought, too, wood for burning and for the carpenter.

All seemed in better spirits for their night on shore.

"Mr. James feared you had been taken by Salvages," sayed I.

"Mr. James fears manie things," sayed Clement. "Mr. James fears manie things."

In the days that followed, I watched for a sign from Clement or Price—or any of the others—that they hadde plans. I hadde, so I think, become painfull at the reading of faces. Either they had none, or they concealed them from me expertly.

These things happened in swift succession: the accident that cost Sweet his foot, the night the shore party stayed ashore and worried James, and meeting Luke Foxe, his ship, the *Charles*.

We hadde been out near four months. Four months of no company but our own. Four months with sight of nought but Ice and Sea and Shoals and Trees and the same twenty-one faces.

But now, a Ship. To see it brought home to us how far we were from all we knew, how we hadde almost, without thinking of it, forgot the world beyond the Bay.

James sent a small party o'er to the *Charles* (our ships were names for sovereigns, Charles and Maria—and here was a meeting of them) with an invitation for Foxe to return the visit the next day for dinner. While they stayed, we were all oddly tuned. None of our usual pursuits would serve. It was as if we waited to hear important news, as if all our ears were turned towards the other ship with tenderness, and hope, and forbearance, as if it were a reluctant lover.

Then came they back, a little smug with drink, cursing the pitching of our ship as it impeded their coming aboard. "The *Charles* is in better trim." We envied them that they had seen other faces, bin aboard another boat.

But when Foxe came next day, we liked our own company more, and even wished to defend our sorry *Henrietta Maria*. He was boastful and competitive and discourteous. Mr. James was merely boastful and competitive.

"I came not to do as any other man, but more than any," said Foxe.

"Time will tell, and God will judge," said Mr. James.

What the encounter told us was that we had not erred in our judgement that passage was not possible this year, and that our Ship was in worse shape than we had thought.

At mast the next day, four men reported sick.

The day after, the weather being calm, we put the ship in better trim, moving a greater part of the coal aft.

Mr. Palmer fell in a swoon three times.

We sailed through shallow ground and could rarely get closer to land than three or four leagues. Weather again rose.

This, like so many other sets of days, seemed to go on forever, repeating and repeating, hard to distinguish one day, many days, streams of days, from other days, streams of days. Untill something worse hit.

When James was asleep, Clement had charge of the ship, which he left, as is wise most of the time, to Price, the ship's Master, and his Mates. Under Clement's charge and Price's watch, near high tide, the ship ran aground. At low tide would not be so dire, but at high tide, we would not be greatly lifted off by any water. James was enraged beyond anything I had seen in him.

They had, the two of them, been drinking. Clement had the helm. Price had fallen on his ass and was so sodden he could scarce stand. James kicked him. He only groaned.

Wardon took charge and the rest of the night was spent trying every set of the sails to get us off, putting an anker astern to pull us off, pushing us off with poles. Nothing worked.

Come morning 'twas clear the only way off was to lighten our load.

What should we jettison?

The coal we had just shifted, was the answer. From now on we depended on wood alone.

Jettisoning the coal was not enough.

What next?

Water. To save the work of lifting them, our water barrels James ordered staved in place and the water pumped out.

Now to try an anker more truly astern.

The anker must go thro' James's cabbin, the window at stern ta'en out and enlarged to fit it, the boat sent out to place it, then all at the capstang to haul ourselves off. The line broke. All fell in a heap, but none were badly injured, thank God. All right. A new anker was sent out. And again I thought we could not keep losing ankers.

Because of the staved barrels, we could not tell if the ship were taking on water. But on the assumption it was, we put those things most essential in the boat—the carpenter's tools chief among these—to safeguard them against our sinking.

Five hours later, after much pumping and lightening and hauling, we were off. Leaking badly. Distraught. Readier than ever to turn towards home. But now, would our ship make it without repairs? When could these be effected?

Price was sick with remorse, Clement full of shame.

With Wardon and Whiterred and my self in attendance, Mr. James said, "Mr. Clement, Mr. Price, I have considered what action to take after the accident caused by your negligence.

"Mr. Price, I have listened to advice as to how to treat you. All of it has merit. I could demote you to the level of mate and promote Mr. Wardon in your place. Wardon himself has no ambitions in this regard, lest you think this thought came from him—it came from me. But in all other cases, you have shown good judgement and care of this ship. Drink is your down fall. Drink shall be taken from you. We have discovered your private cache. The Steward has stores under lock and key."

Price hung his head. Put his face in his hands.

"For the sake of us all, for the sake of the men, you must let God forgive you. We will have a service and the general confession. When from this you rise, you will be confined to your Cabbin with Mister Billson by for physick for three days, after which time, assuming you show your earlier good judgement, you will resume your post as Master of this Ship."

"We must live with each other. We have a year, at least, ahead of us, with no other company. We must tune our hearts and minds, our will and goodwill, towards our survival. We will not survive as enemies." This was James's first overt suggestion we would o'erwinter.

To the present, and this April day. Cole is still lifted to his work each day and can do less and less. I have watched him with plane or mallet, the slow return to resting, the gathering all his will into the movement to follow, the stroke, the slow return. He works now most by directing Hammon.

Clement has taken it on himself to lead the search for wood Cole can use. He still seeks to redeem himself, recognizing how he'd put all our lives in danger. His cocky preening is gone. The wood must have certain qualities for knees and other for beams. The trees here are straight but spindly, with rarely a trunk greater than five inches across. One tree will make then one plank, or, if we are lucky, two. Clement wraps his feet in woollen bandages, wears four woollen coats one on top of another, a Monmouth cap, and his face wrapped with more wool. He takes with him Leggat and Rance and Nick, who has grown, his beard starting and his voice a-dropping.

James keeps on with his celestial observations, observing the sunrise and sunset and the meridian. He has been painful with the glasses that they be turned a-time. And yet, knowing our latitude, 'tis not hard to reset the glasses upon calculation.

Price, after running us aground, and being cut off from his own supply of drink, after a few days fell sick of it, and had the sweats and shakes. I sat by him in the small space of his cabbin. He would try to rise from bed to beg drink. "You must not," sayed I, pushing him back. "Mr. James has forbid it. Remember your error."

"God!" he cried. "Have mercy."

He would quiet for a few minutes, the shakes coming and going, and then be taken o'er again.

Once, he awakened, sat up, and showed the plainest terror on his face at some vizion that came at him. He dodged, put his arms up to protect his face.

"Get them off me! Get them off!"

Nothing was on him, it was a phantasy.

"Their mouths, their teeth." He dodged the creatures who plagued him, then swiped desperately at his neck. "They swarm me. Get them off!" He brushed his hands against his face. "Beetles." He spat them out. He threw them up. He screamed and writhed as they turned into maggots, into snakes.

And then flies flew from their maggot homes and swarmed his whole face and he curled into the tiniest ball and moaned as if his guts were coming out his nose.

I held him down, held his arms, kept him from harming himself. At last he lapsed into sleep. It was best when he did. I dozed off myself then, remaining partially alert and ready for the next round. One time when I so restrained him, he fell not asleep but into a fit of violent tears that convulsed his bodie, as if bodie and soul were at war. "O God," he cried. "I am a worm. I am fit to die." When he had somewhat settled, I drew away, but he pulled me back into an embrace and let not go. "Billson," said he, "Billson, how can I face them?" and wept more and clutched me a long while yet.

"Billson, you come before me strangly. I seem to have lived all this before. How familiar is your face. You put me in mind—forgive me—of my sister. She had a face like yours. A little monkey."

And with that, I knew him. I wondered I had not seen it before. He was the blue-eyed mariner of the *Diamond* I have told you of. But so changed by the years I had missed the remembrance. Did he know me? That was the question. He had then bin my protector and friend. But his protection had come at a cost, which you can guess. I liked not the thought of reviving that cost.

The moment passed. He wiped his eyes and slept again. Two days and two nights of this followed. He took a little pottage and small beer and at last he slept twelve hours. The day after, the Sabbath, he made his confession, as did we all, but his he almost shouted, as if he wanted to bruit all his true contrition.

Then he was back at his post.

In the days that followed I kept one eye and ear upon Mr. Price to see if he knew me as I knew him. If he did, he gave no sign of it.

By now we were in the SE corner of Hudson, his bay, looking for a place to winter. Mr. James hoped we might find the mouth of the River of Canada, and harbour there. Instead, we lumbered thorow shallow waters and small islands. One day in October with a light snow falling we had need of firewood and vetches for our sick, so ankered and sent the boat ashore. I stayed aboard with Sweet, whose strength was waning. He tried to get adeck once each day, to say that he had. That day he sent them off in good cheer. Cole had made him a crutch that he waved after them.

All day the men laboured, wading to the chest thorow half-frozen water that impeded the boat, filling the boat with wood, finding no vetch, wading back, loading the wood on board. Hour after hour while the snow thickened until we could not see the bow of the ship from the stern, they waded and sought and gathered and lifted. Leggat was so froze he lost the use of his limbs and had to be lifted like the driftwood into the ship. We had a brazier in the gun room where Sweet lay, to keep him warm, and there we brought Leggat, stripped him of his wet clothes, and wrapped him in dry ones, where he shuddered and shook, teeth clacking. Sweet sang, which soothed him.

On deck, they huddled about the galley fire, drinking the sack James had allotted them.

On the morrow, after prayers, with snow piling up on deck and sails frozen above, James announced at mast we would go no further, but winter there.

"Our labour of yesterday is in vain?" said Rance.

"We are still not warm from it," said Barton.

"I may ne'er be warm again," said Leggat.

"God save us," said Ugganes.

"The weather has turned against us. We have not the harbour I had hoped for, but we may find no better," said James. "On this island we will take shelter."

The move ashore—removing all the stores we would need, building a house to live in and one to make a pinnace in would take weeks.

In the meantime, Mr. James hoped we might have some good hunting ashore and sent out a party under Clement, including Barton, Leggat, and Marsh after deer or foule or what they could find.

Another party went ashore with Cole to build our houses.

I remayned with Sweet, and betwixt attending to my patient put my hand in where it was needed in bringing up stores and bringing down rigging.

Once the frustration of the day's needless work was got over, we turned to our tasks with fresh heart. What we did now was new. Its newness made it easier, tho' the labour itself was just as hard or harder.

Sweet had a store of wood to feed the brazier. He had his flute to play. We caught bits of song above the wind as we got the sails off the yards and thawed them to fold them. Men's hands froze and grew clumsy.

"Hands out of your pants, Crossin," sayed Palmer, when Crossin warmed his hands as they loosed the sail from the yard arm.

"They're useless without warming," sayed Crossin.

"Your cock's hot enough one touch should do," said Palmer. "Back to't."

The house builders stayed ashore. The hunting party stayed out the night. Those few left aboard made our task seem too large, and our bodies seem wrong in the landskip. The rightest thing seemed to me that we all die and leave this place alone. But Sweet's flute was a reminder of life's sweetness, of summer, and warmth.

And I had you to remember, to keep me alive.

Next evening, the hunting party returned. Everyone a-deck saw Barton was not among them. Sweet was up on deck for soupar, in anticipation of the return.

"Where is Barton?" said he, as they drew alongside. "Does he stop with the others?"

"Let us get aboard," Clement said, "and we will tell you."

Their going was slow and difficult, the snow being waist-high. They took turns cutting trail. The dogs, after the first few miles, would not go ahead to break trail. They followed deer tracks, lost them, found them, lost them, spied some in the distance, across a lake, shot, missed. Carried on. Came upon the deer again in a clearing in the forest. Barton shot and hit, but did not kill it. Now they followed the injured deer through the forest until it was dark and they could go no further. They had gone too far to return that night, so spent a miserable night doing what they could to stay warm. In the morning, the deer's tracks were covered with fresh snow. They resolved to return to the ship, keeping an eye out for game. On gaining the lake where they had first shot at the deer, which they had skirted afore, Barton declared he would cross it, it was froze hard enow to carry him. He got a quarter mile across, and then disappeared. They went after to fish him out, using caution, but found him not. He hadde been there, and then he was gone. Leggat had been watching and could not get over it, the way he hadde hadde his eyes upon him and then he was gone. He kept saying, "I was watching the whole time and he did not fall, he went not down, there was no downward movement. He disappeared." Leggat snapped his fingers.

"Ah, Jesus," sayed Sweet. "Himself to the end."

When the others had returned to shore, and after we'd had our suppar, and I'd checked his wound, which now wept very little—but whose weeping froze—and he had quieted so I thought he slept, I heard his grief.

He was still well enough then to rise from his bed a little each day and use some crutches the carpenter had fashioned for him, and go sit by some ice that needed picking out with a handpick for a few minutes at a time.

At night, Sweet told stories about Barton, and drank, and sang, and wept, and slept earlier, and wakened later, until some weeks later he rose not from his bed. A day later, he awoke not, tho' he yet breathed. The next day, he breathed his last.

Mr. James read the Service for him. We set him in the boat, and took him out to sea, where his bodie was consigned, and sorrowed.

Too much befell us and too much work we performed once we were on land to recount it all. We took off the sails and used them for the roofs of our houses. One of the houses burnt down. We built another. We had to decide what to do with the ship. What we had been looking for was some protected harbour, as in the mouth of a river, or a protected shore where we might careen her and haul her out of the sea. Instead, she was moored in shallow water with no protection. When the sea ice froze, it might break her then, or if not then, it might move her with it as it moved over rocks, and in the spring when the ice broke, so to might she break apart. James wished to drill a hole in her and sink her so she might ride out the winter below the ice. Mr. Cole liked not this plan but had no better.

Why had I sailed? I was in a fury at myself. I had sailed! What fool was I! Where were you? What had followed my departure? All this time I had been reassuring myself with a vizion of Heard receiving my letter, and understanding what he had seen, and marvelling o'er it, that he had not known, and cursing me that I hidde from him my true nature (as he would have it—for myself, I knew I had ever shown him my true nature, as I had lived it).

To move ashore was a massive undertaking that took a month of heavy work. For a time, the greatest subject twixt James and Cole and Price was how to preserve the Ship. Left where she was, she'd be crushed in the ice. Sunk, she'd be beneath it, and safe. But could she be raised in Spring?

We watched from shore, as Cole cut a hole. Down she sank. The boat with Leggat rowing Cole and James and Price came towards us as she dropped. Our hearts sank with the ship.

And then, as they ever do, rose again.

"We will surely die ere we reach home."

"Until then, what can we do but live?"

Our two priorities were gathering wood for the carpenter, to build a pinnace, and wood to keep us warm.

Our relations changed. James was a better leader ashore than aboard. He maintained authority. But we became more equal.

Each man had his own shifts, into and out of despair. What choice had we?

April 17. My Love. I fear we will not live. 'Tis this fear that starts me writing. At least I have spoke to you in my mind before I go.

Here are the reasons death feels so near. Our ship is sunk a mile off shore, as I have recounted, in shallow waters where ice buffets it. Our carpenter lies near death. He can no longer rise to build the pinnace that might, if we fail to raise our ship, carry us home. The cooper, who has been his apprentice, continues, but our tools are bad and broken. The carpenter is only the sickest of the sick, he is far from the only one. The Boat Swayne we have feared for his life for months now.

Mr. James writes his account of our journey to wrap up and leave here that any who follow might find it. His will be full of our stoicism, his own wisdom, our sundry misfortunes, God's mercy.

Mine will be something else.

We had yesterday our first warm day in six months, a day when a man may stand in the sun and feel its warmth on his face, a sensation we had all forgot. We are thin and sick and our joynts are swole and sore, but all who can make it a point to rise each day. When a man is down and has not got up by soupar, we crowd about him and chant, "Rise, rise, rise ye sailors rise," untill he makes it to his feet. Or so we did until the first man—'twas Palmer, the boat swain—rose not even then. We lifted him to his feet so we could say he'd done it, but he fell away in a swoon, and we laid him back down. We had no heart the next day to do our chant onlie to see him rize not, so let him lie. Then to our surprize, he took some broth and rose of his own accord. Then we began again.

Mr. James had read in Cartier, his account of his travels, that a certain concoction boiled of spruce or balsam worked against scurvy, but we have not found one that works for us. We had gathered vetches as late as we could but by the middle of October they had died beneath the snow. Teas I have made from dried leaves and needles and salve I have made from the same may have some small effect, it is hard to tell. Why are some men more afflicted than others, when all have had the same diet and treatment? Age is one difference, but it is not all.

Yesterday, another day of cold, six of twenty of us rose at dawn. Another six rose to take their dinner, such as it was, as their mouths are only fit to take broth and softened biscuit or porridge. Up at dawn were myself, James, van Rijn, Clement, and the two boys. Their youth helps them. In James it is that he is an example to all. In van Rijn, that he must feed us. And I, that I minister to the ravages of this disease the best I can.

And today, this glorious sun.

It melts, by God, it melts, cried van Rijn from without. Come, feel the sun on your face. We roused ourselves, all but Palmer and Cole, and came out in the sunshine, to blink and glory in it. Wardon is as sick as the other two who stayed abed, but comes out draped on the shoulders of Rance and Hammon.

God be praised, sayed James.

There we all stood in the clearing outside our house, sad, broken sticks of men with blackened lips, sores everywhere else, and old wounds re-opened, tears in our eyes at this small sign of hope, that seemed all the more cruel for bringing hope back.

Snow melted from the trees and from the roof of our house, making ice daggers.

Let us bring out Palmer and Cole, sayed I. They should feel this.

Then took four men each a corner of their blankets and carried them out into the sun, where they shielded their eyes and cried out as if we carried them to Hell. But then, their pupils shrunk down, they seemed to take heart, as we did.

Since Easter, in anticipation of such a warm day as this, we had bin repayring our pry bars and shovels to be ready to dig ice out of our ship, so off went the men who could to do't. I stayed with the sick, with Will to help me.

The sickest among us are Cole, Wardon and Palmer. They can scarce turn over in their beds but must be lifted and turned and must be set upon the pot. Little better are Mullins and Snigge. Ugganes has been working on the pinnace since Cole cannot. It is almost ready for planking. Ugganes does not want to give it up, but if we can raise the ship, it is wasted work to keep on with the pinnace. Our biggest want is planking. The trees have been so frozen all through the winter that they cannot be worked without a fire to thaw them. So first we must find a dead tree standing and not under the snow and bring it down and light a fire by the tree we want to cut to thaw it enough to strike with the ax.

At the end of the day, the crew returned with the news they have recovered our anker, but not yet the rudder, which is more important, for without it we go nowhere.

But they are in good cheer. Something greater to do than care for the sick and gather wood is better tonic than anything in my chest of physick.

James says there is water inside the ship but knows not if it comes from within or without.

Marsh, who made himself known early on for making bets on every small thing, has not offered any bets on whether we shall find our rudder or raise our ship. By these things we live or die.

[Undated]

Dear Joan,

We have been hit with a great gale of wind and snow and hail. 'Tis worse than if there had bin no good weather at all. I have no will to write. Death looms near. My love for you is all that I am. If I go out, where goes it?

———

CURIOSITIES

May 1. Joan, Joan. It hails and snows when at home the maypole is raised. Will this winter never end? I wake in the morning feeling I have not slept for all the moans and cries. Price is plagued by nightmares.

What is goodness? Is it obedience? Love for our neighbour? We have faced greater hardship than we have known. To labour in this cold is to dwell outside time.

The purpose of our sailing. The men do not question. They eat their next meal. They shit it out. The companionship of each other is enough. The care for each other is delicate.

The young men dream of spoils and glory. The young men [sentence unfinished in manuscript]

Our journey is entirely futile. We are buffoons. Look at us drop through the snow.

When we do, we are. When we do not, we are not. We are empty vessels.

What is the worst of our extremity? Leggat burnt his frozen foot. He could not feel it was burning and then he was in agonie. Something in this stands in for the whole.

James is confident in God, that God directs us, that God loves our King, that our Country is great and shal be made greater by our travelling through these lands and claiming them. We toast the King, God's representative on earth, the head of our church. We may as well toast him from the Moon and say the Moon is ours. The land has given us nothing. It might have given us more, but our muskets jam or misfire. 'Twould be easier to hunt with bow and arrow than with guns that fail us. Why did we pack no bows, no arrows?

We ne'er saw a white partridge but we fired at it and missed. Once, almost by accident, two birds were hit. When pluckt, they were as lean pigeons, that is, a quarter of a meal for one man. We have shot at and missed: white bear, deer, grey foxes, white foxes, brown hares, white

239

hares, geese, swans, weasels, and otters. We have shot and killed some handful of foxes, that gave us nice fine furs.

Will tried making a bow and stringing it with fox gut, but putting it to use in winter, the gut broke and then the wood, so it was no use.

We wrap our hands in great mittens. When the flesh is frozen white and loses sensation, it must be warmed ere long or the flesh dies and turns black and I must cut it away. Hammon has lost his nose this way. Now he keeps wool across his face. "I am better for it," says he. "I had too much nose."

The dogs Mr. James brought to hunt deer sink as we do into the snow and are no good to us. If we had not meat enow we could not conscience feeding them. But we have barrels of it yet, yea, even for the dogs.

Joan, today, May 4, James and I a-hunting. Geese and cranes. Snow wet, great shallow ponds filled with foule and none brought down, not a single one. I am wearie.

Joan, today, May 6, Wardon breathed his last. Buried him on top of sandy hill.

May 13. I give you news, Joan. Yesterday morning as I did the rounds of the teeth, Whittered said to me of my vigour (which is feigned) and beardless cheek, "You are like the fairy folk who age not."

At this Price, beside him, looked at me again, and sayed of a sudden, "You are the lad from the *Diamond!*"

What did I? Feign surprise? Lie? Say I am not? Conjure up again my dead twin that it was he, not I, who had been aboard the *Diamond*?

But I waited too long and now had to pretend to recognize him just this moment. To this end, I turned my eyes on him and let myself see him again as if for the first time, let myself recognize him, let myself show the recognition on my face.

"You were called George, then," said I. "Wherefore George?" His name that I knew now was Arthur Price.

He shrugged. "Some jest I have since forgot, just as you were Little Tom." He exclaimed again in wonder, clapped me on the shoulder. "How took it me so long to know you? This lad was a passenger aboard the *Diamond*," he said to the room, "that I sailed on to Virginia and that was in the great storm. His parents died in it. And he lived. Signed on as ship's boy. He was my shadow and acolyte that voyage."

The revelation gave us days of novel talk, of reminiscence particular to me and Price and the *Diamond*, and then our reminiscence sparking each man's own reminiscence of similar events and climes—tempests at sea, St. Elmo's fire, Virginia, our ways of ending up where we were.

Even as the talk went round of the marvel of our not knowing each other until now, even as we gave our tales of the *Diamond* and of Virginia, and heard everyone else's tales, none of them knew what Price and I knew. What import this recognition might have. I knew it, and Price knew it, and it was a weight in the air. Price had now power over me, to reveal my birth.

That day and night, and again earlier today, I caught him gazing upon my face more than was his wont. Should I avoid the chance of being alone with him or to seek it out?

At last, I went upon an errand to see if any vetch had grown in sheltered groves or south-facing slopes, and he came with me.

We walked in silence for a long time as fast, given our sore hips and knees and ancles and toes, as we could go, to keep the bugs off.

"Did you know me sooner?" he asked. "You seemed not surprised when I knew you."

"Not at first. Not for a long time."

"Am I so changed?" asked he. "You are changed. You were a tadpole. But I am the same man. Older, I know, but the same."

In contemplation of my answer, I responded not.

"No, you are right. I am not, I am not the same man. I am grown ugly, in and out."

"I see no ugliness in you," said I. "In or out." I wished by saying it to make this true. "What will you do?"

He knew I meant, How will you use this knowledge that I was born a girl that once you kept close so long as I put my hand to your yard when you willed it?

"After the shoaling," he said, "I might have used it to get me drink. But now." He left off for a long time. "By God, Little Tom," said he. "What to make of you. Thou'rt not quite a lass. This whole time, I have known you a man. And you have bin a man. But now I know thou'rt not quite a man either.

"It was after the shoaling you knew me," he said, that idea sounding in his head right then, "when I said you put me in mind of my sister. I was used to say that on the *Diamond*, wasn't I?"

We walked on. I had no fear of him for my person. I had, almost, pity alone.

"The shames of my life roll over me," he said. And he wept. "I am a sad carcass of a man. Why did Wardon die and not I?"

I saw he wished me to embrace him as he wept, and in that embrace to let him loose himself. I say I had no fear (we were all in such extremitie nothing that might happen as it might in ordinary times), but I knew that he might in his self-pity let himself do that his better self would not. I let him weep and walked on.

I had walked for two or three hundred yards, skirting a pond, keeping my eyes out for the green of new growth, when I stopped to see if he was following. He was. I walked on. In another few hundred yards, he had caught up.

I had it in my mind to say, "I am past caring, Price, what you do," but it was not true. I thought of what seemed the worst that might happen if he told James and the rest of the men, to see the change in them all. And to be used by them, that was a danger, too. I almost preferred death, which seemed not so far off, in any case, given we had just buried Wardon. But if I lived, I might see you again, which hope was enough. You. Joan. The strength in the bend of your neck. Your eyes.

"Little Tom," Price said. "Mr. Billson you have been and Billson you remain. Our chirurgion. There is nothing to be gained from discovering you."

I turned and looked him in the eye as if to exact a promise. Tiny flies made clouds between our two faces and around each of our heads. They crawled down our necks. They bit us behind the ears. Suddenly they were intolerable, and we were two men hopping in the madness of them, swatting blindly, asking our poor legs to run. "Where do they come from?"

Tonight, Price sleeps aboard the Ship, though she is not raised. To the rest, by laying his head there, he shows his dedication to the *Henrietta Maria*. To me, that he intends to hold true his promise.

He has stayed true, Price, thorow seven nights. One small good amid our misery. Pinnace undonne, Carpenter near death, cooper scarcely better. No Rudder. Flies like clouds of petty demons. And James has van Rijn sow peas. He maintains hope. He is an idiot. He is a god.

I want to write you every minute, but my hand likes not the pen. I take it up and there it sits. I am in a fog, a dream. Old Nut is in it, and you, and Mary Dance, and you, and Ned Hazelwood, and you, and my father, and you, Lady Margaret, and you. Someone calls me. I wake. There is the pen in my hand. I put it down. I go to them.

[Undated]

And now Cole has died. His work, there in the Shop, framed and ready to be planked. The work of his Bodie there in the Wood, in the wondrous shape of this fine Boat. Wasted. His Life. Wasted. On this Journey we could have returned from last year.

Price, returning to the Ship after burying Cole, and looking about her in the water, he found Sweet, the gunner, face down amid the ice, come in from where we had let go his body far out to sea, strangely untouched by his six months in the ice but that his skin was loose. His face more youthful than the day he died. How can this be he is better dead than alive?

We buried him on the hill with the others.

Dear Joan,

God be praised. On this 24th day of May, Hammon has found and recovered the rudder. The ice melts.

Dear Joan,

May 31. Vetches have raised their heads from the earth. We will live a little longer.

Dear Joan,

A day after vetches up, it freezes. A month past, I asked if this winter would end. No, says Winter. I am endless. It is June 7!

We tried and failed to hang rudder. No one can stand in the cold water long enough.

After a week of vetches morn and eve, one third of the crew is up and about, the other rousing. Emptying ship as much as possible so as to raise her.

I hardlie dare hope, but hope I do, my hope a slender candle-flame in a gusty, capricious wind, this hope: I shall see you. In the flesh, not in my minde!

Dear Joan,

Another week and now are all men on their feet and their teeth strong enow to chew.

As the snow melts, it leaves pools on shore. The days are hot as I have ever felt. The men throw themselves in the pools for relief. How is it we have gone from the bitterest cold to this heat in so few dayes? How is the sun so hot and so cold? How go we from day's heat to night's ice?

Out of nowhere come tiny biting flies that follow us in clouds. Behind them come whining mosquitos. Then horse flies like cavalry. We are maddened by them.

Thunder and lightning. But the rudder is hung! Hope burns brighter.

Dear Joan,

June 24. Ship is raised. Our houses have been disassembled, and everything taken down to the shore in preparation for loading and sailing. James takes meridian measurements. He has put portraits of king and queen along with his account of our expedition up on a cross he had made from a tree.

Yesterday, off goes James to look out from the Watch Tree one last time, taking Will. Each month, he has set a signal fire in case it be seen by Christian or Selvedge. (That we have lived makes him hope against reason Hudson may have done so. And he would inquire of Selvedges if there is a River or Sea towards Canada.)

James climbed the tree. Will set the fire, not calculating the wind, nor the dryness of the brush. The fire blew back toward James's tree, catching while he was still in it, so he had to leap from the lower branches, and the two of them run, while the fire spread as we had not known fire to spread.

From the shore, where we stood loading the boat, we saw it creep and then run and race and flow like a flood. It blew through where our houses had been, eating up what had been our town as if it wanted us gone, wanted to obliterate all trace of our having been there. And who can blame it.

The dogs howled and ran in the water, where they trembled and kept up their howls. Will stood between the two of them, trying to give them comfort, himself full of woe.

Now we are aboard our Ship. The light fades. The fire burns across the hills. Tomorrow, we sail. Tomorrow, I sail to you.

Anne's Note

So ends Tom's Hudson Bay account, much of which can be cross-referenced with James's own account, published in 1635. I am still awash in wonder that it exists.

My partner, meanwhile, pointed out a serious omission. Like me, she is in awe of the leaden packet, its stains and wormholes, its hidden message, but she is skeptical of any narrative from a European expedition that states or implies the absence of Indigenous people. Too convenient. Too terra nullius. A narrative that says, "Look, there's nobody here, let's take it."

Tom's account does reinforce what James's reports—in eighteen months, the men on that ship did not meet any Indigenous people. But, as my partner would assert, just because the Europeans did not meet Indigenous peoples, it does not follow they were not there.

It seems likely that the people of Waskaganish, who live on the east side of James Bay, would have been aware there were Europeans camped on the island (named "Charlton Island" only after James spent a winter there). The area is flat, and the

James party kept fires going constantly. They lit signal fires regularly, in case they should be spotted. James seems to have both hoped to meet, and feared meeting, the people who lived in these lands. Did the people of Waskaganish see these fires and choose not to explore their source?

An internet search for "Cree oral history 'Thomas James'" turns up some leads. One is a book by Cree storyteller Louis Bird, published in 2005, *Telling Our Stories: Omushkego Legends and Histories from Hudson Bay*. The Omushkego people live on the west side of James Bay. One tale features a man called Cut-Away Nose who's a bit strange, and doesn't know any stories, and gives away his food to a young woman who worked beside him on the caribou corral hunt, and says he's from far away, where there are stone buildings and different forests with different animals. Bird also tells a side-story that mentions two ships making thunderous noises at each other. I can easily imagine this to be Luke Foxe and Thomas James meeting and firing their guns in greeting. The larger account is about watching a European crew whose ship has been stranded at the highest tide of the month and can't get away until the next highest tide in another month's time—at least, not without help. The people send one man to see if these strangers are threatening or not, and, finding they are not, the people help them, and make some trades, the best of which is a steel-headed axe.

These are some stories I found, and there must be others. It seems entirely likely that people on both the east and west sides of the bay would have been aware of the presence of the Europeans on the island.

In imagining Tom—and James, and Price, and Cole, and Hammon (who turned into a Cut-Away Nose himself), and Palmer, and Wardon and all the rest of them—on the island that winter, I now also imagine people on both sides of James Bay lifting their heads when they hear gunshots, exchanging a glance, and going back to what they were doing.

There's much more to write on this—as my partner would say, too—but for the purpose of this tale, I send you back to Heard's Confession, as sent to Aubrey, and to The Memoir of Lady Margaret Long, as found by me that day in Somerset. (As there is some duplication in their two narratives, I have edited each slightly to give minimal overlap.)

The True Confession of John Heard

*T*HERE WAS NEVER A DOUBT in my mind that what I had seen—Tom Barrows, unmanned by Joan—was the truth. He was entirely naked. His chest was a man's; he had no dugs. His broad shoulders and muscled arms were there, his compact Bodie, his strong legs. Tho' he was but short of stature, he was all Man but for that one absence, of his yard.

I was the more surprized at Joan, that she should be a Witch and have donne this. She had untill now counterfeited so well a modest womanne.

She was taller than he, her figure womanly, and wanton. In her face was a madness I recognize now as Lust. It was fully evident to me, in this look I was seeing for the first time was cunning and sorcery, of which Barrows was a victim.

If Joan be Witch, was an infection in our very Parish. And if Joan, how not Lady Margaret herself? Unless she, like Barrows, was bewitched?

Lady Margaret argewed against us from the start, laid claim that Barrows was no man but a woman, which, as the evidence of my eyes gave me, was patently false. The question remained. Was she an unknowing dupe of the Witch Joan? Or was she complicit?

253

But first let me tell you what transpired. I walked away from the gatehouse. The rain had let up as suddenly as it had come. God signalled to me in this way. If I could do nothing in myself now, coward that I was, I must go to the Magistrate so that he may take action. So went I home and saddled my horse and turned to Sir Herbert Hopton, near Shepton Mallet, which journey took me two hours, but he was not at home. I then composed a letter to him and left it there for his return.

As I rode home, I reasoned Joan must be seized ere she cause further malefice. I must engage Isaiah Gough, a yeoman and Constable of Chew Magna, with whom I had some agreeable acquaintance, so to his house I repaired. I found Gough at table.

"Mr. Heard. What news?"

"I come to engage your service as Constable," said I.

"On what matter?"

"It is not fit to be spoken of before your Wyf and children."

He wiped his mouth and came away from the table while the children clamoured and his Wyf endeavoured to hush them. The oldest boy rose from his seat and followed untill the nurse plucked him by the sleeve and pulled him back.

In a closet I told him what I had seen.

"I am amazed," said he. "I had not known it possible untill you came from Bavaria. Here. Here. In this place. I am wholly astonished. And then, I am not." He lifted his brows here to communicate his meaning, then whispered it to confirm. "Lady Long." He nodded sagely. "Well." He slapped his knees. "We arrest this Joan, then?"

"Arrest her and alert the magistrate he is needed."

We then went to Gough's deputy to join us in the arrest and then took ourselves to Longwood, where we found Lady Long at home, and Joan, as she told us, from it. I trusted not she told the truth.

We stopped first at the gatehouse. 'Twas empty. I expected nothing else, but in my mind I saw again what I had seen before, the full nakedness of Barrows, the hair alone at his crotch where his yard should be, the look on his face of surprise and consternation when he saw me and where my gaze was trained. I firmed my resolve and rode on with my companions up to Lady Long's door.

We were admitted. Lady Long was alone, no Joan by her side as was her wont. She asked our business.

"We are come in the name of the King to arrest Joan Palmer," said Gough.

"On what charge?"

"Witchcraft."

"You mystify me."

I explained what I had seen.

"You saw them before you naked? Together?"

I allowed it was so.

"Embracing?"

"Not embracing, but standing one before the other. Three or four paces between them. Barrows was as rooted to the spot. Onlie when I broke the spell by my entrance did they shift."

She widened her eyes at me and then berated me. We had to interrupt her and press for the person of Joan.

"She is not here," said she.

"Come, Lady Long," said Gough, "let us have her."

"I tell you, she is not here."

"Where then is she?"

"The full extent of my knowledge is: not here. I know not where she is."

"Whither has she gone?"

"I know that neither."

"She is your servant, Lady Long," said Gough. "You are her mistress, Lady Long. You must know where she is."

"She has long been her own mistress, and I do not."

"Where might she be?"

"My knowledge has not increased from when last you asked me."

And so we were forced to leave and seek her elsewhere. But before we went, we sent the deputy around to the kitchen to ask of the servants if they knew Joan, her whereabouts.

Where was Barrows? With Joan? In what place? Had he decamped for Bristol?

We repayred to my house and learned Barrows had collected his belongings and walked off. The servant who saw him do so said he went towards Chew. Was he alone? Yes, he was.

We then asked in Chew did any see him?

No, came the answer from the fellow we had asked, a man repayring a cart wheel outside his shop, with another man by that spoke to him as he worked. Why, the question. We believe him bewitched, the answer. I made a hasty calculation, or rather, I made no such a one. I was full of the moment. I told the men what Barrows had suffered. Immediately it was apparent that this news would spread as fast as any gossip has ever spread. I counted this a good, as it would aid in our securing the Witch.

The three of us went separate ways to ask had either Joan Palmer or Tom Barrows been seen.

We got no answer that satisfied us. None that saw them walk together. None that saw Barrows go anywhere but Chew. We told everyone. Their dread was great.

Where had the two gone? They had not vanished into air, or, anyway, Barrows had not. Who knew where Joan might have spirited herself? Tho' ever I suspected her with Lady Long. They knew themselves discovered.

It seemed likeliest that Barrows should take himself to Bristol, to the Physitian's Hall. We had no better guess than that Joan had gone with him. We determined the next day to go to Bristol to apprehend Mistress Palmer.

On the way there, who did we meet upon the road but Mistress Palmer herself, walking with long strides toward Chew, as brazen as you please.

"It is convenient we meet you, Mistress Palmer, the very person we seek."

She looked me hard in the eye until I 'gan to feel it an Evil Eye, as the Spanish have it, and sign the cross to ward it off. She had some hidden meaning in her eyes that gave me unease.

"Where is Mr. Barrows?" we asked.

"Do you not know?" sayed she.

"Would I ask if I knew?" sayd I.

"I understand you not, Mr. Heard."

"We come to arrest you," sayd Gough.

She scoffed and walked on. We must turn our horses to keep pace.

"In the name of the King, stop," cried Gough. "Seize her," he sayed to his deputy, who rode beside her and seized her shoulder as he dismounted.

"What is the charge?"

"You know very well."

"That I do not."

"You are a most damnable Witch," sayed I.

She lookt amazed, a most creditable feigning. "You have lost your wits," sayd she. She shook off the deputy's hand and resumed walking toward Chew Magna. The deputy had some reluctance to regain hold of her it seemed.

"Seize her," sayd Gough. "Where's your rope?"

He dismounted, took a length of rope from the deputy's saddle bag, while the deputy seized Joan's arm.

"You are in earnest," sayed Mistress Palmer, in wonder. Truly, Satan had made her a powerful counterfeiter.

She made no struggle as they tied her wrists. "What have I done? I have done nothing. Mr. Heard, what is your part in this? Why shame you me this way?"

I saw before me her Lust-crazed eyes as they had been in the gate-house. "Foulest servant of the Divell," sayd I, "you know your crimes."

She swore she did not.

"You did most feloniously unman Thomas Barrows."

She lookt at me as if I were mad, but sayed no more.

Where to hold her? We had no gaol and had little cause in either Chew or Norton to hold prisoners. Therefore thought we of an edifice that could be lockt and guarded, either the church or the tithing barn, or there was a barn of Gough that could serve, which is where we took her, and then sent word to Sir Herbert Hopton.

We passed some few people on the way to Gough's holding on the road to Norton Hawkfield. Word now would spread wider. There we put her into the barn with the deputy as guard, and got Gough's labourer to serve in like regard. Gough's children were full of curiosity and when they learned their barn held a Witch, they were full of scorn and daring to see which could taunt her the worse and not by her be cursed.

Now that Joan's person was secure, it must be examined for the Divell's mark, for which were needed three good women of the parish. And as this could not be her only crime, a survey must be done of her neighbours to know if there were any other complaints of her. Mistress Gough could be one, offered her husband, but when it was put to her she feared she could not do't. Her husband asked who else should be asked.

Into Chew Magna we went. We approached Mistress Whitwood, wyf of William Whitwood, weaver, goodwife Eliza Pringe, and Elizabeth Ridman. I described to them what must be done. She must be stripped of her clothes and each inch of her skin examined to find the Divell's teat where he or his imps did suckle. Upon finding one, they must test it with pins to see if it were sensible, not letting her see where they tested.

Next we went about Chew, inquiring of households if any had a complaint. What we found was a great deal of speculation about Lady Long, her doings, and Joan Palmer only by association with Lady Long.

Susanna Veale, who had the news of every thing afore her neighbours we went to first. There with her already was Jane Grimsby.

"Is't true that Joan Palmer has been taken prisoner as a Witch? Joan Palmer?"

"Most regrettably true, Mistress Veale."

"For magicking a man's yard?"

Now another of her neighbours joined in. "I wouldn't mind being able to do that."

"Tempt not the Divell with your jests, Mistress," sayd I.

"Mr. Heard saw it himself," sayd Gough.

"Saw it not, you mean."

"Have you complaints of Joan Palmer?"

"She has not ta'en my yard," sayd Mistress Veale.

"Jest not, I say," sayed I. "The foulest danger of a Witch lies less in the harm she does her neighbours than in the peril wherein she puts their souls. Where one Witch is found, there can onlie be more, for Satan is ever pressing her to bring souls to him, away from God."

"There you be, then. 'Tis not Joan Palmer we suspect of witchcraft, except in the service of her mistress. Her mistress, she is out at night, taking measure, says she, of the moon and planets. Says she, says she. Consulting with Owls. Who knows what other dark things."

"Has any bin harmed by her?"

Mistress Veale gave a shrug.

"Think you she has given her soul to the Divell?"

"She goes to Church like everyone."

Jane Grimsby: "Her neighbours do not complain."

"Her sheep died not the year others had a blight."

"Last year was a bad harvest. This year a late springe. Is there a witch among us?"

"She takes Communion."

Another neighbour: Her fortune has not gone ill almost since Joan Palmer came. Mayhap they both made a pact with the Divell.

"My old mother was cook there," sayed Goodwife Grimsby. "Lady Long was always wanting help with strang alchemy. Boil me this, strain me that, she'd ask. Mam was suspicious at first but when she had been there a year or two it concerned her not. Lady Long showed her what transpired when this was added to that, and her suspicions were allayed."

"Mayhap he tried to have her by force. For that, she'd take a man's yard, I don't doubt."

"I'd take a man's yard for that. Who wouldn't?"

"You make the curate blush, Susannah," sayd her friend.

I got the same answer from Martin Edgel, a waller, about her sheep thriving when others did not, and her wool fetching fine prices.

From another villager: Joan Palmer spoke sharp to my husband once and later he got a boyl.

From Edward Mill, who worked at Lady Long's some ten years since: Once I goosed her, innocent enough, and she fixed her eye on me just like a witch. Next day, toothache.

Many had stories like this but none would come and depose before the Magistrate.

Some had stories of kindnesses Joan had donne or gifts Lady Long had given them. She gives a good feast, I heard more than once.

Of twenty villagers, almost all had suspicions, but none would stand forth.

"Fear you not a witch amongst you?"

"You fear enough for all of us," sayd one of 'em as my back was turned.

As I walked off, I heard laughter, directed, I knew, at me. After all I had been through and all the efforts of my life, 'twas the same as walking to the village school. I was destined for ridicule.

I must take it as Job, and let nothing shake me. Yet I was shaken.

The Memoir of Lady Margaret Long

*C*AME KNOCKING AT MY DOOR the stripling curate, John Heard, and his neighbour, Isaiah Gough, a florid, self-regarding, self-important, and stupid man, with a mournful, complayning wife and various odious children, who was serving his turn as Constable. He brought with him his groom and dog. At the door he told French he had a pressing matter upon which to see me. I had him brought into the room in which we did estate business, and bid French stand by.

"Mr. Heard, Mr. Gough," sayed I. "What is your pressing business?"

"Lady Long," sayd Gough, "I have had report of Mr. Heard here that your servant, Joan—"

"My companion, Joan."

"You may not be so eager to call her companion when you hear what she has done. Your *companion*, has, I know not how, 'tis beyond me how it might be done, she has, she has cast a spell to unman Heard's friend Barrows."

"Make yourself clear, sir. I fail to understand you."

His jaw flapped and his cheeks reddened. "Heard, you tell her."

"Joan is a most damnable witch and has by her craft and her pact with the Divell caused Barrow's yard to disappear."

"Caused Barrow's yard to—" What meant he? "Saw you Mr. Barrows naked?"

"The two of them together I saw naked, she a terrible Eve and he a—"

At once I understood. "Mr. Heard, you credulous ninny!"

"My Lady!" sayd Gough.

"Fool! Idiot!"

"Nay, my Lady, you go too far, my Lady."

"Where is the nose upon your face, Mr. Heard? Is't here?" I pulled at my chin. "Here?" I slapped my forehead. "Joan is no witch, Mr. Heard. Your Mr. Barrows ne'er had a yard."

Gough sayd, "She must be brought before the magistrate. We must secure her person and bring her."

"You must do nothing of the kind. She is no witch. She will do nothing but live and breathe."

Gough, his face, was full of confusion.

"Let us have her before us," sayed Heard.

"She is not here," sayd I. I had not seen her since morning, when she and Mr. Barrows had gone, as they said, for a walk. I had stayed back to meet with Mr. Lifton about our sheep and their shearing. I had grown worried something had befallen them, and had sent out sever-all of my staff to find them, to no avail. As evening drew nigh, I thought they had run off together to get married. I was in Choler with them, heartsore, afraid.

But this was not to be borne.

Gough's man lookt to his master, who looked at Heard, whose jaw clenched.

"Take your accusation," sayed I to the men. "Take that and that alone."

They made further objection, insisting Joan be brought forth.

"Do you say I lie, sirs? Do you accuse Lady Long of untruth? Get gone from my house."

French followed them to the door. They asked him where Joan was. "Think you my mistress lied? She is not here," sayd he. He watched them until they were on their horses. "I have a premonition they will skulk around and ask the kitchen," sayd he. Thither we both hied. And thither they came, the deputy and Gough's groom, merrily calling out to the kitchen if Mistress Palmer was about. "I have not seen her. Why?"

"I see you come to ask of my household what you disbelieve from me," I sayed, which startled him that he knew not what to say. "Take your leave."

Then had I to meet with the household to quell gossip.

At last when I was alone, "Joan," sayed I, though she was not there to hear me, "I thought I could give you up, but I find I cannot. I could do't before you were discovered, when I, like everyone else, took Barrows to be the man he seemed to be. You would be marrying a physitian, a well-favoured man, curious and ingenios. Now, I am struck all of a wonder. How did I not see't? His stature, the size of his hands, the beardlessness of his cheek, the timbre of his voice—they all point to his being womanne and yet I saw them not. I am envious of him. I could do that. Think you I would make a good gentleman? I trow I would."

I wrote to Sir Herbert Hopton, the magistrate, and sent the letter straight away. "You will hear presently—you may already have—from a young divine, lately come into Somerset, and disappointed it is so dull, having few Witches, John Heard, of the parish of Norton Malreward. He accuses my companion, Joan Palmer, of, by witchcraft, causing the Penis of his friend to disappear. To write it out pains me the more by the clarity of how absurd is his accusation. Heard is young, has been in Bavaria (where lies much madness), and has a witch-mania, its fervour exacerbated there. Joan has lived with me for more than twelve years, and I assure you, is no Witch. Heard discovered Joan and Thomas Barrows, whom Joan had known from her infancy, naked before each other, and so convinced was Heard that his friend was a Man that he concluded not the truth—that Thomas Barrows was not Thomas but Thomasina—but that Joan had magicked away his Yard."

As the evening whiled away with no appearance of Joan, nor Mr. Barrows, I wondered if they hadd gone off to be married. My heart ached. My mind ran untrammelled this way and that. Joan, do not leave me, ran one refrain. O, Joan, come home. And then: This accusation is absurd, it can go nowhere. And again over the wonder of Tom as Mr. Barrows, how he carried it off. How I might. But I could not.

Where were they? Why did they not write? How could Joan have left me? Without a word. So ran my thoughts that sleepless night. To distract myself, to give myself something to do, I began my account of Joan, her life, burning the lamp all threw the night to write it.

On the morrow, mid-day, I learned Joan had been apprehended by Heard and Gough on the road from Bristol and was being kept by Gough. I took myself there post-haste.

"Where is Mistress Palmer?" I demanded of Mistress Gough, her husband being from home.

"She is in the barn, my Lady."

"She must be released immediately."

"O, must she, my Lady? A witch. Released. No, she must be held, and examined and tried."

"Show me the Barn."

"'Tis not hard to find."

Went we round to what was less a barn than a cowshed, a low stone building with one square window, through which two boys, Gough's sons, tried to throw stones, missing more often than not. By the door stood Gough's deputy. He made no move to curtail the boys but seemed to encourage them.

"Be gone," roared I at the boys and they scattered.

"Lady Long," sayd the deputy.

"Release her," sayd I.

"I am charged to stand guard," sayd he. "My duty is to the law."

I roared with impotency now, then collected myself. "Then let me in."

He looked uneasy but did as I said. Simon, who had driven me, remained outside with him.

The day was the first bright day of May with the sun shining and warmth falling down. In the barn was cold and damp. I had seen Joan but two days before. So much had changed in that short time. I almost knew not how to approach her.

Wordlessly, we clasped each other's hands. "Joan," I whispered.

She saw my despair. "My Lady."

"That they have you here."

"That they have me at all."

"Tell me. Tell me."

She lowered her eyes. "You know," said she. "I think you know."

"You showed yourselves to each other," I said. "And Heard burst in and saw 'twas Thomasina he knew, not Tom."

"But he does not believe 'twas Thomasina. He believes I took Tom's yard by magick."

"Did you not tell him Tom is not Tom?"

"I could not."

"You must."

"He would have to live in skirts."

"As you do. As do I. I told Heard. You must tell him."

"He is too firmly convinced."

"His accusation is absurd. What witch has taken a yard?"

"He examined one in Bavaria that sayed she had."

"How would she do't? He is an idiot in a curate's cloak. He is a boy. He is a ninny."

"He has convinced others he is in the right."

"It cannot last. What of Tom? Where is he hid?"

"Aboard a ship and sailed," sayd she.

"He is a coward."

"'Twas I that begged him to go."

I became aware again of our surroundings. "'Tis not right you should be held here. 'Tis too mean for you. I will speak to Gough." I rose to do so, though I knew not whether he had returned.

"Stay," she bid me. It warmed me, that "stay."

"I mind less where I am held than that I am," sayd she.

We walked about the space to keep warm.

At last we heard the approach of a crowd.

Came through the door Gough and Heard and Mistresses Whitwood, Ridman, and Pringe, who greeted me with surprize that I was there in that low place.

"My Lady Long," sayd Gough.

"Mister Gough, what is this?"

"Mistress Palmer must be examined," sayed Heard. "These good women come to do their duty."

"Mister Heard, no. This absurd accusation must go no further. There is no truth to't. Your Tom Barrows ne'er had a yard to be taken. Tell him, Joan."

Joan was silent.

"She responds not, my Lady. She does not corroborate."

His self-satisfaction was abhorrent.

In anguish, I cried her name. "Joan, Joan. Do not do this. Tell the truth. God wills it. You save Tom nothing."

"I am no witch, as the evidence will show."

Mistress Whitwood: "There is not light here for us to see."

Gough: "I will send for more lanthorns."

"I cannot believe you are proceeding. I assure you, she is no witch."

"Pardon, my Lady," sayed Heard. "Your word is insufficient."

Again I implored Joan to speak on her own behalf. Again she would not.

Gough and Heard retreated outside the shed. Heard had sayd a prayer that was an admonishment for the women to sober justice and duty to God. "Thou shall not suffer a Witch to live."

The women came inside again.

Mistress Whitwood, "I am sorry to do this, Mistress Palmer, God knows." She turned to me, but spoke to Joan. "Lady Long would preserve your modesty more by stepping out."

"There is not much left of my modesty," sayd Joan. Then did she take off her skirts and her shift and other undergarments until she stood naked.

"Art thou cold?" asked Eliza Pringe.

Joan nodded.

"Well, sit upon that stool and we will work as quick as we can."

They examined first her back, where were severall moles and pimples. They held up her hair and searched her neck, behind her ears. Goose flesh came up on her skin. I could see it from two paces off, even in the dim light. She shivered, and I saw her shoulders shake with silent weeping. They examined her chest, lifting up each Breast. Then they required her to stand, examining her backside where again were moles and pimples. The moles they pricked with pins and waited to see if she flinched or made a sound. She began to shiver more. Then came a spot they pricked and she made no reaction.

"Feel you this?" they sayd and they pricked her not.

"Nay, I feel nothing," sayd she. "I am too cold."

"Feel you this?" sayd they again and pricked her.

"The pin is like a flea," sayd Joan. "It jumps."

So they went down her legs to her feet, and the warts on her toes, which were insensible, as warts sometimes are.

Then they allowed her to dress again. They have found nothing, sayed I to my self. I let my breath out.

"We have done," shouted Mistress Whitwood. The door opened. The light blinded us. A year, it seemed, had passed since I entered. Out went the women. Up went a clamour of voices as if half the village were outside the hut.

"It is too like Old Nut," sayd Joan.

"But you can speak, my Love, where she could not," sayd I. "Speak. I implore you."

Heard and Gough returned.

"Lady Long, 'tis time for you to take your leave."

"I will not," sayd I.

"You must," sayd Gough.

"Mistress Palmer should be alone and free of your influence while we examine her."

"Mistress Palmer should have me by her side to guard against your ill usage of her."

"We are not here to use her ill but to have the Truth and redeem her Soul."

So the argument went, untill at last their seeing how firm I stood, they withdrew. I left Joan not before eleven of the clock and returned with the Sun, when I found Gough and Hurd had been questioning her all the hours I lay without Sleep. I had better have stayed.

Sir Herbert Hopton was a tall man, Deaf in one ear, a smile always about his mouth, with an inclination to do as he list. He had a great appetite for Musick and Falconry. He was disposed to laughter and to argument, oft-times, thought I, for its own sake. He was prone to look down his nose at me, at which I bristled. "You have an amusing little wife," he was wont to say to my Husband. "She is a good deal more than amusing," returned my Husband. Nevertheless, I counted him an ally. He arrived with his Secretary an hour after I had banished Gough and Hurd from the barn. Hearing him arrived, I walked out, too.

"Lady Margaret, in what strang circumstance we meet," cried Hopton. "Yet it is always a kindness to the eyes to see you. Fare you well?"

"Fare I well? As far from well as any can stray. I pray you are nearer it."

"I am full of curiosity. Where are they keeping this ingenios Witch?"

"In a stable," sayed I, "and she is no Witch."

"The complaint must be heard. Which is Hurd and which Gough?"

Those two men were spilling out Gough's door toward us.

"The stripling is Heard."

"Good morrow, Mr. Heard, Mr. Gough. I am come to hear your complaint."

He went with them back into the house. I made to follow but was rebuffed. Went I instead to see how Joan fared.

She drowsed in the hay. "They have kept me up all night, asking, when did Satan first come to me? In what form? How long have I been a Witch? They ask it kindly, they ask it cruelly. Do not lie! Stop you counterfeiting! Thou art a Witch. Say it. Confess it. Make your peace with God."

"Oh my sweet," sayed I. "Cruel as well as fools. Sir Hopton has arrived. Let us pray he will see the absurdity of their Charge and you will be released ere long."

She was worn out but furious, too, to be held like this, and humiliated by a reedy blinkered Boy and a puffed-up Yeoman.

Soon Gough, his deputy, came down to bring Joan to the house. She recoiled in the brightness of the May morning. Gough's children burst from the house, squawling and squealing, the boys chasing the girls, then spied Joan. "The Witch, the Witch," the boys cried, driving their sisters toward us. The girls screamed and dodged. "She will get you," they cried. "She will get *you*," sayed one sister. Their nurse now appeared on the doorstep to call them in, but they paid her no mind. Next came Mistress Gough, yelling at the nurse she was no use, and at the children, who paid her no more mind than they did of the nurse until the nurse came at them. As soon as she drew near one, the others scattered. One boy she caught by the collar and slapped his bottom. The eldest repeated his taunt of the day before, calling me Lady Witch and Joan my servant. "You are caught now, vile Witches, and will be hanged."

"Who do you call witch, boy? Stop thy tongue, insolent pup! Mistress Gough, take care for your children. They run wild."

Mistress Gough hushed her son but glared at me.

Sir Hopton spoke first to Heard, thus.

Hopton: Is a naturall explanation possible, Mr. Heard, not a supernaturall?

Heard: No, by God, I assure you.

Hopton: Lady Long believes your Mister Barrows no man, but a woman.

Heard: I know with a certainty he is not. I have known him since boyhood.

Hopton: It is easy enough to have the truth of it. Let Mr. Barrows be brought before us.

Heard: That cannot be. He is not here.

Hopton: Not here? Where is he?

Heard: I know not with any certainty. He may be in Bristol. He may have sailed.

Hopton: Find him. You have no crime if you have no victim.

Heard: . . .

Hopton: Now let us hear from Mistress Palmer.

Joan looked the worse for her two nights in the stable, but held herself as straight as she could as Hopton asked her name and parentage and circumstance before he got to the matter.

Hopton: Mistress Palmer, you come before me on a most serious and solemn charge, made by this curate, John Heard, that you by witchcraft did take the yard of Thomas Barrows and make it disappear. 'Tis the strangest charge I have yet heard, and if true, most execrable and heinous. What say you to this charge?

Joan: My Lord, I did not.

Hopton: Is it true, as Mister Heard has it, that he came upon you and Mr. Barrows in the gatehouse of Lady Long?

Joan: It is, my Lord.

Hopton: Naked?

Joan: Yea, my Lord.

Hopton: How came you and Barrows to be naked in the gatehouse of Lady Long?

Joan: We are betrothed.

Hopton: And has your betrothed a yard?

Joan: . . .

Hopton: Look not to Lady Long to answer my question. Lady Long says he has not, that Thomas Barrows is not a man but a womann.

Joan: He is a man.

Hopton: Are you a witch, Mistress Palmer?

Joan: I am not.

Hopton: Take you communion each week?

Joan: I do.

Hopton: Are there any other complaints of this woman? Mr. Gough, you have made inquiry in the parish. Have any come forward with complaint?

Gough: Not directly.

Hopton: If any have a charge to make, let them make it before the end of two days. Let a search be made for Barrows, and in the meanwhile, I entrust Joan to the company of her mistress, Lady Margaret Long. Untill Barrows is found, and examined, or untill further evidence comes forth, I will go proceed no further against Mistress Palmer.

We then packt up and went home, most happy and unhappy. Our way went through town, where all eyes were upon us. I waited to say, "You told not the truth, Joan."

"I could not speak it," sayed she.

"What will you say when Tom returns and is asked to show forth his yard?"

"I will write him to say, Come thou not here, I will meet you."

"You would leave me, then? Though I love you and ever have and ever will? More constant than Tom, and closer, not to say higher born, and richer, and altogether better?"

Tears came into her eyes. "I would it were not so," sayed she softly.

Then I took her in my arms and we wept together. "There. Let us dry our eyes. Thou art free."

I liked not stopping in Somerset with the eyes of the neighbours upon us, and decided to go to Surrey, to a small holding I had there, near my parents, my Mother yet living. We kept to ourselves the few days it took to prepare ourselves for departure.

We were just climbing into the carriage when up rides Gough with a large retinue, and behind him half the Village on foot.

"What is't?"

"Lady Long, we arrest you in the name of the King," says Gough, "for most feloniously bewitching my son to death."

Now came forth all my household to see what was the matter.

"God bless your son's soul, Mister Gough. I am sorry he is dead. But lay not the blame at my feet."

But he would not listen to reason. Further, he had enflamed the crowd, who would not rest untill they saw me taken.

This was a terrible wrong being done, a great injustice. Now they had complaints of me of their own, that I had turned their milk when they had not paid rent, that I had lamed their horse after it had crossed the path of mine and got tangled in the traces.

They blamed the slow spring on me, the rains, a storm of thunder and lightning that had cracked a great tree that killed three sheep as it fell. These, the very neighbours I had greeted at church with kindness, condescencion, and goodwill.

"To Sir Hopton we go, my Lady. Stay in your carriage. We have men to ride before and after it."

I knew not what to do. I was incensed. "We go to Surrey," sayed I, "as we purpose."

"I am the agent of the King," said Gough. "Therefore, in the King's name, I take you to Sir Herbert Hopton. Your higher estate shields you not from the Law, my Lady."

"This is a base, false accusation."

In the end, we had little choice but to go as Gough would have it.

As we went, the crowd grew raucous. Our way led us again through Chew Magna. Of a sudden, a heavy rain fell, and came a roar from the Crowd, the carriage jostled, and rose a cry from Simon, who drove us, and another from the footman. Our doors opened and the crowd—Martin Edgel and his son, James Veale and Susannah, his wyf, John Ransom, and many more, labourers whose names I knew not, laid hands upon both myself and Joan, drawing us from the carriage. The rain soaked us, then pelted us as it turned to hail.

What madness was this? Did they mean to hang us?

"The hail is their choler!" cried one.

"Put me down," I cried. I named them by name, but Susannah Veale sayd, "I stop up my ears against your Magick, I hear you not."

I struggled mightily. "How dare you lay hands on me," sayed I. "This is not justice. Let me down or know you will yourselves be charged. You seize a Gentlewoman and your better."

"Do not threaten, Witch," sayd Edgel.

But two labourers who held me turned sheepish and put me down. I saw then John Powdry, the schoolmaster, had come amongst them, crying, "What is this ado?"

"She is right," sayd Ransom, now, under Powdry, his eyes. "Let justice be done by Law and not by our hands."

Now they argued amongst themselves, but they had put me down. Mr. Gough had not good control of his horse, who skittered and would not mind him. He called out that we be let go, but the Crowd cared little for his cries.

The Crowd that had Joan continewed on. They had reached the river. I could not see full well, but it seemed they had cast her upon the Water.

Gough got control of his horse, Simon had wrenched himself free of those that had seized him and stood by me, and Gough and his Deputy went after those that had ducked Joan. They clearly thought as little of Gough as I, but they were fools to think of ducking her in the river, for it was shallow and they proved nothing.

At last, all hands were off Joan, who stood in the river to her waist, coughing out the water she'd taken in.

Powdry named their Names as a warning he knew them, and that Gough should take report to Sir Hopton.

The frenzy had gone out of the Crowd.

We went on.

———

We had another two hours to get to Shepton Mallet, and Sir Hopton's house. For an hour I stayed wet with the rain before drying out. Joan, in her wet skirts, shivering even beneath the carriage blankets, was not so fortunate.

"I thought not to see you again so soon," sayed Sir Herbert at our arrival. "How now?"

"This buffoon of a Constable will enlighten you. He has not enlightened us."

"My lord," said Gough. "These two witches have conspired to kill my son, as retribution for the witch Palmer's arrest."

Sir Herbert's eyes grew large and he turned to us in wonder. Our own wonder was as great, but in ours was more fear that any might believe this true.

My self: "Preposterous! He has died some other way."

"Lady Long did bid my son hold his tongue and one day hence his tongue so swelled that it stopped his breath." Gough wept. "He is dead, my Boy, my eldest, unnaturally, most unnaturally."

Hopton: God speed his Soul to Heaven.

Me: I am sorry the Boy is dead, as I have said, but I had no hand in it. I have lost children and know how it enflames the brain and consumes the soul. To accuse me of Murder is too much. I know not what caused the boy's tongue to swell, but 'twas not I.

Hopton: What says the Doctor?

Gough: He died ere a Doctor could be called.

Hopton: His body must be examined for another cause of Death.

Gough: The cause of it is here in front of you. It is known these two are Witches.

Hopton: It was not known a week ago.

Gough: It has been known for years, or suspected, as everyone in Chew Magna will tell you, for they were full of accusations when we passed thorow.

Joan shivering beside me recalled me to her state. She had not dried. I conveyed this to Sir Herbert, insisting that her dress be changed. Hopton dismissed Gough with the charge that he engage Mr. Broughton to examine the boy's body. He himself would take charge of myself and Mistress Palmer, and then return to Chew to learn from Broughton what he had found.

Joan's dress was changed; her chill lingered.

We remained at Sir Herbert's in a strang state, guests, but not guests.

Broughton rode down that evening. "The boy died of a bee sting," he sayd. "He had trapped it and tried to make it sting his brother." He slapped his knees. "A very parable, is it not?"

"A natural cause," sayd Hopton. "As Bernard advises."

"God be praised," sayd I.

The Goughs clung to Witchcraft as the cause, sayd Broughton. Mistress Gough insisted she had bin stung a dozen times without harm. How then should her Son die when stung once?

He had explained most are not killed by it, but some, their tongues swell, and they asphyxiate unless a hole be cut in their windpipe. Galen, sayed he, tells of an Egyptian pharaoh that died of bee sting.

"Mistress Gough maintains 'twas Lady Long who directed the bee to sting," sayd Broughton. "That the bee was her familiar."

"I was with Lady Long when she bid the boy hold his tongue," sayd Sir Herbert. "She sayed and did nothing other than was meet to the occasion. I will take this case no further."

I hastened to tell Joan the news. We were Free.

The True Confession of John Heard

*A*FTER SIR HOPTON'S HALF-HEARTED EXAMINATION of Joan Palmer, I went at his direction to see if I might find Tom Barrows. I wrote to Tradescant on chance Barrows had gone there, but got no swift answer. Not knowing where else to search, I went to Bristol, to the Physitian's Hall, where I heard Barrows had come some weeks before, but he had not been seen there since. I inquired of the Chirurgions. There was a Captain James, I'd learned, preparing a voyage Northwest to China. I sought him out. He had a chirurgion, said he, but his name was Nathaniel Billson. Having pursued these inquiries, I was at a loss.

I returned to Norton Malreward, to my usual tasks. I addressed myself to my next sermon, on sorrow and faith. My texts were the story of Balaam, and Israel among the Moabites; St. Peter; and St. John on the disciples trying to understand Jesus when he sayed, "A little while and ye shall not see me; and again a little while and ye shall see me." I thought of Balaam, not seeing what his ass sees, which is the Angel of the Lord with a sword in his hand, and his ass saves him, and he smites his ass when it is he that is wrong and the ass right, and thought of

Barrows, blind to the danger of Witches. I was the ass, and warned him. But this would not work for a sermon.

I turned my thoughts to St. Peter, his letter: "Abstain from fleshly lusts, which war against the soul," which put me in mind again of Barrows and Joan as I found them. And then: "Submit yourselves to every ordinance of man for the Lord's sake; whether it be to the king, as supreme; or unto governors, as unto them that are sent by him"— this would do better for Lady Margaret, who refused to give up Joan to the agent of the King. I'd speak on "the ordinance of man."

I thought I must find some paper to put my thoughts down. Upon the table in my closet was a sheaf of paper, and drawing it near, I saw a letter lying there betwixt two sheets. I inquired of the household when it had come and who had received it, but no one would own up to it. Then I opened its cover and read.

There, in the first few lines, was the truth from Tom Barrows's very hand: "Now you know what I have long hidde. I am a maid."

I felt pinned, like a Moth in a collection. I could scarce draw a breath. Tom a maid. I could not see it.

Everything fell away. The floor under me, the walls around me, the very World itself. I was in a daze, I know not how many minutes or hours, but in them I lived again the whole length of my age.

Little by little did my mind begin to clear—tho' in truth, it cleared not fully for years—and I understood that Joan had not done what Barbara Kurzhals had done.

Lady Margaret had the Truth of it.

Tom had ne'er had a yard. I had only thought so because he pissed from it and pulled at it and protected it as other Boys.

That Tom was not Tom but Thomasina took longer for me to understand. She had counterfeited so completely! *She* was the Witch, thought I. I had bin bewitched. Had she gi'en me a love potion to make me admire her so and yearn for her favour? Had the Divell aided her? How could a Woman be so completely a Man? I could not conscience it.

I went over all I knew of her—her Latin, her tumbling, the strength of her arm, her skill at fighting. That first fight when she let me off so lightly! A maid! I burned with shame.

I burned, O, I burned.

They were Witches together, thought I, Tom Barrows and Joan. Thomasina. The very name came to sound like a Witch's name.

I was a gull! A simpleton! A fool! The blindest Baby!

Lady Margaret had tweaked me rightly. The nose upon my face *was* as plain.

Horror at my error suffused me, sickened me, enraged me, fuelled me. I wanted to kill Barrows. I felt my*self* unmanned.

The Witch of my childhood I still believed a Witch. The Witches of Bavaria, they, I knew, were Witches. That a man's member may be taken or hidden, I knew was possible. I *knew*. It had not been, here. But it *had* been, there. So I fervently believed.

I have since come to disbelieve it all. But then . . . Then I believed it still.

I knew not what I must do. Reveal my shame? Poison myself, that I live no more, but dwell forever in Hell, which I deserved?

Say nothing (as I could make no change to what was already done)?

The laughter I had thought trailed me through the town was what I had told myself it was not.

I had not thought myself ambitious, but I found I was, for I believed if I spoke what I now knew, my hopes of preferment were over. What Harm I had done myself already!

I knew not what to do.

Nothing was the main course. Do nothing. Joan had been released. Do nothing.

But I burned.

I should be whipped. Excoriated.

Barrows should be whipped. Barrows should be slapped in stocks and made to confess his . . . her . . . sin, her most impertinent, unnatural sin. *Was* she a Witch? She had ever professed there were none.

I shoved the Letter back beneath the paper it had lain under.

I told myself I must write my Sermon.

Balaam was asked to curse the Israelites. Instead, he blessed them. Three times Balak asked him. Three times he said he could do no other than the Lord commanded.

We can do no other than the Lord commands.

What commanded the Lord of me now?

I threw my head in my hands.

The sky was dark. Thunder rumbled. Then great Hail stones rained down.

I prayed.

'Twas time for dinner, but no one had called me for it, and I had no appetite. I wished to see no one, only to be alone and to pray, but at last Hannah bellowed from below to me to come eat.

Where is Susan? sayed I.

Gone off to Chew with the rest of 'em, sayed Hannah.

Gone off to Chew?

To see the Witch.

Mistress Palmer?

You are not abreast of the news, sir. Lady Long.

Hannah then told me they had word from Joan Dix, who worked for Isaiah Gough, that his son Daniel had died, his tongue swelling in his mouth so it stopt his breath. Mistress Gough called it Lady Long's doing. She had told the boy to watch his tongue when he spake 'gainst Joan Palmer, and now his tongue swelled, which was her revenge.

Mr. Gough had gone to arrest her, and all the household had gone off withal, to see what she made of it.

My mind was divided in two. With one part, I knew I had bin wrong about Barrows and therefore wrong about so much else I could not even begin to name it all, ergo Joan Palmer was no Witch, and Lady Margaret neither. With the other, I accepted all three were Witches, conspiring in our midst, in league with the Divell, who came and went as he list to sow filth and dissension. If they had not done what we charged them with, they had done something, and must be rooted out and punished.

Gough would go arrest Lady Margaret and take her before Sir Hopton.

Let him, thought I. Sir Hopton will dismiss this charge as he dismissed the other. And that other part of my mind thought, Let her be charged, let her be hanged, let the world be rid of all Witches.

I was recalled to practical concerns by Mr. Smallridge making sounds he was hungry.

Who remains? sayd I. Who will serve dinner?

You and me, sayd Hannah.

Who will lift Mr. Smallridge?

You and me, sayd Hannah again. Come.

What can they all be doing in Chew? They should not have gone.

So I told them, sayd Hannah.

The two of us drew Mr. Smallridge to his feet and felt his thin hand tight on our arm as he shuffled into dinner.

I had not the stomach for food. The movement of Mr. Smallridge, his spoon to his lips and the dribbles down his chin, made me sick.

I rose from table.

If Joan had not taken Barrows, his yard, did it follow Joan was no Witch? And if Joan was no Witch, did it follow Lady Margaret was no

Witch? Was I bound by God to tell what I knew? Tom Barrows wished
me to do nothing. To let him sail and return, if God willed it, and marry
Joan and go on as he was. This I could not do. He must, *she* must, be
exposed. But if exposed, so, too, was I.

I went across the road and into the Church and fell to my knees and
prayed to God, unto whom all Hearts be open and all Desires known.

I prayed for Forgiveness. I prayed for Wisdom. I prayed for Humility.

I stayed upon my knees until they ached. Then I stayed longer. I
prayed.

At last, I rose weary in Soul and sick in Mind, no closer to deciding
a course of action.

Soon returned our staff from Chew. Each told a different tale, but
the larger one was consistent: Lady Long had bin in choler at her arrest;
the Heavens had hailed, which they took as a sign of her anger; then
a Crowd, led by Ned Seaver and Martin Edgel, came forward and took
her from one side of her coach and Joan Palmer from the other, and
took them to the River to swim or duck them. But then came John
Powdry from his school and scolded the Crowd and the tide turned
and Lady Long was returned to her coach, but Joan was already thrown
in the river, where they learned nothing, for it was too shallow to swim.

Those in our household came back as if from a feast or holy day,
full of Spirit and mirth.

And they spoke to me as to one who feared and reviled the Witches
and would be pleased they were coming to Justice. And still I sayed
nothing, did nothing. Like Balaam, like Peter, three times was I offered
the chance to speak. Three times did I refuse that chance.

I soon learned Hopton had directed Broughton examine Gough,
his son, that he see if a naturall cause for the death be found. The sting
of a bee had done it, said the physitian, and the boy's brother testified
a bee had stung him—he had been trying to trap the bee and have it
sting his brother—and after that his tongue swelled. Mistress Gough

maintained the bee was Lady Long's familiar and had acted upon direction from its mistress. Was't possible? I knew not. But Sir Hopton released Lady Long.

Tho' they had pulled her from her coach for her reputed crimes, no one from the village would stand up before the Magistrate and make the same claim. Witch or no, she was free.

I delivered my Sermon, I know not how.

I went through each day in torment, too great to describe. I freely drank the wine in Smallridge, his buttery.

I went nowhere but to church, across the road, and back.

Then I heard Joan Palmer was sick, and then that she died. I called to mind all my encounters with her, not solely the one in the gatehouse, but all those before, when she had seemed modest and gentile.

God had called her to Him.

It was years before I saw my own part clearly. Had I made no accusation, she ne'er would have bin plucked from the coach nor ducked, from which her cough and fever followed, from which her Death followed.

Lady Long removed herself to Sussex. The tenor of life settled back down into its dull regularity, but I could not settle my Self in it.

I grew Melancholick, Argewmentative, and Dissolute.

I had assurance the parish was mine upon the death of Mr. Smallridge, the current, dottering Rector who dribbled his soup, but I knew not if I wanted it. Norton Malreward? A backwater. And a reminder that I was laughed at. That thorow my error, a woman died. That the World was not as I had known it.

And then that choice was taken from me, for I was passed over. I might stay on as Curate, if I wished, but I did not. Better a curacy elsewhere where I was not known. And so I began a chain of curacies, until not even the worst parish would have me, until I became the man I am now—faithless, infirm, telling my Tale for Drink.

God save you, if a God there be, Mr. Aubrey. I am dead, and my Soul condemned to Hell or Oblivion long since. This Packet, this Confession, now goes to you.

Anne's Note

I have read this confession again and again, and always take an involuntary pause here, always dwell in this moment of disbelief. Joan's death. It can't be real, can it? It's hearsay. He wasn't there. Heard wasn't there.

But I must give you Tom's last two letters before I say a word more.

Letters from Hudson Bay, Never Received

*O*CTOBER 22, 1632.
Dear Joan,

Wonder of wonders, I am returned to you.

The actual event of our arrival was greater and lesser than that I had imagined. I wept tears that against all expectation we had made it. We were alive! Never more to sea would I go. In my imagining, you were always there, in the crowd, waiting to greet me.

But I had lost the habit of imagining other people. They exist! In the hundreds and thousands. Those fifty or hundred who saw us and ran alongside as we drew into Bristol, gathering more on the way. Women! Children! I was not prepared. I could not imagine going amongst them. I scanned for your face. The crowd mobbed the wharf. Where were you? Where were you? We had been spied afore our arrival. Word had gone ahead, but you, in Chew Magna, would not know. Of course you were not there.

The investors, fat and clean, so it seemed to me, awaited. Mr. James did not want it given out yet where we had been or not been. But how could we not tell them. Had we gone through to Japan, surely we would have bruited it as soon as we could. To say nothing was to say we had failed. For the first time, I had small understanding of James's desire to do his utmost to get through, to be able to return, head high, and say, We tried, and it cannot be done.

We moored and unloaded, but that was not the end of it. If left there, moored, the ship would have sunk at her moorings, she was leaking so badly. She stayed afloat only through constant pumping. All of us had taken turns at the pumps, every last man, though it fell most upon Leggat, who could indure beyond any of us. His strength was nothing to look at, and he could not lift what Rance could, but he could keep on when all else had quit. As soon as we had got the greater part of our cargo out of her (Leggat pumping the while), she was towed where she could be winched ashore and careened. We ran after to see the state of her. Her keel was ragged and shorn, her cut-water plagued by gouges and gashes. Had I seen her like this ere I had sailed in her, I'd have said she'd not float. I trembled with the knowledge of what we were spared. There were so many times we should not have lived and yet did. 'Twas hard not to be like James and see God, his hand in our manie escapes. Why did God want us home? Why should we be blessed? Which among us was the good man?

I walked up from the docks and it came back to me, walking down the same street 'fore embarking, with you, your high forehead and love blazing as if you were the very Sun.

I want nothing more than to walk into Chew and straight to your door. But I am afraid. Will I be seized? Made to give up my life, my freedom, my profession? Severed from you forever?

I must know what answer gave John Heard to my letter! I had hoped for a letter from him. I had hoped for a letter from you. Neither greet me.

I am in agony to see you again.

This brings you all my love.

Your Tom

———

October 23.

Dear Joan,

I have had no reply from you, none from Heard. The boy I sent tells me at Longwood the house was closed and none living there but a man to watch over it, who said nothing of your whereabouts. At the rectory in Norton Malreward, he learned that Smallridge has died and a new Rector is in the living. Heard has not bin seen since he had left the curacy close to Lady Day. I will write next to Tradescant to see if he has knowledge of him.

Lady Margaret has holdings in Sussex. I must—

I am interrupted.

O, Joan, what has befallen you? I knew I was wrong to leave you. Truer, I *feared* I was wrong to leave you, and hoped I was right. As soon as I sailed, I regretted my choice. Better you and I sail to the Low Countries, or Virginia, better we lose ourselves in London. But I had sailed, there was no changing it.

Through only a few careless questions of news at Chew Magna, I learned at the Inn where I lodge something of the astonishing events of last year, that Lady Margaret herself was accused of witchcraft after her maid had bin accused of taking a man's yard by magick.

A roar of disbelief came from those that had not heard this before, including some others of James's company, a round of incredulous laughter. For me, I was turned to stone.

Heard had taken the evidence of his eyes and made something else of it.

I had to counterfeit curiosity to mask the terror that suffused my heart. Had you bin tried? Were you dead, hanged, while I was a coward at sea? Were you both—you and Lady Margaret—dead, because of me?

"What came of it?" I asked. I thought my heart might spill from my mouth.

"Naught came of it," said the Innkeeper. "Naught but disgrace for the curate that accused them, naught but a tale to tell at an Inn, for the laughter and shivers it brings."

"So they live?"

The Innkeeper shrugged. "If they have not died. Lady Long removed to Sussex or Kent."

I breathed again.

The room divided. The greater part mocked the accuser, a stripling curate, as they called him (who can be none other than Heard). Others were in thrall to the dread of the crime, to the power of Witches to work awful magic. They were like little boys.

Yet others did not believe any of it. There was never any such manne. There was, there was, but he disappeared. First his yard and then himself, scoffed one. Nay, 'tis a tale and only a tale. Nay, he was a real man, I knew him, his name was Thomas Barrows. I peered at this fellow. If he knew me, I knew not him. I was glad to be under the name of Nathaniel Billson.

It seems clear enough. I must find you in Sussex or in Kent.

Anne's Note

That's it. That's all I have.

The way Heard writes to Aubrey, saying that Joan died! It's almost an aside. Yes, he takes responsibility for it. There's that. But we don't see Joan go. We don't know what happened. We can only surmise that the chills Lady Margaret describes led to an infection, and this killed her. Such a small death, so ordinary.

I mourn anew for Lady Margaret, this new loss. And for Tom, who stayed alive in order to see Joan again, and never saw her.

Still, I retain this one doubt: there's no record of Joan's death.

And the very fact that Tom's letters were in Bibby's archive means they must have been in Lady Margaret's possession. And if they were in Lady Margaret's possession . . . Tom must have found Lady Margaret.

If Tom found Lady Margaret, I can imagine the rest.

Tom's discovery of Lady Margaret in Sussex—
    (She had aged, it seemed to me, ten years. *"You,"* she sayed with contempt.)

Lady Margaret's fury at Tom for taking off instead of staying and accepting his fate. Her refusal to see him, at first. His persistence—

("My Lady, I am returned from the frozen regions of Hell itself, where but one thought kept me from the brink of death or madness, and that thought was Joan."

"Go back, then. Go back to your hell. She may be there. She is not here."

"Not here? Then where?"

Lady Margaret looked at me without answer in such a manner that I understood at last that Joan was gone, truly gone out of this world. There was also in that look a suggestion that I was to blame, but I kept this understanding at bay while I took the blow. I had survived. I had come home. To nothing. I felt as dust. I wanted to be dust, blown from a shelf.

"No," I cried. "This is your revenge, to have me think her dead when she is not."

"O, no," said Lady Margaret. "It is not my revenge. It is only true.")

Their joint sorrow. Weepy apologies, confessions, regrets. A long stretch keeping company with each other as they go over and over what happened, what they lost.

And then: settling into their joint lives. Lady Margaret taking up her desire to don trousers, at least on occasion, at home.

Tom and Lady Margaret living out their days together.

And if I can imagine this, why not imagine Heard was wrong? That Joan lived. That she and Lady Margaret faked her death, and moved to Sussex, and renamed Joan, and recast her history as Lady Margaret had been doing in her head ever since recognizing how smart she was, how much her equal. That they lived there, in Sussex, quietly, leaving eggs in the nest now, watching the nestlings grow. Where Tom found them, one cold November day, in the Downs, near Fulking, and they wept to see him, after all they had been through.

Each of them alone, and together.

ACKNOWLEDGEMENTS

This book took a long time to write, and many people and organizations helped me. Thank you to the Canada Council and BC Arts Council, which provided grants in the early days that allowed me to travel for research and gave me time to write. One of the places where I went was Canterbury, to consult the Cathedral archives and especially to visit the King's School, still in operation, where Peter Henderson is the archivist. I spent a wonderful day with Peter touring the school, learning its history, integrating its geography, accessing its library and copying maps of the abbey's gardens during Tradescant's tenure there. Thank you, Peter.

My employer, UBC Okanagan, gave me time to write in the form of summer research terms and study leave, not to mention a rich working environment replete with supportive colleagues and cool students. Sean Lawrence regularly sent me articles that shed light on my time period. Thanks, Sean.

Significant chunks of the novel were written at the Leighton Studios at the Banff Centre. Copyedits were done at Cove Park in Scotland. They are both beautiful spaces to spend time alone and with other artists and to see the world and the project in a new way. Thank you.

305

Upon inquiring at Macleod's Books in Vancouver about books on witchcraft studies, I was delighted to be taken to what I think of as a "secret storehouse" across the street from the shop, there to plunder a collection from a former UBC professor, including Montague Summers's *The Geography of Witchcraft*; *Witchcraft in Tudor and Stuart England* by A.D.J. Macfarlane; *The Trial of the Lancaster Witches* and *A Jacobean Journal* by G.B. Harrison, among others. Thank you, Macleod's.

I deeply appreciated writing on witchcraft and the witch craze by Malcolm Gaskill, James Sharpe and Lyndal Roper, among others.

For material on the Tradescants I drew on Jennifer Potter's *Strange Blooms*, and Mea Allan's *The Tradescants*, as well as *The Diary of Elias Ashmole* and Tradescant's own *A Viag of Ambusad*.

My list of sources is much, much longer than the space I have here, and to name only a few is to leave out the majority. But I want to acknowledge the importance of the work of historians, biographers and the curious throughout the centuries. Thank you. Certain people delighted me by their very existence, like Joan Thirsk, who wrote the eight-volume work *The Agrarian History of England and Wales*, from which I learned that Kent, the area I had chosen as a base for Tom and Joan, was the only region in England *not* to use a common field system. Sadness: I wanted common fields!—but I still give thanks for Joan Thirsk and her ilk.

I am deeply indebted to Dr. Jonathan Clark, from Concordia College in Minnesota, who sent me the transcript and translation of Barbara Kurzhals's trial. It was a key resource that unlocked the book's Bavaria section. But I made up stuff, too. If there are historical inaccuracies, they are mine, not his.

Big gratitude is due to my friends Marg Scott and Leslie Walker Williams, who read the manuscript when I was stuck and asked key questions that set me on track again. I'm grateful for Michael Hathaway's curiosity, which is vast, and which inspired so many great conversations about science and nature. I had similar diverting conversations, though this time about art and books, with Jake Kennedy and Marlo Edwards. Thank you.

Chris Willcox and Amy DiGennarro, thanks for *Mr. Wilson's Cabinet of Wonder*.

Allan Westwood, thanks for "Gory Deaths in the Iliad" and *Rats, Lice and History*.

Michelle Benjamin is one of those people whose modus operandi is to lift up and support the work of other people, which she has done throughout her long career in bookselling, publishing, arts organizing and promoting the arts. I can't thank her enough for that work and for her encouragement of me personally.

My conversations with my editor Lynn Henry are unfailingly fun as well as rich, insightful and rewarding. Thank you.

Melanie Little is a dream copyeditor, wise, thorough, thoughtful, kind. Thank you, too.

Cindy and Kaden, you've been right there beside me all these years, cheering me on unflaggingly. Thanks. It means the world to me.

ANNE FLEMING is the author of *Pool-Hopping & Other Stories* (Raincoast, 1998), which was shortlisted for the Governor General's Literary Award for Fiction, the Ethel Wilson Fiction Prize, and the Danuta Gleed Award, as well as the much-praised novel, *Anomaly* (Raincoast, 2005). She is also the author of a middle-grade novel, *The Goat* (Groundwood, 2017), which was a Junior Library Guild and White Ravens selection, shortlisted for Italy's Premio Strega, optioned for film, and named one of the Top Ten Children's Books of the Year by The New York Public Library and the *Wall Street Journal*. Anne Fleming lives in Victoria, BC.